HOUND DOG
THE APOSTLE

JEDEDIAH CLYDE

SAMWALKERWORKS

SAMWALKERWORKS

2150 Lewis Avenue
Arcata, California 95521
samwalkerworks@gmail.com

Cover by SAMWALKERWORKS

ISBN: 978-0-578-31193-7 (print)

Printed in U.S.A.

Dedicated to the Big Blue Bullfrog.
Thanks for the warning.

1

I am traveling in a wagon pulled by a 20-mule team to a meeting of an extraordinary committee of which I am the chairman. I have no idea when I will arrive, but certainly much later than the members expect.

No doubt I will be pelted with complaints. The members of this committee are among the most arrogant specimens of humanity that ever graced the Earth. Czar Nicholas for example. For him every second of his time is more precious than all the gold in Krasnoyarsk. Even though he never does anything.

And Mickey Mantle, who uses his 555 foot home run over and over as a metaphor for the will of popular power expressed in an elected autocracy. I can never understand why anyone argues with him about it. Just let it go.

Then there is Oppenheimer. Insufferable. We remove all artifacts from the walls before he arrives; yet he still insists on identifying the origin, age, and place in cultural development of each one just from the markings left on the wall by the mounting screws. Sometimes I wonder if he is just making this shit up. How would anyone know?

We have Regina Bismarck Smith, a descendant of the Chancellor. She inherited his lust for authority. At every meeting she asks for plenary power to coordinate defense of the committee against armed assaults on its prerogatives and that a mobile strike force be put at her disposal for that purpose. Each time the members unanimously agree and move on to other business.

Our vice-chair is Molly Davidowitz, a retired actress, known for supporting roles in the moderately successful films *The Babe Who Blew Up Baltimore* and *Show Me The Greens: The Fuzzy Zoeller Story*. She also was renowned as the very strong-willed administrator of a charitable foundation called "Stand Up for Tomorrow". With her peerless powers of persuasion she raised millions for the foundation, even though no one seemed to know its purpose.

Molly is fearless and does not shy from provoking hostility, which can be dangerous with some persons. Like the James brothers. Molly questioned their preoccupation with gold bullion over greenbacks. "Maybe you'd like a little taste of silver," Jesse snapped at her, spinning the cartridge on his .45 and aiming it at her head. Fortunately, Frank intervened to explain that occasionally they need to shoot someone to complete a job and they preferred not to waste a homicide for currency that is susceptible to declining value from inflation.

We usually have a guest at each meeting. Last time we had Hugh Hefner. What was left of him anyway -- after decades expending more sexual energy than any other mortal man ever has. Two ravishing beauties arrived carrying a gold velvet robe with a smoking pipe hanging between the lapels. They asked where we wanted him and deposited the robe on the guest chair.

Out of the robe emerged what looked like a poorly preserved mummy head with a pipe stuck between its lips. With a leap of faith I said "How do you do, Mr. Hefner. Thank you for coming." The pipe nodded. That was Hef's contribution to the meeting. Meanwhile his entourage hovered about, mercilessly distracting the chairman.

Today we are fortunate to have Marina Oswald. To discuss her new book containing previously undisclosed facts about the assassination of John F. Kennedy. Her most intriguing revelation, and the one I am most eager to question her about, is that the man in the photos holding the rifle was not her husband Lee. It was Don Knotts, who Marina claims was the real assassin.

The committee answers only to a set of mysterious corporate officers whom I have never seen. They monitor our meetings electronically and disrupt our proceedings if we stray even slightly from the esoteric format they prescribed.

Take the meeting we tried to have with guest participant Robert Fulton, inventor of the first operational steamboat. He was about to begin his presentation when one of the officers suddenly declared that we had not satisfied the required preliminary sampling procedure. No one knew what she was talking about. Fulton, who had to travel there through spacetime utilizing only an 18th century steam-powered gondola, was frightened by the disruption and could not continue.

The officers also are fanatics about security. For access to a meeting we must pass an absurdly rigorous screening process. We are placed naked in a concrete vault, where an electronic body scanner searches for cellular abnormalities, nervous anomalies, and subversive mental content. Urine, blood, snot, saliva, and stool samples are extracted. The sentinels might require us to identify Homo Australopithecus among photographs of hominids, to chisel the chemical formula for aluminum sulfate into the wall, and/or build a tugboat with Legos dipped in linseed oil.

A motorcycle cop is hovering alongside the wagon signaling for me to pull over. "You are violating Traffic Ordinance 4.343 by taking a full 20-mule team through a 14-mule maximum zone." He writes up a ticket and orders me to exit that restricted roadway at the first opportunity.

I did not know. This is my first experience traveling by mule team. Before I became chairman of the committee I traveled by motor car, like most people.

One of the lucky few at my high school to have a car, I drove a modified Studebaker Daytona convertible that came to me when my grandfather died of a heart attack while trying to have sex with one of his companions at the assisted living center. The only addition it needed was an amplifier so I could blast FM radio beats across the blocks between my house and the school.

I wanted people to notice me. Especially the female people. Way too shy and timid to approach them directly, I figured a bass boom they could feel would attract them to at least ask for a ride. But the only girls who ever rode with me in that car were not the kind I dreamt about.

It was not that they were ugly or fat or smelled bad, although some were and did. They were vulgar and mean. Treated me like their chauffer, ordering me to drive by the convenience store so they could buy cigarettes or along the parkway where they shouted obscenities at other girls hanging out on the sidewalk.

The worst of it was that after the first time I let them ride with me they claimed a right to do so whenever they pleased. If I hesitated one of them would wrap a chain around my neck, yank my head close to hers, and, breathing Camel tobacco smoke at me at close range, snarl "how 'bout it?"

As a result of my apparent willingness to be the chick posse's chump I never developed a positive reputation among the girls I would have preferred to know. Even after I stopped driving the Studebaker, so the nasties would leave me alone, it was too late to cure the injury to my image. Hence I remained a lone nobody for the rest of my high school career.

I drove the car to Diller, Ohio for my first year at Jane Mansfield University, hopeful that it would bring me better luck there. We did not make it. About 100 miles out of Diller the engine began to smoke. The car lurched to a stop. A leak had drained the oil pan and my driving it so far without oil had disabled the vehicle to the extent that repair was not worth the cost. The Studebaker was towed to a junk yard. I arrived at JMU in the most miserable condition possible: Carless.

Which meant loveless and sexless as well. Without even fancy wheels to make up for a lack of masculine charm, my prospects for romance fizzled even amidst an abundance of alluring coeds.

I had to thank the dormitory for the few acquaintances I did acquire – all male. Dorm living was too close and personally intense for someone to survive without making any friends. And I was pretty much a regular guy. I drank as much beer as the next one, wasted as many hours staring at sports on TV, did my laundry three or four times a year, talked about girls like I was the expert.

None of the courses I took sustained my interest beyond the second week of each semester. It did not help that they were all required. And two weeks, twelve hours of class time, in an introductory US History class, just to cover the mercantilist roots of the Louisiana Purchase? A term paper on the structure and function of the endoplasmic reticulum? A group research project and presentation on the symbolic use of pronouns in the works of Zane Grey? For me college seemed to be all about indulging the professors' obsessions.

After struggling through two semesters to a C- grade point average, and enduring the humiliation of one too many "no thanks" from the ladies, I gave up. Stayed in Diller. And looked for a job.

The only offer I received of any kind was to be an unarmed security guard patrolling an eight-unit strip mall in the Broccoli Crown area of Diller. So for two years I was a uniformed presence outside Knottseau Dry Cleaners, Scrambler Insurance, Horatio Fong's Chinese and Irish Take Out, Day and Night Pharmacy, The Law Office of Melvin Mussolini, and Dusty and Useless Electronics.

I also watched over a stand-alone fast food dispensary called Cooked

Meat Express. I routinely bought the Cooked Meat Power Lunch Combo: Racoon ribs, coyote liver, and a basket of smelts – all cooked. Hence the motto they used in what little advertising they did: "We cook our meat".

When I first started the job I was compelled to get there by taking the city bus, which required two transfers. It also required much more patience than I had to wait in line for the regular elderly passengers to scale the steps into the bus, search in their purses for coins to pay the fare, argue with the driver about the amount, having forgotten the ten fare hikes that had occurred since they were only charged a nickel, and contend that as seniors they should not have to pay anything, in fact that the bus diver should pay them to ride on his bus. I needed a car.

So I was susceptible to the lure of the Sears Silver Special, the only automobile model Sears ever sold. There was a Sears store in Diller that featured an adjoining car showroom displaying the two models of the Special available instore. Two more models were offered, but only through the catalog. One afternoon I stopped at Sears to buy some socks and for the first time entered through the showroom.

Catching a glimpse of the Silver Special Coupe glistening there on a rotating platform with a sexy model at the wheel, I was entranced. And after the sales associate acquainted me with all the Special's special features, after I test drove it halfway to Akron and back, and after we settled on a price that was only a couple of thousand more than my credit limit, which he cajoled the credit department into increasing just enough to cover what the college fund my grandfather also left me did not, that baby was mine! The sales guy even threw in the two pairs of socks I needed.

That thing was hyper cool. A two-seater with some extra space behind large enough for a briefcase. Six cylinders of internal combustibleness, a hi-fi system booming bass beats that could be felt for blocks, and unique vinyl upholstery that had the look and feel of real leather. Before and after work I would cruise around Diller, again trying to catch the eyes and ears of the ladies.

Unfortunately, that was still all I caught in those days. Not one babe asked to join me in the Special, and I remained too shy and sullen to invite them. Moreover, I had no physical magnetism that could overcome my inept efforts at smooth talk. But providing pretend security for the strip mall would have a surprising consequence.

For the most part the job was pretty dull. Eight hours of watching people and cars. The only stimulating aspects were the conversations I had every day with the myriad specimens of humanity that frequent strip malls. Having nothing else to do, I was always available for a chat with the drag clown waiting for the cleaners to finish starching his bloomers, the Fongs' cooks who would come out periodically for fresh air and cigarettes, Mussolini's secretary out killing time while her boss met with a sexual predator client in their tiny office, the 110-year old living fossil showing me the RCA vacuum tube she needed for her Philco Model 90 Cathedral Radio. By the day I threw my uniform in the recycling bin I could talk about anything with anyone.

The only noteworthy day in my tenure at the strip mall was my last one. A week past my two-year anniversary on the job an incident occurred that inspired me to find a different occupation. I was leaning against one of the concrete planter boxes chomping on a Snickers bar, when I saw a woman running towards me, waving her arms and shouting "robbing the pharmacy". Like that had anything to do with me, I thought. Then I remembered, horrifyingly: I am the security guard.

Acting only on stupid impulse, I ran to the front of the pharmacy just as two dudes in ski masks burst out the door holding gym bags in one hand and pistols in the other. One of them saw me, stopped, and jabbed the barrel of his gun into the side of my head. The last thing I remember is how foul the guy smelled, like a clogged toilet in a public bathroom. Lucky for me, he did not pull the trigger. Instead, he knocked me unconscious with the butt of the gun.

I came to on a gurney in the emergency room. A cop asked me what I remembered about the incident. Only the smell. So after they arrested someone I was called as a witness – to testify about the smell. It turned out the guy was fired the morning of the robbery from a temp job at the waste treatment facility, after he opened a valve that released sewer gas into his work area.

We are now traversing a Walmart parking lot, trying to reach Jed Clampett Boulevard. Clearly none of these shoppers moving out of our way has ever seen a 20-mule team in the flesh. Some are staring at us with wonder. Most are colored with anger that anybody would dare desecrate that hallowed ground with multiple pounds of mule shit.

I am getting hungry. I will offer a passerby cash to obtain food. Really hungry and late for a meeting. Twenty bucks if she will stroll over to that KFC and get me a three-piece combo. She's not sure. Look, I'm ready to trust you. You could just take my money and disappear. Ok she'll do it. I hand her 40 dollars and off she goes.

Here she comes. Bless her heart, she is carrying a big bag with the colonel's face on it. She ordered extra, figuring that maybe other people at the meeting will want some. Will she ride with me for a little bit? Declining the invitation, she passes on and out of my life.

But she leaves me with a bucket of Kentucky Fried Chicken, hefty tubs of mashed potatoes, baked beans, sauerkraut, ferret blood chowder, scrambled pterodactyl eggs, and a few other items I did not even know KFC offered. Plus about 50 dinner rolls, a two liter bottle of Dr. Pepper, and a giant wad of plastic ware, napkins, salt, pepper, and packets of transmission fluid. I have at it. I will eat it all. Screw the others.

2

W hen I had recovered from Stinky's tap on my head, and was cleared to work, I left the strip mall behind and took up a new profession: Auto sales. Del Baxter's New & Used. A thousand cars spread across expanding acres outside town, a chain of flashing red, white, and blue lights separating new from used, spotlights reaching the stratosphere even through fog. Chevrolet, Buick, GMC, Hyundai. Previously owned from Buicks to Volkswagens.

My interview lasted little more than ten minutes. Del and the two sales managers did not waste a lot of jibber jabber trying to determine whether someone had the stuff for car sales. If I could sell cars I had a job; if not I would be gone in ten days.

Turned out I could. I found that "guarding" the strip mall had evolved my personality, that I could be as gregarious as I needed to be if the result was worth the effort. I had developed the skill of charming my fellow humans, colleagues and customers alike. With this charm came the power to convince, to gain trust, to project sincere confidence in the product. To sell.

I was even a match for the old-timers. Some of them had been there since the place was a two-acre patch of dust offering only used vehicles, before Del finally landed the GM franchise, opened the new car lot, and grew it into the magnificent automobile temple it was when I came on board.

The secret to successful auto sales, I grasped instinctively, is building trust. By communicating my good intentions to the customer, and making him or her feel comfortable hanging out with me, it meant that much more when I inevitably declared: "This is the car for you". I became a master at convincing the customer that I believed in the vehicle under consideration and that I would buy it myself -- if only "the wife" would let me.

Selling used cars was much more problematic than selling new ones. There was no mystery to a car just coming off the line. The true condition of a vehicle that had been driven 50,000 miles or more already , however, was known only to the previous owner and the mechanics who performed the Del Baxter

Special 55-Point Inspection and Miracle Restoration.

What exactly these mechanics did, how an automobile coming out was different from the same one going in, was never disclosed during my time there. It was not like I could offer a customer a document that identified every defect found by the inspection. All we could say was that Del's veteran mechanics inspected 55 different components of the vehicle and "restored" any they found that were defective.

My own confidence in a particular vehicle was especially crucial to selling a used car. My practice was to ask the mechanics to confirm that they performed the inspection and restoration properly for that vehicle and were not deliberately concealing anything. Then I would convey to the customer my trust in the honesty and integrity of "our guys": regular, hard-working fellows with loving families, respected in the community as mentors and models for our youth. I did not think it relevant to disclose that some of "our guys" had prison records or that one of the local garages was known as The DB Pit, allegedly the center of a stolen car parts operation and host to weekly crap games.

The most frustrating aspect of selling new cars was the constant pressure to sell added features. Del required all the sales representatives to offer car buyers the added features. We were evaluated, however, on how hard we tried to convince. I did my duty. And happily pocketed the extra commission.

Special coatings, for example. Casual conversation during test drive: Man, sure is smoggy today. Have you heard the latest report about how caustic the industrial chemicals in the air are becoming? And the rain and snow is getting more and more corrosive. Not to mention what is coming in now through the depleted ozone.

Then at the late stage of a sales transaction: I know you will want to protect your new beauty from all the crap we have now in the atmosphere. I highly recommend one of Del Baxter's ultra resistant protective coatings. They are formulated to protect the vehicle from industrial chemicals condensing in the atmosphere, rain and snow that is becoming increasingly corrosive, and satanic waves from outer space entering the atmosphere through the depleted ozone. A smart automobile consumer will not drive his new wheels off the lot without one.

I deliberately avoided ever seeing one of the coatings applied, as I feared that the spray cans labeled C1, C2, and C3 hidden in the supply room might have something to do with the process. Sometimes, to be a good salesman, it is better not to know.

Del's Double Down Sound Kit. Why make do with only five speakers when you can enjoy the soul stirring experience of ten? An electronic anti-theft device. When armed, this thing shoots 4,000 volts into anyone touching a door handle. The Eco Mask. An electric plug on the side that has no function other than to make other motorists believe you are driving an electrically-powered car and turn signals that spell out the words "I Drive Green!"

Test drives could be trying experiences. A husband or boyfriend, who tagged along with wife or girlfriend to ensure that the wily salesman did not take advantage of his naïve little lady, would then become jealous and hostile during the test drive when he thought I was too fresh and the woman too receptive. Occasionally, this worked in my favor: for example, if she pulled the trigger on a deal just to spite the overbearing dude.

Some customers drove like they had just learned to drive, accelerating and braking almost simultaneously, hopping us along the road and taxing my neck muscles. Or so slow we became the object of other drivers' testosterone-fueled fury and the suspicions of police wondering if we were blazing up a blunt.

Some test drivers, on the other hand, inspired by newer engine power and the freedom to taunt danger in someone else's car, channeled Richard Petty and pushed the car at full throttle, disregarding all traffic laws -- and the life of the salesman sitting beside them.

After my first year I was setting Del Baxter records for selling cars. Customers were referring other buyers to me and later returned for another purchase. My confidence for connecting with people of all types grew steadily.

Working as a car salesman also finally ignited my social life, including romance. I met my first wife at the dealership. Jennifer was a customer, although she never bought anything. After her first visit she came three more times, asked for me, and we went on a test drive. Then she invited me to Starbucks for a cup. I took her out for dinner at Denny's. We talked about getting married and then we did. Not a very romantic tale.

I really was out of her league. She was ten years younger, in fabulous physical condition, radiant olive skin, dark eyes, and loads of charcoal colored hair. We enjoyed a healthy sexual life for the first year or so and it seemed probable that she would conceive a child. Not that it mattered to me. I had never particularly cared about having kids. She talked a lot about it at first, but after a while she lost interest in the prospect.

So the relationship grew old prematurely. The triple bacon, garlic, muskox cheese and toe jam burgers I feasted on several nights a week did not help. She had a very sophisticated palate: delicate crepes filled with honey, saffron, goat cheese, and salmon. For me, it was either the burger or the Mexican Hungry Man frozen dinner.

She finally decided I was an incurable loser and took off for Southern California, hoping to hook up with the film industry, as a screenwriter or director or something. After struggling for a couple of years, she succeeded as a producer of television documentaries, mostly for the Real Shit channel. Her piece chronicling the daily life of a mail carrier working for the United States Postal Service is a classic.

Except for while I was happily married to Jennifer, my romantic life while I was selling cars consisted of dates with an extended series of different women. Some became sexual partners; most did not. After Jennifer I gradually lost my desire and my vitality and, as the months and years passed, my enthusiasm for selling cars.

As we approach an intersection police lights are flashing and a crowd of onlookers is milling about. There are persons lying face down on the strip of grass bordering the road -- handcuffed. Must be a drug bust or a bank robbery. Hey there, what happened here? Protest, she says. Protest about what? Animal rights.

Protesting animal rights? Excellent! That's a protest I could participate in. Damn these animals. Who do they think they are? "For far too long we've tolerated animals and their egocentric bullshit," I yell out across the waves of heads. "It's time we put an end to their arrogance. Animals have no rights!"

There is even legal authority on the issue: *Willie v. Wells Fargo*, authored by the horribly distinguished jurist and game show host Brendan Boozer. The case held that even though an orangutan walks into a bank wearing white Italian leather slip on shoes, a pinstriped silk suit with a gold silk bow tie, and carrying a briefcase full of cash, he is not entitled to open an account.

Those who can hear me above the hubbub are looking at me disdainfully, shaking their heads and calling for the police to "do something". As I prepare to hurl passages from Justice Boozer's opinion at the crybaby nitwits who are approaching the wagon a gaggle of roosters begins to crow behind them. Roosters clamoring for recognition of their rights. And the people hear them. They forget about me and call out to the roosters: We hear you.

I may have dropped a spoiler there when I brandished some legal expertise. Yes, it is true. I went to law school and once upon a time I was a judge. However, my path was a bit unconventional.

3

W hile still with Del Baxter, I decided to see if I could complete college and launch a more prestigious career. Smelter County John Glenn Community College Campus No. 15 offered an accelerated associates degree program. I was astonished at how many credits transferred from my very mediocre year at JMU.

With that academic experience under my belt, and now wise to more efficient methods for passing courses, I enrolled and did not stop until I had that AA degree in hand. The common objective of these methods was to pass the class rather than trying to learn something. There was a shortcut to success for virtually every course I took.

Using my newly acquired charisma I was able to hook up with other working students, some of whom inevitably knew someone who had already taken the course. Most of the teachers also worked other jobs full-time, so they did not put much effort into developing new material. Hence, it was not too difficult to obtain and memorize just the information the exams asked for. Sometimes I even got hold of previous tests on which some helpful former student had scribbled answers to the questions.

Another tactic that worked well for me was to schmooze the teachers. I was a master at ingratiating, at feigning genuine interest in a subject dear to the teacher, and creating a rapport:

You know, Ms. Diggerman, maybe some day I can work on an excavation. Must be exciting to spend hours picking through pebbles and sand in hopes of stumbling upon an ancient Mayan tongue depressor.

Gosh Dr. Saltbags, the theory of unconscious intelligence bias in inter-professional colloquy is fascinating. Where can I learn more?

Hey Mr. Taftmaster, your course on the influence of footwear on municipal political campaigning has really inspired me to volunteer for election work.

This routine would pay off with very favorable evaluations of my efforts, at least for the subjective components of grading, like participation, papers, and essay exams. Because I wanted only to pass the class, with a C or better, the objective part of the grade was almost irrelevant.

Now and then, of course, this tactic backfired. For some reason, perhaps because of the very lovely young instructress, I signed up for beginning French. Amelie Chevrolet was her name. During the first class meeting I was daydreaming about how enjoyable it was going to be sweet talking my way through that class. Did not work out that way.

Amelie was receptive to my disingenuous declarations about how eager I was to learn French. She even suggested the possibility of one-to-one work outside of class. The consequence of this auspicious beginning, however, was that she demanded more from me than from anyone else. She would frequently call on me and expect me to know the answer. She would hand back my written tests with red scribbles all over them, whereas I could see other tests that showed hardly a mark.

After a few weeks of this treatment I confronted her about it. She explained that the other students were there just to pick up the credits; they did not really care about learning the language. On the other hand, I had expressed eagerness to learn it, so she felt the need to make sure I got the most from her instruction. I hung on and earned a C. I did not learn much French.

Once I had the AA I moved on to Beef College, located in Beef, five miles outside Diller. Beef also had an accelerated program, and, once again, I was pleasantly surprised at how many credits they accepted from my previous schools. By taking three courses each semester I was able to finish in 18 months.

Almost immediately after starting Beef I faced the dilemma of picking a major. The choices were limited, Beef being a very small institution. After a little research into what major would be the easiest to complete, I chose Popular Culture Studies.

We watched movies and television shows, read magazines and newspapers, and listened to music. The only somewhat challenging work was completing research papers on culturally influential people. I wrote a paper on Johnny Carson. It consisted mostly of excerpts from the transcripts of a few *Tonight Show* episodes.

My thesis was that Johnny established a benchmark for late night programming, which all subsequent shows have attempted, but failed, to reach.

This failure was the root of an anxiety spreading through society over the possibility that *The Tonight Show* with Johnny Carson was the peak, the culmination, the climax of human development, and rendered all cultural activity since mere futile and fake imitations. Never again, I argued, would members of a studio audience join their voices together as one powerful awe-inspiring chorus, to ask with such conviction: "How cold was it?"

The professor pronounced my paper "superb". He shared it with his colleagues, who concurred. The result was that I barely had to lift a finger in each class I took thereafter. Just a few "brilliant" comments in class was enough to satisfy the Popular Culture Studies faculty that I deserved a degree regardless of my academic performance. I coasted to the conclusion of my undergraduate education.

Meanwhile I continued to sell cars for Del Baxter's New and Used. Without proficiency at greasing wheels I never would have survived. The grueling work and school schedule would have done me in. The guys at the dealership generally supported my efforts, but the management watched me closely to see if my dedication to auto sales diminished as I progressed in school. Eventually it would. For the time being, however, I felt secure enough to take the next step: law school.

I enrolled in the night program at the Ricky Nelson Institute of Cosmetology and Law. The schedule was pretty similar to what I was used to by then. Classes two nights a week. About an hour a day, more on my days off, reading cases and study guides and sometimes writing stuff.

The teachers were not exactly great scholars. Or teachers for that matter. Most had graduated from law schools even lower in prestige. One old-timer would recite the supposedly hypothetical facts of a case, then ask us how we thought it came out. Usually one of my classmates would know exactly the right answer. After class, when we asked her how she figured it out so quickly, she disclosed that the facts were exactly the same as an episode she remembered of *Perry Mason*. I was astonished -- that anyone remembered an episode of *Perry Mason*.

Like me, the other students worked full-time day jobs. One guy taught high school US history and was an assistant football coach. He would arrive for class with a frightening expression of pure hate, then argue with the teacher about some arcane issue, like whether *Roy Rogers v. Cowpunchers Anonymous* really stood for the proposition that bestiality was a mitigating factor in animal cruelty cases.

Unfortunately for the quality of our legal education, disruptions like this were common. As were the tendencies of the teachers to wander off track into reminiscences from their days of actually practicing law or, in some cases, serving as judges.

One lady repeatedly regaled us with the story of her one great trial victory, which denied recovery to a well-known chef suing her client for libel. The client had written a guest column in a culinary newsletter accusing the chef of using bulk wine produced in the San Juaquin Valley of California to make his signature Coq au Vin, instead of the ten-year-old Napa cabernet the chef claimed. According to our teacher, the two protagonists waged a vicious war of recriminations, one calling the other an idiotic son of Eskimo whores and the other calling the first a desperate and cowardly insect.

In defense she set out to prove that the accusation, even if false, was not libelous because the bulk wine was equal in quality to the Napa cabernet. After enduring scoffing the likes of which had not been heard in a court of law, including blatant ones from the judge, who fancied himself a connoisseur, she arranged a blindfolded taste test for the jury and the judge. Many bottles of both wines were consumed before the jury gleefully stumbled back into the box and delivered a drunken verdict for the defense.

Somehow I managed to persevere through the long days and nights of selling cars, driving to the school, sitting in class, gathering with my classmates at the Bamboo Broiler & Bar for a few rounds of post-class discussion, and staring at case reports at home until I fell asleep. Not sure how much law I learned. But after five years I graduated.

Our commencement speaker was Ron Popeil. I do not recall what he said. However, I made good use of the goat scrotum cooker he gave each of us as a reward for all our hard work.

The bar exam was supposed to be difficult. Ninety-five percent of Ricky Nelson graduates failed the first attempt. I got lucky. One afternoon a guy showed up at the dealership looking for a new Regal. We went out on a test drive and the subject of the bar exam came up. He told me that he flunked it twice before learning the secret from one of the examiners with whom he shared a bottle of premium scotch. If I got him a good deal on the car he would clue me in. I did and he did and I passed on the first try.

The secret: Key words. To streamline their task the bar examiners some time before had devised a system of looking just for certain key words. If they found enough of them the candidate passed, regardless of how well he or she handled the rest of the exam. I wrote a load of bullshit sprinkled with key words and got my license.

Good thing I hung on with Del, however, because almost a full year passed before I earned my first dime as a lawyer. A customer needed a lawyer to appear with her at an unlawful detainer hearing. I took the case and when I got home looked up the answer to an important question: What is an unlawful detainer?

Her landlord's attorney told the judge she had not paid rent for six months. I told the judge the landlord had been peeping in her window, probably taking pictures, repeatedly entered the premises without permission, ostensibly to make repairs but really to intimidate her into providing sexual favors. I said he probably was a known sex offender and demanded authority to search his residence for photos or videos. I had no reason to believe any of this was true.

The other lawyer looked at me like I was an unruly teenager. His client, however, spoke to him and, after an intense whispering attorney-client exchange, they announced that if my client would agree to a reasonable schedule for paying the back rent over the next year they would drop the matter. Done. Client was happy and I got my first fee.

The only other work I did as an attorney did not turn out so well. One of my colleagues at the dealership asked if I would represent his brother in what was supposed to be a routine divorce proceeding. The brother wanted to avoid large legal fees. Not quite routine: The wife demanded both houses, both cars, both alpacas, the entire stock portfolio, and the couple's collection of assegai spears.

Marital dissolution proceedings are form-intensive. I determined which forms were mandated by the code for use in that specific situation. I must have completed and filed fifteen of them.

At the hearing before the judge, however, she noted that Form FA144.68b was missing. This form was entitled Respondent's Declaration of Notice to Interested Parties of Intent to Squabble Over Possession of Personal Property in the Custody of Third Parties. The judge admonished me like she would have a third grader, explained that the form was required for her to make any rulings on my client's claims, struck all of our papers from the record, and awarded the wife everything she asked for.

I told the client we could appeal. A week later he said it was not necessary because he and his wife had reconciled. Did my failure to file Form FA144.68b save their relationship? Maybe – at least for the year or so before they split again.

I never was able to make a living as an attorney. My law degree allowed me to hang a diploma on a wall of the house in which I was imprisoned after acquiring title in the marital settlement, to talk a little legal jargon with customers who could appreciate it, and occasionally sign my name to demand letters someone else had prepared. That was it. Meanwhile, I was growing older and beginning to see myself 80 years old and senile and still selling cars for Del Baxter's New and Used.

Then I met the Honorable Olivia Holmes.

A flock of steel-beaked crows is dive bombing the team. There must be fifty of them. What do they want with my mules? Screeching out of the sky like Stukas, lining up a target, and attacking. It's not fair. The mules are defenseless. And not happy. They are stamping their hooves and braying in anger and frustration.

But the crows don't care. Crows never care. The most arrogant, insolent, incorrigible, and insensitive species of animal on earth. I remember the kind of wiseass crap Heckle and Jeckle used to get away with. Someone needs to take crows down a notch or two. I holler at them. They glare at me as if to say be glad we don't come after you.

So now we are stopped again. I have a crisis on my hands. I am not one to panic, but this seems like the time for it.

4

I had not sold a car for two weeks. My friends were ignoring me because I had become such a downer. One woman after another declined my invitation to see Shrek 11. Mortgage payment three months overdue. My life petering out into loneliness, poverty, and oblivion. As I left work one evening the new car sales manager told me he and Del wanted to meet with me in the morning. Jesus, I thought, am I going to get fired?

Driving home, I was depressed, anxious, and bitter. Deciding not to stop at Shorty's for a drink, because it was Renaissance Poetry Night and I was not a renaissance poet, I drove on. Not towards home -- just aimlessly along familiar and unfamiliar streets, past evil couples conspicuously and malevolently flaunting their happiness, assholes whistling while they strolled carefree along the sidewalk, jolly young men dressed in the latest styles slapping each other on the back and stopping to watch the ball game on a TV displayed in the front window of an appliance store. It was more than I could take. I determined to stop in at the next bar I saw and order doubles.

The Liquid Justice Lo_nge. The name appeared in dim white and blue lights with the third u burned out. A couple of blocks off was a small building that looked like a courthouse. Later I learned that it housed the 3rd District Municipal Court for the City of Glenn. My meanderings that evening had taken me into a new jurisdiction.

So I stopped in for some double liquid justice. I sat my ass on a stool at the elbow of the L-shaped bar and immediately whimped out by ordering a Coors light. About half of the ten stools were occupied.

Just around the elbow, on the stool closest to me, was a woman wearing a crimson jacket with the collar turned up to cover part of her face. She was sipping on a martini and reading some kind of journal. Maybe a few years older than me, her dark brown hair was expertly styled sweeping back from her face in the manner of Patty Duke in *It Takes Two*. Two patrons passed and said hello to her on their way to a table. One said "Hello judge." The other said "Hi Olivia". She responded with a terse good evening.

I was not there to socialize, so I paid no more attention to the woman until another patron, this one not so friendly, approached her and began berating her for something that had happened earlier in the day. She was visibly annoyed, but polite and trying to retain dignity.

Having no dignity, I told the guy that he should leave her alone. I was in a hostile mood already, so I did not care much what happened. They both looked at me like I was insane. A tense moment passed while the guy screwed up the meanest face he could and I stared straight into his unsteady eyes. The bar tender hovered close, and several other patrons appeared ready to help. Finally the dude huffed and puffed and left.

Thinking that I had poked my nose where it was not invited, I finished my beer, ordered another and a double shot of Quervo, and watched the TV that was showing highlights from the professional bowlers tour. I did not need to hear the broadcasters: "Wow, that's a strike. Wow, that's another strike. Wow, that's also a strike..."

Eventually I realized the woman was watching me toss down the double shot and order another. She thanked me for intervening. With a wistful smile, she told me that normally she would go to a place a lot farther away where people did not know her, but today this is as far she got. I responded that my circumstance was the opposite, that I had come farther than I ever had before in search of liquid justice.

That is how it started. We chatted and drank for two hours, until neither one of us was fit to drive. I learned that she was Olivia Holmes, presiding judge for the 3rd District Municipal Court for the City of Glenn. Like me, her one marriage had ended with no kids.

Olivia learned that I was a car salesman, new and used, employed by Del Baxter's New and Used, that I too was divorced with no kids, and that, oh yeah, I had a law degree. She was most intrigued by my current occupation, having purchased two vehicles from our dealership, a Hyundai Sonata and a slightly used Pontiac Firebird. Both transactions were handled by our new car sales manager himself, Bud "Ball Buster" Jones, who most just called Buster.

I told her of the meeting the next morning with Jones and that I expected to get fired. Did not have the drive to sell any more, I said. Maybe it was the law degree. Although I had not done much with that.

Eventually I faced the dilemma of how I was going to get home. Risk driving under the influence of tequila and Olivia Holmes? Even if I did not get arrested or kill someone, I would never find my way back. Sleep it off in the car I guess.

What about her? Turned out one of the people she knew offered her a ride. Lucky lady. Then, when she found out my plan, she asked if I wanted to crash on her couch and come back the next day for my car. The gentleman was a gentleman and accepted his new passenger with nary a raised eyebrow.

My memory of the rest of that night is pretty much gone. I woke up on the couch, declined breakfast, rode back with Olivia and our friend, parted pleasantly with both, and, close to being late for work, drove straight there, not caring a whit how I looked.

Meeting. Not fired, but on probation. One month. If production did not improve I was out.

That was a rough month. I tried. Or at least I thought I did. Selling cars under that kind of pressure, however, is difficult at best. Shoppers can sense the hard sell and they do not respond well. My numbers did not improve. By the third week I became resigned to failure and more or less gave up. Which, ironically, resulted in a few sales. But not enough.

Then one afternoon, about 5:30, as I was beginning my final week, there she was. Olivia Holmes. Talking to Buster and asking for me. She took me to Starbucks. I was in such a vile mood that when the barista asked what she could get started for me I said "get started on this" and grabbed my crotch. Olivia was cool. She even stifled a smile.

That bad, huh? she said when we were seated in an obscure corner. Last week. Been doing this for a long time. Used to be good at it. Maybe it's the place. Can't get hired at the Johnny Bench dealership? To tell the truth, I am mighty weary of this work. Probably shows. Probably why I cannot sell any more. Pretty sure I told you I have a law degree. Nothing happening there either.

She was sympathetic, but not to the point of really caring. Instead she went off on her own problems, personal and professional. Whined about how hard it was to find romantic partners at her age and with her position. I suggested she try a dating service. She was not amused. But then came to the point and invited me for dinner at her place.

Two days later I arrived wearing my JMU sweater, which actually hung loose on me when it should have been extra tight considering how long I had had it. James Madison University? she guessed. I corrected her. She did not believe me, but did not pursue the matter.

Dinner was delicious. The two bottles of wine we consumed were as well. A 1998 Forest Lawn pinot grigio and a recently bottled root beer-infused merlot. I retasted them afterwards on her lips while we languished on the familiar couch kissing and cuddling and deciding that I should spend the night.

Olivia and I started seeing each other two or three times a week, usually at the Hans Holbein Hotel in Scruffsberg, a five minute drive from Glenn. Our relationship at that time was predominantly sexual, but we did have some scintillating talks about her work, or more specifically her complaints about the work, and occasionally about my work, or the work I used to do, since I was no longer with Del Baxter and, in fact, was unemployed and worked only to the extent of visiting the bank to deposit my unemployment check.

One cold foggy evening Olivia surprised me with the happy (for her) announcement that she was pregnant. Whoa, I said. She was supposed to be taking birth control pills. Must have missed a few.

She immediately launched a campaign to get us married. I could sell my house, crawl out from under the mortgage, and move in with her. I would get benefits, health insurance, etc. Maybe I could even jumpstart my legal career.

But I did not want to get married. I had a number of objections. First, there was the religious conflict. Olivia was catholic. Not a particularly active catholic. She never went to mass except on Christmas, Easter, and Saint Sinatra's Day.

With a few caveats, she accepted the Pope's infallibility and hoped that our child would be raised catholic. The wedding would have to be in the Mary of Tyler Moore Cathedral and feature a full-scale mass, complete with life-sized balloon replicas of Jesus, St. Augustine, Knute Rockne, and the Pope.

Olivia assumed that I was not religious and thus would have no reason to object or not to promise the priest a catholic life for our child. Unfortunately, she was mistaken. I was raised as, and was at the time, a member of the Burlap and Barbed Wire Assembly.

A simple faith, its tenets were set forth in 1922 in an anonymously-written pamphlet modestly entitled *Burlap and Barbed Wire*. Our core belief is in the sacredness of burlap when joined with barbed wire. Thus, at an early age I learned how to make humanoid figurines from the two materials and to worship them mounted on a large piece of foam board at the front of whatever meeting place we used at the time.

As I contemplated Olivia's proposal I could not recall what, if any, marriage doctrines our faith professed. But I was not going to disregard the foundation of my spiritual life without study and reflection. She would have to wait for my decision.

Because she thought I was joking she first became angry, then began to cry. I assured her that I truly loved her, that I really wanted to marry her, and that I just needed a couple of days to figure things out.

Strange as it may seem, the religion issue was not the biggest obstacle for me. My problem was that I had no enthusiasm for entering an arrangement where I would be so dependent on her. It may sound cliché-ish, but I did not want just to sit around in the living room all day watching reruns of *Dateline* and pretending that I was doing something to start a legal career that I knew damn well would not start. Realizing that fairness to her required it, I determined to come out with my true fear the next time we met.

So I did. She said she understood. And there was no more talk of marriage that day.

At our next rendezvous, however, she had the solution. I understand that you want a job, she said, and preferably a legal job. Yeah, but -- She had one for me. You can be a judge, just like me! I thought she was mocking me and I protested. How could she be so callous and cruel to an unemployed loser who loved her?

But no. she had it figured out. First, she would take me on as an un-paid clerk to help out with various tasks, like research on cases pending before her.

There was no limit to the amount of research that could be done on any given case, so she could keep me busy while I learned the ropes and schmoozed with the courthouse staff.

After I acquired enough of the judicial drill and charmed anyone who might have objected, she could hire me officially and no one would question it. A few months further on she would be planning for pregnancy leave, which would create a temporary vacancy in one of the three departments of the 3rd District. She would then declare that I was to be her replacement pro tem, subject to agreement by counsel in specific matters that I could hear and decide them. And voila, I would become a judge .. just like her.

Not as confident in my aptitude for politics and self-promotion, I balked at the idea, then endured a whole lot of female vitriol and bitter tears before I gave in. After all, I finally concluded, what did I have to lose?

The crows finally have had their fill of mule particles. The black cloud lifts from the team, drifts off to the north, and now is fading out of sight. We will soon be on our way again. However, my arrival for any part of the meeting is growing doubtful. Probably the officers will direct Davidovitz to chair the meeting in my absence.

Bound to be a nasty cat fight between her and Oswald. The Czar will summon the palace guard, Bismarck the non-existent strike force. Mantle and Oppie will intervene and suffer disfiguring scratches. I must be there to moderate. But the team does not appreciate the urgency.

Dusk is descending. Ghosts gather out in the heavy air.

5

For some time we were careful to avoid any open acknowledgement of our relationship. I showed up at the courthouse one day and told the clerk in Olivia's courtroom that I was hoping to get some experience without pay. I left my slightly exaggerated resume with a request that it be forwarded to Judge Holmes, as I was a great admirer of her work.

"*Slightly* exaggerated" may itself be slightly exaggerated. I could not very well fake the name of my law school, although that certainly would have been expedient. But I did describe my extensive experience in the field of unlawful detainer, my work drafting documents pertaining to contract disputes (between me and two clothing retailers I accused of selling me, respectively, defective suspenders and a hat that shrunk when I washed it), my analyses of property distribution in the context of marital dissolution (my own), and my exhaustive study of court procedures watching *Matlock*, *L.A. Law*, and *Night Court*.

Olivia told her clerk to bring me into her chambers. After fifteen minutes of canoodling, she escorted me out and casually informed the clerk that "this nice young man" would be lending a hand here and there to learn some of the legal ropes.

So for almost two months I showed up every day in Department 1, just after the lunch recess, and chatted with Betty, the clerk, and Joe, the bailiff. I asked Betty about her family, photos of whom adorned her intelligently cluttered desk adjacent to the judge's bench, and for more details about her and her husband's recent vacation trip to Nashville, where they took in the Grand Ole Opry and saw Ferlin Husky, Skeeter Davis, Red Bean McDonald, the Clausewitz Cousins, and an Iron Maiden tribute band called Made in Iron.

With Joe I talked football. What did he think about the Browns' second round pick, a Chinese linebacker known at Zhengzhou University as The Slicer? Joe could barely contain his disgust at the choice. He was painfully mystified especially because the team had the chance to get Tiny Williams, a 450-pound, six foot nine defensive tackle from Cornflake College in Battle Creek.

Then I had a brief conference with my girl friend, aka Judge Holmes, to get my assignment for the day. I usually spent the afternoon in the modest law library the court had. There I found court decisions and statutes relevant to the issue I was given, read briefs and other papers filed in a case, and wrote up little memos for the judge. Most of the issues were miserably mundane, just questions Olivia had contrived so I would have something to do.

Sometimes, however, she gave me more interesting assignments. Like the Dr. Slappy matter. David Slappy, D.D.S., a dentist practicing in the City of Glenn, had decided to diversify. He converted a portion of his office into a massage parlor – without informing his landlord, let alone getting permission, and without obtaining the required license.

Furthermore, so his neighbors in the professional office building they shared claimed, Slappy was in violation of the spirit, if not the letter, of understandings, if not rules, restricting the occupants to activities consistent with the practices of professionals. The landlord, the city, and the neighbors ganged up on Dr. Slappy and sued to enjoin his operation. He countersued, alleging that they were wrongfully interfering with his business rights and trying to stifle competition.

The law firm handling the matter for Dr. Slappy was one that I would deal with multiple times in my career at that court: Lizard, Blizzard, & Gizzard, a City of Glenn institution. Another local firm, Mottle & Bando, represented the plaintiffs. Courthouse rumor had it that Mottle and Bando were really the same person. The only lawyer from the firm who ever appeared while I was present called himself Parley Poppinberry, so I could not affirm or deny the rumor.

The judge asked me to find authority on enforcing a restriction acknowledged by practice, but never written, limiting the activities a tenant of a professional building could pursue. A seemingly relevant opinion popped up right away. *Chester v The Hot Stuff House*. 1887.

Chester was a mortician who leased a space in a structure appropriately called The Professional's Building, which housed a couple of medical doctors, a lawyer, an accountant, and an architect. The building's newest tenant, and the subject of the controversy, was The Hot Stuff House, a brothel.

The accountant had sublet his space to a Madam Lucy Taft, who converted it to an "office" of prostitution. Immediately upon getting wind of the project, Chester, the mortified mortician, retained a lawyer named Rufus Taft to bring legal action to stop it. Madam Taft hired her brother, and Rufus' cousin, Reginald Taft to respond.

Reginald Taft's defense rested on one simple proposition, which he repeated again and again in papers and oratory: What could be more suitable for a building dedicated to professional activities than the world's oldest profession? The trial judge dismissed the suit without explaining why. The appellate court affirmed the decision on the ground that the term "professional", unless defined specifically otherwise by law, agreement, or custom, could not be interpreted to exclude the services of a brothel.

The futility of my work was demonstrated when Dr. Slappy, unhappy with the dismal revenue he received, closed the massage business before the judge made any substantive ruling. Only the lawyers gained anything from the action.

After about seven weeks of this unpaid work, Olivia hired me to do the same thing, but for pay. A couple of weeks later she started taking the wraps off our relationship – allowing her to be seen walking with me to the parking lot, sometimes having coffee with me in the cafeteria. Three months into the project she finally let it be known, first, that we were an item, then, only a few days later, that we were engaged. No one seemed to care.

Before anyone could notice a baby bump we used a lunch break to visit the county administration building and have an official there tie our knot. I put my house up for sale and moved in with her.

Meanwhile, I was becoming a very familiar face, and, I might add, a popular one, around the courthouse. And I fancied up my resume by publishing an article in a local bar journal: "Unlawful Retainer: The Pitfalls of Taking Exotic Reptiles as Deposits on Fees". In addition, Olivia had me fill in for her on the bench a few times when morning sickness made her late for routine scheduling conferences.

Finally, Judge Holmes announced that we were married, that she was pregnant, and that in 30 days she would go on maternity leave. Rather than allowing the temporary vacancy to float in limbo while the process of weeding out contenders dragged on, she stated, somewhat imperiously, that Judge Snodgrass would take over as presiding judge and that I would fill in for her as a judge pro tem, subject to agreement by counsel in specific matters. Then we held our breath waiting for the hue and cry to commence.

It did not. No one cared. Many of the lawyers to whom the judge had served justice multiple times were just happy that she was going to be gone for a while. Our friends in the courthouse community congratulated her on the coming birth and sympathized with me for stepping into the muck.

So I became a judge and a father within successive weeks.

I quickly found that the worst aspect of judging was having to sit for an interminable time listening to and observing a parade of attorneys, who were mostly either pathetic and groveling or sickeningly pretentious and pompous. This latter group arrogantly assumed that I would be an easy mark for their superior savvy. Hence I made a point in the beginning of disabusing them. When one of these specimens swaggered to the counsel table and preened for whoever might be watching I determined to rule against him or her no matter the merits.

Your honor, my client will be in Milan for the next six months meeting with officials from the Frank Netti Museum of Renaissance Numbers Rackets and cannot possibly appear for a deposition before the trial.

Your client is hereby ordered to appear for deposition one week from today at the office of Hatch & Snatch, and to produce every document he has ever laid eyes on, including, but not limited to, spelling quizzes from the first through fifth grades, lists of camping items he may have compiled as scoutmaster, and cards he received for every birthday from the first to the most recent. That is all.

Another case: Your honor, we have supported defendants' motion with spreadsheets, blue prints, schematic diagrams, electronically formulated models, computer data bases, digital readouts, product specs, functionality demonstration videos, statistical spectrometer salivation surveys, and certified findings by the American Board of Causation and Consequence Examiners, along with detailed and voluminous declarations and reports by fifteen of the most distinguished experts in the relevant fields. The plaintiff, Mrs. Brown, submitted only her own two-page, patently self-serving declaration.

Counselor, your motion is denied. That is all.

I relished the power. Especially the greatest power a judge has, one that can originate with him whether or not the parties have brought a dispute: Contempt. Maybe I used it too freely. Maybe some of my citations were overly harsh. But I was not going to take any crap in my courtroom.

A little old lady, there for moral support of her sister who was contesting an eviction, had the audacity to nibble on a Butterfinger bar in open court. Contempt! Three days in the slammer.

A young boy about 15 was there waiting to testify, if needed, in a petty shoplifting case against another young boy accused by Taft Family Pharmacy of sampling more than the allowed three bottles of cologne. This miscreant demonstrated utter disrespect for the law, the judge (me), and the sanctity of the proceedings by not muting his smart phone before someone piped through it a few bars from a horrible version of the Thong Song. Contempt! Four days in the pokey and 20 hours of community service helping disabled Salvation Army veterans apply for South American travel visas.

On the other hand, it was not like I meted out rough justice to everyone. I could be compassionate on occasion, especially if the defendant's plight struck a sympathetic chord with me or if his public defender was one of the hot babes recently transferred in from Columbus.

One dude, sneering and scowling and menacing even in shackles, his scarred face and tarnished gold teeth contrasting with his clean and bright orange prison jumpsuit, tried to stare me down from the safety glass enclosed holding booth.

The deputy district attorney read the charges: Multiple premeditated homicides with multiple special circumstances, which included being as evil as the devil, cooking and eating the victims' small intestines, shouting Francophobic epithets as he went about his grisly business, and violation of the county ordinance governing disposal of human remains.

While I was wondering how he could have consumed the small intestines of multiple people in the time span ascribed to the crime, the small intestine being one long ass organ when unwound, the luscious fox defending him finally found the file in her stylish leather briefcase.

Looking up at me, nervous and breathy, she said "Your honor, this man has been treated so unfair. I mean – like - the charges are all trumped. And the evidence is – like - weak. No one saw him eating. He loves the French people. And – like - the police took him before he could dispose the bodies. The media your honor. We want to change the venue."

I ordered a change of venue. We needed to give the guy a chance. The prosecutor hissed. But the defense attorney said "thank you your honor" so sweetly I was considering whether I could invite her into my chamber for a "conference". But in the nick of time I remembered that I was married and, in fact, had a newborn baby girl waiting for me at home.

We went through a bit of a tussle deciding on her name. Olivia wanted Mary or Margaret or Mary Margaret. I preferred Darlene or Dolly or Dolly Darlene. We settled on Angel.

Olivia was pretty cool through most of the delivery. I was in awe and rendered dumb and stupid by the magnificence of the slimy procedure.

At one point between contractions she saw me staring like a zombie between her legs like I was trying to see up inside her vagina. That's when she lost her cool. She called me an ignorant bag of human excrement, a little festule rotting the air with the odor of never washed armpits, a horrid demon reveling in his wife's agony. I had been warned, but ...

Finally, she screamed for me to get the hell away from her! So I left the room.

Only to be summoned before I even got to a vending machine. Olivia was sobbing with remorse and pleading with the staff to get me back. "Now you're in contempt", I cracked, trying quite unsuccessfully to lighten the atmosphere. This pattern continued for two more hours until the final shocking upheaval scared me senseless and ended with cries from a tiny creature who was as mad as her mother had been earlier.

I hear tell that back in the day the climax of birth was customarily signaled with a maternity nurse calling out "It's a boy" or "It's a girl". Nowadays we parents already know the gender way ahead of the time.

In fact, by means of implanted micro-transmitters sending video data into the ether and hence to an online server, we had the opportunity, if we cared to take it, to see on a laptop every second of Angel's development in the womb from the moment she left her microscopic phase behind.

More amazing still, with the image was posted every digit of information there was on the structure of her DNA, RNA, NBA, QNA, and all other biochemical signatures from inside the nuclei of her cells. If we had requested it, the technicians could have told us what color her hair will be, how tall she will be, whether she will need braces, how well she will be able to hold a tan, whether she will develop a natural golf swing, and whether she will disagree with her parents about the benefits of privately run prison systems.

So I passed out cigars at the courthouse. Even lit one up while hearing a motion. Just because I could. Except that I couldn't. Joe told me I was violating multiple ordinances and that it would be his duty to arrest me if I persisted. That was that.

Meanwhile, even as I was celebrating the birth of an Angel, I was making rulings that brought death to three unlucky souls. The intestine eater was not one of them. His case had been transferred. The new judge sentenced him to five days in the electric chair – cooking slowly, voltage increasing hourly.

One of my capital defendants was a 62-year-old man who claimed to be the Roman tribune Gaius Gracchus. The hairdresser he had stabbed to death, the defendant believed, was actually his ancient enemy the consul Lucius Opimius, who had ordered the murder of 3,000 of his followers. Justifiable revenge, he cried. Insane, said his attorney. Insane, said the psychiatrist who evaluated him.

Not insane, said the cross-eyed professor of historical transmigration brought in by the prosecutor. The tribune knew that it was wrong and unlawful to kill Opimius, regardless of whether he deserved it. He, of anyone, knows that one cannot take the law into one's own hand.

I could not refute this logic. So I declared that *damnatio ad bestias* was in order and sentenced the defendant to be locked with a hungry grizzly bear inside a handball court.

I imposed my other death penalty on a woman. Her name was Alex Atkinson. She was accused of slashing a dude's neck with a broken beer bottle during a brawl at a dive bar out on Highway 9. The guy died after five days in intensive care. A private attorney came in from Diller to defend her with the allegation that the victim died only as the result of mishandling by the paramedics and hospital staff, which resulted in a fatal infection of the neck wound.

I called this the Charles Guiteau defense, but the hotshot lawyer had no idea what I was referring to. His client did. She sneered at him disdainfully before delivering a well-informed summary of Guiteau's claim that the doctors who treated James Garfield caused his death with their unsanitary probing of the wound, which triggered the infection from which he eventually died.

I had to hand down a death sentence just because the lawyer was such an ignorant, arrogant, egocentric prick. Otherwise I might have accepted the defense, despite the utter lack of evidence to support it.

The third person who died as a result of my ruling was the husband in a marital dissolution with custody matter who killed himself after I ordered him to pay enormous spousal and child support, along with support for the pets, the in-laws, the neighbors, and the PTA.

In that case I was repulsed by both the lawyer and her client. The lawyer because she was a self-important, self-righteous, self-absorbed feminazi bitch who showed me disrespect every time she appeared, for example by showing up in tight jeans that barely contained her three-hundred pound thighs. In written messages to staff I called her The Porkupine.

I do not recall much about the client, the Porkupine having filled my memory screen and blocked all related recollection. Maybe he was not such a bad guy after all. Just hired the wrong lawyer.

Anything the ghosts are planning to do to me is deserved. My mind is pretty fuzzy right now, but I imagine I can hear voices, calling to me from the netherworld, from purgatory if you will, where their souls must remain until their appeals to the higher powers are complete.

No doubt the higher powers will not issue a reckoning for them that does not include one for me too. I should strip myself naked, stand atop one of the mules, raise my arms in supplication to whatever deities happen to be on call, and plead for mercy, and forgiveness.

I am the target of vitriolic remonstration coming from all sides. Corpses drifting through time, an ethereal finger snaking off long and lizardly, pointing to me, marking me, accusing me. Mad mules plotting a coup, one in particular, four rows out, had my eye on him, troublemaker, rest will follow his lead, in league with the phantoms, the rattlers, even the jackrabbits coming to take a share.

Mutated scorpions suddenly possessed of thought, one thought – me --
driven by a species anomaly to swarm, against me. The tides, the waves of
miserable flesh, yellow and bloodless, dancing death to my face, the blind bats
hurtling through darkness from hundreds of miles over bush, concrete, and
blacktop to shriek their maniacal pleasure as they converge, on me, to lacerate my
ears, tear skin from my cheeks, pierce my eyeballs. Now the crimson lightning,
multitudes of millisecond streaks closer and closer, illuminating awful faces
burning with exquisite anger.

I am lost. I do not know where I am. I am afraid, trembling, shivering,
terrified. I try to stop the team, but they are paying no attention. They continue
the march, only not in the direction I instructed. They are veering to a new
direction and I am helpless to do anything about it.

I have lost control. Of everything. I curl into a fetal knot on the floor of
the wagon and choke out panic-stricken pleas for deliverance.

6

My tenure as a judge lasted all of about seven months. Until Olivia grew tired of cleaning Angel's ass ten times a day, having her nipples gnashed and clamped by Angel's powerful gums, reading news reports about the vicious food fights between members of the British royal family, and having to listen to Mrs. Bighead from next door complain about the specialty grocer not ordering enough canned mackerel for her yearly pelagic fish feast.

When she told me one day that she was ready to return I wondered what that meant for my judicial career. I should have known. Judge Holmes was welcomed back with a huge hullabaloo, complete with balloons, banners, the release of 50 doves (probably should have done this outside, to avoid the avian hysteria, chaos, and diarrhea that resulted), remarks by Judge Taft visiting from the 2nd District, Tanya Taft Teasdale, the district attorney, and Larry Lizard from Lizard, Blizzard & Gizzard. I went home to clean Angel's ass ten times a day, spray milk from a bottle on her face and sometimes into her mouth, and dream of the power that had slipped through my hands.

Olivia knew I was not happy and worried a lot about it. But in the circumstances one of us had to be depressed and hopeless. Better my worthless ass than her golden spirit. So I accepted my fate as cheerfully as I could and dedicated myself to our wonderful little girl.

I was not much better as a father than I was as a judge. At least I sincerely tried. It was easier at first than it was later, mostly because she could not talk back. So I usually could calm her, and even convince her to sleep, by prattling on and on about whatever topics seemed ripe: South Asian economic policy, the foolhardiness of the Reds trading for a 49-year-old knuckleball pitcher who was rumored to be injecting a new youth serum that enhanced performance but produced hallucinations, and why in heck the specialty grocer had such an oversupply of canned mackerel. I had a captive audience who did not complain about it.

After a couple of months her awareness increased to the extent that I could make her laugh by reciting New York Stock Exchange reports in a Donald

Duck voice. This led to her making noises with her mouth, one of which sounded something like "ufu". Soon she was using this term repeatedly, especially in conjunction with my efforts to amuse her, and it dawned on me that this was her label for me. Other babies were calling their fathers "dada" or something similar. My daughter called me "ufu".

Olivia was not impressed. In the evenings when she came home the two of them shrieked and squealed and screeched and clucked. But for Olivia the idea that any of Angel's homemade sounds signified me was ridiculous.

Judge Holmes typically brought home a satchel of papers to work on. Once the explosion of greetings subsided and whatever lame food I prepared was consumed, she would retire to her home office until it was time for the nightly *News One Must Think Oneself a High Brow Intellectual to Appreciate*, breaking only to purr and gabble over Angel going to sleep in her crib. The romance had pretty much evaporated from our marriage.

But Angel and Ufu became quite a pair. Even when she started speaking an established language and could easily have said "Daddy" or "Father" or "Sir" she continued to call me Ufu when no one else could hear. It was a joke between us, although we never talked about it.

The neighbors would see us every day, weather permitting, walking nonchalantly along the sidewalk, Angel first in a stroller, later hopping or skipping, sometimes even walking. There was always wonder to be seen: robins in their infamous Communist vests, seagulls tangling over the remains of a double bacon cheeseburger, crows pretending to be stupid while diabolically plotting their dastardly doings, lilacs, sunflowers, and flytraps belching satisfaction, the goofy Dietrich kid, who tried to hide when he saw us coming then jumped out to scare us, provoking a squeal from Angel followed by a fit of giggles. I never asked the kid the question that troubled me: Why?

This placid life continued through the four years before my Angel heartlessly deserted me to start kindergarten. You're really going through with this, I whined while walking her to school that first day. I laid guilt on her like a wet coat. Made no difference. She even had the nerve to say "Man up, Ufu, you got this".

Home that day, and many many of those following, was the most lonely, desolate, depressing place I had ever been. And those were the longest hours I ever experienced. I felt like someone who is *lost* but does not even know where *found* might be.

I slept too much. I read legal notices in the newspaper. I watched *The Wild Boar Show*, *Name That Field Marshal*, and other game shows. I shopped for handbags, skin cream, and 666 ways to rekindle your man's libido. After an hour of "What's in your Beauty Bag?" I almost cried because I didn't have a beauty bag. I even wrote blistering diatribes to the specialty grocer about the canned mackerel situation.

In sum, when Angel was gone at school it seemed like my life was empty of anything to value, and I was hard-pressed to restore my outlook by the time she got home. But god forbid if I should ever even once let her sense my despair. Only ten minutes of Angel was enough to cheer my mood. So whether we were drawing funny pictures together or I was helping with her homework all was very well.

Of course the summer after her first year was paradise. Angel was there almost 24 hours day, only gone during the few hours she spent at another girl's house, her first friend. I called the girl Jezebel.

Olivia actually took a week of vacation and we went on a trip to a new theme park that had just opened in Forksville, Pennsylvania. Called Forksville Fantasyland, it described itself as the doll capital of the world and did not disappoint. Never have I ever been, and never will I ever be, in the midst of so many dolls, thousands, of styles too varied to summarize, of every nationality and ethnicity found in humanity.

There was Barbie House, which should have been called Barbie Estate, its size eclipsing any three "houses" I ever saw. Live teenaged Barbies guided us through all thirty rooms. Each had multiple displays of everything Barbie, including a dazzling array of Barbie fashions and accessories, from shoes, dresses, and swim suits to make-up kits and Barbie Brand Tampons. All available for purchase with the Fantasyland Credit Account we opened on arrival.

When I asked about Ken, however, they sent me down a long narrow staircase to a cramped chamber in the cellar, where a single Ken doll stood on stool holding a sign that said "That's just how it is." Yeah Bro, I said and climbed back up to heaven.

Heavenly was how Angel felt about the place. Olivia too if she had admitted it. But our stay eventually ended and we drove back home in the 19-foot U-haul truck we needed to haul our purchases. And then summer waned. Angel went off to first grade, leaving Ufu once again alone and intensely despondent.

Olivia tried to help. One night she made the mistake of suggesting I get involved with the school, the PTA, volunteering, or something. Notwithstanding my protests that I was not cut out for it, Olivia set me up to try it. The experience was a fiasco.

Back to school. Angel's teacher: Mrs. Buzzard. Crass, juvenile parents -- like me – snickering at the name. Until she stood up from her desk, glared over us with the scowl of a viking, and said "Good evening. I am Helen Buzzard" (BuZZARD: emphasis on zzard).

During her presentation she announced that anyone wanting to be Room Mom should let her know. Olivia elbowed me. I whispered that I am not a mom. She scoffed, raised her hand, and asked about a Room Dad, which Buzzard was quick to adopt as her own idea. My embarrassment only worsened when Olivia volunteered me at the conclusion of the proceeding.

Three other people, all moms, also threw their names in. Which meant an election. Which meant my pride was at stake. So I launched a campaign.

I spread a rumor that one of the moms had been fired from a daycare center because she talked about her sex life in front of the children. Loud enough to be heard by many, I asked another when she and her husband had left the Communist Party. And I made it known that, unlike *some* parents who want to be Room Mom, *I* took *my* daughter to Forksville Fantasyland. My tactics worked; my competitors withdrew, and I became Room Dad.

I commenced my administration by broaching with Buzzard some ideas I came up with for enhancing the children's first grade experience. I even prepared a memorandum and a power point presentation. She indulged me briefly and said she would look at what I had done.

But when I asked how many hours each day I should plan on assisting in the classroom she politely but firmly told me my assistance would not be necessary and that she needed to finish preparing her lesson plan. She added as I indignantly exited that the room parent's customary duties fall more into the area of fund raising for supplies and the like.

Olivia noted that one of the fund-raising methods she had heard about was to convince local restaurants to host a night for the classroom and donate some portion of the proceeds. This seemed to be more up my alley. So I went after it. I set out to visit every place that offered food within five miles of the school until I found one that would do it. I scored on my fourth try.

The Penguin Club. Perfect name. Owner Frank Valentino was only too happy to help. He was pretty sure one of his little cousins went to the school. But he asked if I was sure his joint would be appropriate and confirmed that the customers would all be adults.

Since I wanted to set this up all on my own I did not mention to Olivia which establishment would host the fund-raiser. Neither she nor anyone associated with the school learned that information until I had arranged the date, paid Frank the deposit he wanted, and printed up some sharp flyers, which I posted around the school and left in the teachers' boxes for their students to take home.

Boy was I excited when Angel brought hers home and showed Olivia. I knew they both would be so proud of me.

At virtually the same moment that I saw Olivia's shocked expression the phone rang, the first of one call after another that night. She stared at me, inquiring, incredulous, trying to understand something. Pretty cool, huh? I said.

She just sat on the arm of the sofa and cradled her face in her hands. What's wrong, Mama? Angel said. Nothing sweetheart. Go in your room for a while. I need to talk with Daddy about something.

"The Penguin Club!?" she stammered, fighting to keep her anger quiet. "Do you know anything about this place?" "Seemed like a decent place when I was there." "I guess the strippers were off duty!"

Now I knew I was in it. I would have learned also from the answering machine if the speaker had been turned up. Before it was full the machine recorded eleven calls. Beads of sweat were dripping from it, so enraged were the callers and so seething the messages they left.

Apparently stripping was only one unpopular feature of the club. When she had calmed enough to talk reasonably Olivia told me the owner, Valentino, and the manager, Saul Weisenstein, had been arraigned before her multiple times for promoting, managing, and facilitating prostitution, operating a gambling house, and drug trafficking.

My immediate response was profound shame. As all the circumstances settled in my head, however, I grew defiant. So what if the Penguin Club has strippers and a bad reputation? Did that disqualify it from raising money for school supplies? Anyone in the school community who had a problem with it should just stay home.

The more outrage I encountered the more intransigent I became. I refused to cancel. Even when the principal officially disassociated the school from the event, I announced by flyers surreptitiously posted around the school that, despite a campaign of suppression by the school gestapo, the event would go on as planned. I felt confident the flyers had been widely seen before they were removed by the authorities. I readied for battle against the PTA goons who would try to bust up the festivities.

Then one rainy day shortly before the date with destiny I picked up a very distraught and crying Angel. Throughout the drive home I tried unsuccessfully to learn the cause of her distress. Finally, when I had stopped the car in our driveway, she blurted out "Daddy (not Ufu), why are you working for that club, that Penguin club?' Startled, I told her I certainly was not working for that club. To which she said that all the kids were saying I was.

Now I was ready to explode. My anger intimidated even me. I prepared to march right over to the school the next day and confront those stinking little liars and maybe take a few hostage so I could unload on their parents when they came to pick them up.

But when I announced my plan to Olivia and Angel that night Angel started screaming at me: "No Daddy. Don't do that, Daddy! Please .." It took many minutes for Olivia (not Ufu) to calm her down.

I could not bear my Angel glaring at me with such hate, and I promised over and over that I would not go through with it. At that moment I knew also that there would be no fundraiser at the Penguin Club and that my career as Room Dad was finished.

I open my eyes. The new morning light is just arriving. As I glance around, moving only my head, I find that I am still curled on the floor, but serene quiet has returned to whatever earth spot I occupy.

I am sensing a presence. A powerful presence. I have a deep, breathtaking surge of awe and anxiety about discovering what it is. Its majesty summons me, draws me, until I can no longer avoid looking toward this omnipotence lurking over the wagon and me.

Now I am gazing at the impenetrable blackness of premium sunglasses fixed on the face of a gigantic state trooper. "Are you ok?" he says crisply. Yeah, I think so. "Can you stand and exit the vehicle?" Tumbling out, standing up to face a decal on his lapel.

"I guess you had quite an adventure last night." Do not remember. Now looking around and seeing no mules.

Trying to make him understand that I am on the way to a very important meeting, of a committee of which I am the chairman, that I already have been egregiously delayed, and that any further hinderance will have dire consequences. No I cannot tell him what the committee is or what it does. It's top secret.

So now I am sitting awkwardly in the back of the trooper's car, trying to find a comfortable position for my cuffed hands and listening to the chatter leaking from his radio. Naughty teenagers exceeding speed limit on Rutabaga Road, tossing litter out windows, and playing 1960s anti-war music much too loud. Available units in the area please respond.

7

My relationship with Angel was not the same. A subtle distance now separated us. Maybe it was me. Maybe something changed in me with respect to how I related to her. Or how I related to myself. All that I could say for sure at the time was that I desperately needed to find something to do, something even minimally rewarding, something that had nothing to do with her. The money was not that important, but I did hope to become financially independent from Olivia.

My first inclination was a return to auto sales. Did not seem too difficult to find a spot with some dealership, assuming that the boys back at Del Baxter's would say a good word about me. But this prospect evoked too much negative nostalgia and a sense of settling among the fields I had come out of.

Besides I was no longer the swinging, hustling, sweet talking young man who charged up Del Baxter's the first couple of years. My colleagues might want to hang out at a sports bar after work, maybe take in the Cleveland Browns' coaches' show, and expect me to join the joculation. I would have to say no thanks, I need to get some rest and drink some tea with honey and lemon to sooth my voice.

Many more possibilities crossed my mind: Actuary, concierge, immigration and customs inspector, bocce ball referee, faith healer, gossip columnist. Nothing inspired.

Until one Saturday afternoon I was being dragged through a department store leashed to Olivia and Angel. They fastened me to a plus size mannequin showing large female underwear while they went into a fitting room.

While I was waiting and chewing on my collar I spotted a group of shoppers huddled around a platform in the kitchenware department nearby. As I watched what they were watching I knew I had found my new vocation: Product Demonstrator.

It would be like test drives. Except that I would be driving. I would show consumers what a product could do, instead of hoping that consumers would figure it out for themselves. My job would be to demonstrate that a product is much more than the audience expects and more desirable than any similar product. Perhaps to make the product seem even better than it really is, but without making any false representations about it. I would be a natural.

A few weeks passed before I was given a chance to show what I could do. A regional marketing company set up a mock demonstration and invited me and some others who had contacted them about getting into the business.

The product was an electric egg scrambler. Crack eggs into the top and they were squirted out the bottom and into the pan scrambled. All we had to do was stand on a platform, operate the device, and talk about it to a group of company employees assembled for that purpose.

Each of the other candidates followed the same drill. "See, I'm going to crack this egg (crack) and release the contents into this shaft. Then I will go ahead and press this yellow button, which starts the scrambling. Finally I will place the device over the pan like this and press the blue button, which releases the scrambled egg into the pan." Finishing with a stupid grin: "It's as easy as that."

As the last would-be demonstrator to show his stuff, I added some new elements. First, ladies and gentlemen, I want to emphasize to you the brilliant versatility of this product. Let's say it's late at night and you can't sleep because you're hungry and craving scrambled eggs, but only for a little snack, not to get filled up, and you don't want to create a mess in the kitchen. Perfect solution: Crack just one egg into the sturdy stainless steel receptacle, touch the yellow and then the blue buttons, and out comes a scrambled egg that just needs a few minutes cooking.

Or maybe you have a whole crew of folks wanting breakfast. This handy device will let you scramble up to eight eggs at once. But the really cool special feature about this product is that it allows you to add ingredients to the eggs. For example, how about some ranch dressing or mayonnaise to make them creamier? Or tabasco to spice them up? Hollandaise, sour cream, toothpaste, gun powder – whatever you want.

The executives treated me like a rookie pitcher who has just thrown a 115 mile per hour fast ball. We signed a contract that guaranteed me a decent commission and I was off.

First assignment: Scampy's Office Supply. Product: The Magic Briefcase. A briefcase that comes with a miniature microwave and a miniature refrigerator, both cordless of course, built in to the interior, plus other fun features. Easiest pitch I'll ever have to make, I thought. This thing will sell itself.

However, at Scampy's I learned to appreciate one of the fundamental principles of product demonstration: You cannot sell to people who are not there. There were five or six customers milling around Scampy's when I started. Only two of them came close enough to hear me say "Good afternoon, Folks. How are you today?"

Yet a corollary principle is that you cannot stop demonstrating even if no one is paying attention. I doggedly proceeded with the show. I pulled a tiny can of soda from the mini-fridge and, with my facial expression only, pretended the soda was cold. I microwaved a burrito and fingered it delicately so as not to get burned, even though it was not even warm.

Did not sell a single briefcase that day. But I remained resolute that it could be done in more suitable circumstances and I looked forward to trying again.

My next performance was more successful. New venue, new product. Inside Millstone Mall, on a 50 x 40-foot rug just outside Firearms & Fitness, a combination gun dealer and fitness equipment retailer, where the product would be sold. When the product was explained to me I was astonished at the inventor's genius. The name alone announced a marvelous innovation: Hunting for Fitness.

The basic kit included a heavy padded vest, to be worn by the person wishing to be fit, and a rifle another person would use to shoot rubber bullets at the first. To avoid getting hit the target had to dodge out of the line of fire. The hunted one thus would be compelled to run, stop, jump, roll, whatever was needed to avoid the hunter's bullets. Great fun. And great exercise to boot.

So we set up something like a rifle range, only with various objects placed randomly around the rug that were big enough to conceal a person. Volunteers donned the vest and I shot at them, chased them from behind objects that obstructed a clear shot, and generally pursued them until they gave up, out of breath and physically spent. It was a spectacle that drew onlookers from all over the mall.

Prospective customers asked questions about safety. Did the hunted feel the bullets impacting the vest? What if the hunter missed and hit an unprotected part of the body? In response I cited the well-known phrase "No pain no gain".

Anyone who will not put up with a few lesions, abrasions and other injuries to get fit deserves to be a flabby loser. Firearms & Fitness sold more than 20 units of the product that day.

Most of the products I demonstrated during the few years I spent at that level were not as exotic as Hunting for Fitness. I worked with more than my share of toasters, probably because I could make any toaster appear to be the only one of its kind.

Ladies and gentlemen, please let me show you this amazing toaster and what it can do. Think about this: I put two pieces of bread in it like this, set the timer to maximum, and when they pop up (chopping the crusty product into pieces) just like that I have salad croutons.

The inevitable comment: Can't you do that with any toaster? My response: Can you? Buy another one if you want to find out. But I can promise with confidence what *this* toaster can do.

Many of my demonstrations featured commonly demonstrated products like juicers, food processors, portable grills, and cleaning agents. Some were related, but off-beat, items. Like The Bleeder, similar to a juicer except that it extracted blood from small rodents and reptiles for use as a replacement ingredient in recipes calling for pig, goat, or yak blood. The Bleeder Feeder, a small cylinder in which the animal could be humanely euthanized before being fed into The Bleeder. And The Bleeder Eater, a high potency spray agent for cleaning the inevitable Bleeder spills.

For the duration of my years as a small-time demonstrator Olivia, Angel, and I continued to live as a family, although not so frequently as a close family. As I said before, the romance between me and Olivia had evaporated, but we remained friends and went about our separate lives without rancor. We came together congenially whenever it was for Angel's best interest, attending parent-teacher conferences, birthday celebrations, at least until the age when parents become irrelevant.

However, neither Olivia nor Angel ever once came to see me doing my demonstrating thing. For Olivia I always assumed this was for lack of time, as well as interest. Angel, I am pretty sure, was afraid to be embarrassed.

Whenever I talked about my work in their presence Olivia smiled and nodded and Angel occasionally glanced my way to show she was at least pretending to listen. But they hardly ever asked any questions and if they made a comment it was always something like "I can't believe you actually did that" rather than the "that's pretty cool" I was hoping for.

For a year or so after I started the new career Olivia continued to tell me about her work, sometimes in so much detail as to indicate that I was the only person who truly listened and was interested. After all, I had done my time in the 3rd District. I could relate to the people and events she described. And I did ask questions or made comments, anything to draw her out and help her release all the mental crap she needed to dispose of. Since we continued to sleep – platonically -- in the same bed, for convenience mostly, many of these conversations took place there and became kind of a pre-sleep ritual for us.

Eventually, however, the ritual began to wither. Olivia's need to tell me about her life seemed to diminish, almost imperceptibly at first, but within a couple of months quite noticeably, and by another month dramatically. She still happily answered my questions about specific topics, but did not spontaneously start any accounts of her day.

About that time she also began coming home much later than usual a few times a week. She would always call to let me know and to make sure that I would be there for Angel and to talk with her for a while. Often she explained that she was getting together with her friend Heidi, whom I had met a couple of times in Olivia's chambers at the courthouse. Otherwise she cultivated my assumption that these late nights were related to work.

After a time, however, I became skeptical about this. Yet I was too much focused on my own still new endeavor to confront her or otherwise bring matters to a head. Content to stay the convenient course and avoid any disruptions of my path or Angel's, I waited for Olivia to come out with confirmation of what I expected was a new special person in her life.

I vividly recall the night she did. She actually brought the person home. Introducing me, she said "This is my husband" and to me she said "And this is my lover, Heidi, who I believe you have met."

The two women exhibited almost a rehearsed nonchalance, yet the scene was intensely dramatic. I could not conceal my astonishment, which they obviously expected. But they did not express any need to explain or to satisfy my incredulous curiosity. They just laid out the facts and silently declared that this is the way it is.

To say that this news stunned me is putting it mildly. I did not see it coming. And I was way more distressed than I anticipated or should have been. Not that the other person in Olivia's life was a woman, but the now confirmed reality that there was indeed another person. It was as if a chasm had opened in my life, a giant empty space where a full third of my known world had once been.

Angel, who was not home the night her mother brought Heidi home, learned about the development the next night when Olivia took her out for pizza and girl talk. She was old enough then to understand the situation, and did not display any noticeable change in demeanor or attitude.

This was due in part to the decision Olivia made, and that I accepted, to continue living together with me and Angel for the time being, and not to go for a divorce immediately. We did thereafter have separate bedrooms. Heidi, who had her own domestic entanglements to sort out, did not move in, but did become a very frequent houseguest.

For several months I wrestled with the mysterious fact that Olivia, who had been married twice to men and was once a phenomenal sex partner for me, turned out to have been a closet lesbian. Or maybe she became a lesbian. Or maybe she was always bisexual and finally settled on women. In the wake of her relationship with me. So because of me she became repulsed by men. This thought was a load. It made me doubt my sexuality.

To prove otherwise, and maybe to spite Olivia, I tried too hard to meet and get intimate with other women. Often a nice looking babe would join the audience watching my demonstration. So that is how I started. Before I tended to shrink from mingling with the customers after the show. Now I waded in and tested the water.

Rachel was a pensive looking woman with dark hair tied in a bun behind her head. She appeared at the back of the audience watching me demonstrate a hand-held container for liquids that also could heat them, to be used, for example, for bringing soup to work or making hot chocolate at a football game. I noticed her because her expression did not change the entire time she was there; she did not even smile at my jokes. I guessed that she was in her late 20s.

Quite open to talking, she said the product was interesting, but not something she would use. We chatted about the job of a product demonstrator and I asked if she was in any particular line of work. She was a messenger. Like delivering letters and packages? No, delivering words. *The* word in fact. The word of the most righteous, all powerful, and loving spirit. She was a messenger for one who was a messenger for God, a woman who had been anointed a prophet by living angels, and was now embarked on a truly holy mission to spread *the* word.

Not exactly my first choice for limbering up my sexual skills, but I could not be picky. Besides, I figured, I might turn her life around with the magic of Burlap and Barbed Wire. We went for a cup of coffee.

I should have known better. I sat there for an hour listening to Rachel drone on and on about the Messenger, the leader of the sect or cult she followed, a woman who called herself Hydrogen. Why? Because it is the first element and its weight is one, the lightest element, and the most abundant. Fortunately for purposes of discussion, as well as proselytizing, the Messenger allowed her followers in casual circumstances to refer to her as "H".

H is the most generous, loving, kind, and benevolent person who ever lived, Rachel said. Rachel had personally witnessed H perform miracles. Such as ..? Bringing bright flashes of light from the sky with a loud roar. But ..? Causing a giant flock of birds to suddenly and simultaneously launch themselves from the ground. But ..? Securing a minivan to transport us mini-messengers with nothing but a promise. Ok, well that one ..

H also is brilliant, a genius. She knows all the capital cities. She can do math in her head. She can speak all the languages of the world. Now wait a minute, that is phenomenal. Have you heard her speak a language to someone who understands it? No, why would that matter? To know if she is really speaking the language. I **know** she is. When she speaks Chinese it sounds like Chinese. It's called faith. To be a follower of Hydrogen you must have faith that what she says is the truth.

From this she went on to compare H with me and what I did for a living. When H spoke Rachel knew it was the truth. When I spoke during one of my demonstrations Rachel knew that it is not the truth, or not the whole truth anyway. At that point I knew my design for sex with Rachel was doomed.

Next I tried my luck with a very austere-looking woman who turned out to be quite pleasant and jovial in conversation. She reminded me of a character from The Waltons, like maybe the librarian if they had one. Confirming my hunch, she said she was a third grade teacher.

Teachers have sex. Or so I supposed. This one even let me buy her an ice cream. But when I proposed going somewhere comfortable, where we could get to know each other, she politely declined because her husband, Guido "White Shark" Alvarez, might misunderstand and cut both our throats.

My quixotic quest for sexual fulfillment led me next to Adriana, a Latina legal secretary and student of Portuguese cuisine, hence her interest in the device I was demonstrating for quick removal of salt from dried and salted fish. She was very skeptical of my claim as to how "quick" the process was with the device. But she seemed to understand and appreciate my intention. After confirming that she was not married to any Guido's, we went to a place in the same mall for a drink.

Adriana dreamed of opening a Portuguese restaurant. So we mostly talked about Portuguese food and the restaurant business. She was so cheerful and easy-going, not shy about touching, and laughed at my jokes.

Captivated, I was beginning to feel her warming to me, and I was mentally planning the rest of a memorable night. Then she happened to mention the name of the firm she worked for: Blizzard & Gizzard. It seemed that Lizard had left the firm to start a new one called Lizard & Brown.

So then the subject of my relationship with Judge Holmes came up, and my brief time on the 3rd District bench, and the whole picture appeared too complicated for us to negotiate. I believe she was disappointed. I certainly was. Enough to end my search for a sex partner then and there. I resolved to remain celibate until I died and went to paradise, where I was bound to find satisfaction at last.

The patrol car has stopped, parked in front of some building that does not resemble a law enforcement office or a jail. What gives? I wonder. The radio crackles: "Do you need assistance with your subject?" Trooper glances back at me and responds "No. He's pretty calm."

Calm? Sure I'm calm. I'm handcuffed in the back of your squad car. What else could I be? But maybe I won't be calm for long. Maybe when you let me out of here I will make a run for it. Maybe you will have to shoot me. In the back. I can see the headline: "State Trooper Shoots Chairman of Extraordinary Committee in the Back".

He opens the door and politely asks if I need help to get out. No, don't worry your red neck about it. He is careless and lackadaisical, not even watching me as we shuffle towards the big red doors. My chance. Run you fool. Does not happen.

Trooper pushes a button to the side of the doors. A loud ringing follows and the doors slide open. We pass through. Hey, wait a minute. I was right. This is no police station and no jail. It's a fucking hospital. The suckers approaching us are wearing blue and white hospital uniforms. There are dumb-struck yokels sitting in chairs watching us because we are more interesting than the drivel in the magazines piled on the glass table before them. A god damn waiting room! What the hell am I doing here?

We enter a small room where a hippopotamus disguised as a nurse is waiting. She asks for my name. John Doe. Why am I here? She answers a different question, one I did not ask: "We're here to help you, Mr. Doe." Two monsters appear dressed as orderlies and the trooper says good by, unlocking the cuffs and reattaching them to his belt as he goes.

"Now you're going to help us help you, aren't you," the bloated boar says, "and cooperate with these gentlemen?" No, I'm going to slam my knee into their nuts ... if they have any.

"We were told that you were involved in some pretty dangerous activity last night. Do you remember that?" I do not know what you are talking about. "Maybe you will remember when you have had a chance to rest. These gentlemen will escort you to a bed and a nurse will come soon with something to help you sleep." Fuck sleep. I want to blow this joint. The cuffs are off, so now is the time.

I flinch slightly to initiate the move and feel the solid human wall blocking me in. They drag me from the room, past blues and greens and whites darting around the periphery, voices crisscrossing the ambience carrying incomprehensible words: metahemostatic speculariphan, hydrogenative oximolotine, disfukergonady, kingojewsndatird.

"Sir, can we get you to put on this hospital gown?" I see, the kind that will leave me exposed so you can fuck me in the ass. I do it anyway and lay on the bed before they can throw me. Straps. Guess that's it. Now they can bleed me at will. Until nothing is left.

Nurse Shapely comes with a syringe. Nastily jabs it in my arm. I ask for a kiss. She laughs. Superb white teeth. Just one kiss. Ok, then open your blouse. Let me see those tits. She is gone, and the monsters are standing over me again.

8

Having failed in my weak experiment with meeting women for purposes of proving my virility, I settled back down into mundane life. This meant doing demonstrations three or four times a week, going straight home afterwards, transporting Angel to and from school, guiding her through the boredom of finishing elementary school and the perils awaiting in middle school, and engaging in friendly but insubstantial conversations with Olivia and sometimes Heidi. But I needed something more.

So I decided that what I needed were some male friends. Some buddies. Chums. Bros. To hang out with in the garage. Maybe fire up some barbeque, drink some bud, get in on some poker games. Toss around nicknames, like Shorty or Mack or Big Fella or T-Bone. We could convoy to the ball park and hound the Indians or the Browns after a rowdy afternoon of tailgating.

I did some research on how to hook up with some buddies. The only helpful thing I found was *Finding Buddies for Dummies*. The ambiguous title did not do the work justice.

From it I gleaned the most valuable advice I ever found on the subject: If you live in the typical American middle class neighborhood buddies are all around you. Barbeque in your driveway with a cooler full of beer close to the sidewalk and the ballgame or Lynard Skynard on loudspeaker and they will come.

It worked. Guys from the neighborhood passed by walking the dog or pushing a stroller with the wife and stopped for some macho banter and a brewski. Then after they deposited the dog or the wife at home they would return for some back ribs, more beer, and conversation. Soon I was horsing around with Bronco, Salty Pete, The Professor, and El Greco.

Before I would be a true blue hard core fella, however, I needed a nickname. My new buddies ruminated in closed session, appointed a subcommittee, surveyed each other and chance passers by, all for the purpose of anointing me with a suitable one. All the while I was telling them disingenuously that it was not necessary.

But then the announcement, a triumphant moment in my nascent stint as a real guy. I was a nervous wreck as the moment approached. A good nickname is not an ephemeral thing. It does not blow away in the wind of time. It sticks. My career as a real dude hung in the balance.

The posse made such a big deal out of it that Olivia and Angel came out to watch, though neither of them grasped the significance of the event. We lit the coals, popped open some brews, and The Professor raised his can. "I am pleased to announce that, after due consideration and inquiries of the citizens concerned, we have resolved that henceforth our great friend here shall be known as Hound Dog."

Excited as a gambler scoring a royal flush, a boy given his first bicycle, a supplicant visited by the holy spirit, it seemed like one of the finest moments of my life. Bombarded by back slaps, fist pumps, and general roughhousing, I reveled in the euphoria of acceptance and the prospect of traveling through the rest of my life as the rascal known as Hound Dog. It certainly would be a challenge living up to such an honorific moniker, but I confidently believed that I was up to the task.

Olivia's reaction was one of bemused disapproval, like an anthropologist watching an indigenous tribe perform a barbaric ritual. Angel was supercilious, as only a middle school aged girl can be. She just could not understand why the man she once called Ufu was acting like such a fool.

And so began my season of macho loutishness. I can describe only a few of the good times the crew and I enjoyed. My buddy Angelo (we called him "Jello") fixed up his garage into a real cool hangout spot, complete with a pool table, dart board, projection television that displayed on the back wall, and of course a refrigerator. His wife even made pastries for us once in a while.

My buddy Robert (we called him "Roberto") used his family connections to get us hooked up with discount tickets. So we converged on all the venues and saw all kinds of competition: baseball, basketball, bowling, snake racing, senior ladies mud wrestling, speed painting.

My buddy Sven (we called him – you guessed it – "Swede") hosted sporting activities in his back yard. We shot some hoops and played brutal matches of volleyball, badminton, and croquet. Occasionally tempers flared, requiring a group meditation circle to calm things down.

Not to be outdone, I hosted my share of these get togethers, including the one that proved to be the culmination of this chapter in the story of my life. The atmosphere in our home was a bit less hospitable to the rowdiness and vulgarity that often characterized the crew's interpersonal communications. For example, Olivia got upset one night when she overheard Salty Pete asking me if I ever tried to take her and Heidi as a sandwich and that he would not mind "tapping" either one. So I was compelled to effect some separation between my guests, on the one hand, and Olivia, Angel, and frequently Heidi, on the other.

But normally this was not a problem, because I only invited the guys over when the ladies were not going to be there. My activity of choice was poker. I set up a couple of tables in the living room, stocked up on refreshments, and kept the game going as long as any of them was willing to fork up the one dollar ante. Twice, as I recall, we played until the sunlight came through the front window the next morning.

One Saturday I worked up something special. Olivia and Heidi went off to some Lesbian Luxury Resort for the weekend and Angel had been invited on a short trip with one of her friends. So I spread the word for my usual poker night. But I wanted to surprise the boys with something new.

I came up with the perfect idea. Stopped by The Penguin Club to see my old friend Frank Valentino about arranging for some strippers. He was accommodating. Although he advised me at least twice that for anything "extra", that is, anything more than stripping, there would be additional charges. No problem. Just the basic stripper show.

Nine guys showed up for the festivities. Blazed up the grill and cooked some pork and beef ribs, bratwurst, curlywurst, and shempwurst, snags, tofu dogs, and slim jims. Handed out a variety of craft beers, including Walgreens' Pale Ale, Valvolene Red Stout, and Luigi Light Lager, along with standard brews like Tsingtao, Icelandic Doppelbock, and Colt-45. My playlist included Marshall Tucker, Allman Brothers, Steppenwolf, Motörhead, Hitler Youth Choir, Firing Squad, Peter Paul & Mary, Tom Dick & Harry, Malignant Maulers, Naked Dudes Farming, Dicks & Stoners, and James Taylor.

The host and all his distinguished guests were pretty loaded before I dealt the first hand at 9:00. Yet none of us ever got too drunk to play. Something about the act of taking up and studying the cards, reading the faces reading yours, deciding whether to meet a bet or raise or call, keeps the drunk mind on track. The same person who deftly manipulates his way to a win on just one pair will, if he were to drive home the next minute, surely crash his car and not even remember it.

So long as our focus was on the cards the celebration remained more or less under control. But the irresistible distraction about to appear would blow it up.

At the appointed hour, 11:00, the doorbell rang. I immediately stood up and told my friends that a surprise I arranged had arrived. At the door I found three women wearing lots of makeup and shimmering red, white, and blue dresses. They said they knew this was the place from the loud music. I invited them in and watched with glee as my buddies' mouths hung open and their eyes almost popped from their sockets.

"Holy crap Hound Dog," several stammered at the same time. I remained cool, suave, the maestro, and asked the ladies to introduce themselves. Gina, Milly, and Jeri. Frank did not disappoint. These were three hot girls. At least so they appeared to ten besotted and horny middle-aged hombres ...

Who, when suddenly up close and personal with real, sexy women were not quite sure what to do, other than stare and make visceral noises. Salty Pete, always the most vocal about what he would do with this chic or that, was frightened at the prospect that something sexual might actually happen, that he might actually be put to the test.

However, the girls knew what to do. Telling us to sit in a circle on the floor, they asked me to pick some appropriate music. This was beyond my capabilities. So I read off the titles of what I had until they agreed on "The Washington Post March" by John Philip Sousa.

This gave me a double surprise. First, because I had never thought of the march as stripping music. Second, because I did not even know I had it. And not just any version: This was a classic rendering by the Guantanamo Bay Maximum Security Band.

And it was so perfect for the occasion. The girls marched inside and outside the circle, slowing removing their dresses and laying them over our heads, so that we became entangled with each other and frustrated struggling through the fabric to see these goddesses as they opened their bras and displayed their unbelievably perfect breasts. I mean these breasts were like what Plato had in mind as representing the concept breast. They were so perfect that only a master creator, be he a god or a plastic surgeon, could have produced them.

Once the girls were fully naked the mob followed suit, so that by a bit past midnight there were ten naked men, shit-faced drunk and howling, and three naked women marching through our – Olivia's – home. Totally out of control, we grabbed cans of beer, shook them, and sprayed beer all over ourselves, the women, the furniture, books, wall art, and, when we entered the bedrooms, clothes and bed spreads.

Then it was time for the orgy to begin. Time to get these girls prone and start fucking. They were willing. They even teased us about it. We should have enjoyed hours of carnal pleasure, of wild gratification, of hard core gang-banging. We should have taken from that scene a delicious memory of wicked sexual debauchery to last our lifetimes.

Instead, each member of the wild posse, one by one in quick succession, passed out and crumpled wherever he was at the moment. It was my party; I should have been the last one to go down. Alas, I was one of the first.

The last thing I remember was opening my mouth to suck a nipple. Maybe that incredible delight was too much for my bewildered senses. Maybe my brain short-circuited and shut down from processing too many lurid images. When I came to I was lying on the floor in Olivia's bedroom, naked except for some panties hanging around my neck.

In the midst of struggling to reassemble the components of my mind I heard the most bone-chilling sound ever experienced by humankind. It was kind of a scream that became clogged as it exited the lungs and came out as a guttural shriek of horror. Panicked gasping and crying followed. Olivia had just come home.

Forgetting my condition, I rushed out to explain. But the scene there defied explanation. Or rather explained itself. The hired professionals had left sometime before, presumably wrapped in garments brought by whoever picked them up, because all of their clothing remained scattered throughout the house.

Olivia was a sight that haunts me to this day. She frequently appears in nightmares exactly as I saw her at that moment. I withered in the force of her loathing scowl.

Hence the immediate aftermath of my stag party was too complicated and painful for me to relate in any detail now. It will suffice to note only a couple of consequences.

No longer welcome in the house, I completed an emergency move to a hotel. There I was soon contacted by Carmella Brown of Lizard & Brown. She advised me that Olivia would be filing for dissolution of the marriage, that she would demand full custody of Angel, and that she would pursue a separate proceeding, if necessary, to recover from me the cost of repairing the damage done to her property. Adding to my grief was an enormous bill from Frank Valentino.

It would take more product demonstrations than any demonstrator has ever demonstrated to amass the money I needed just to pay these charges. Yet, even though I was physically sick from wondering whether I would ever see Angel again, desperation is a potent fuel. It powered me through hundreds of products and even onto the next level.

Dr. von Bonderman is here evaluating me. He says they need to know whether I should be transferred to the Plankton Psychiatric Institute and Casino. He is going to ask me some simple questions to test my cognitive faculties.

First question: Who was the first president of the United States? John Hancock. He frowns, says that's incorrect, and pulls out a pad of transfer orders. Ah but it is correct. Hancock was president of Congress under the Articles of Confederation. Von Bonderman does not like to be shown up. He flips open a book with better questions.

Second question: What is the annual median temperature in Christchurch, New Zealand?   Do you mean including every year since recordkeeping began or over a more discreet span such as a particular decade? Book does not provide that clarification, eh? Next.

Third question: How many divisions of infantry did Lieutenant General William Birdwood command during the Gallipoli campaign in World War I? Including the attached Indian Brigade and the ANZAC division that contained some mounted units? Nothing about that either.

So tell you what doctor. How about I ask you some questions. Where is the geometric center of a sweet potato? How many minutes does it take for a potato bug to get there? Who discovered the Butt Crack of Yokohama? What is the chemical formula for talcum powder?

He interrupts me: "Tell me about this committee you mentioned to law enforcement." What about it? "Well, what is the name of it and what is its purpose?" Name and purpose are top secret. "Then how about identifying some of the members?" Nicholas, Mantle, Oppenheimer, Bismarck, Grandpa Jones, Dredd Scott, Lucretia Garfield.

He interrupts me again: "There is something in the information I was given about mules. Can you tell me what that's about?" That's how I was traveling to the meeting we had scheduled for yesterday. 20-mule-team. Ponderous way to go. I do not recommend it if you must be somewhere on time. "Where did you get the mules?" Mule Teams & More. He scribbles on his pad and leaves.

9

Once the dust and the legal actions had settled I was on the hook for an exorbitant sum. Ironically, when Frank Valentino learned that Olivia was suing me he wanted Carmella Brown, her lawyer, to represent him too. My lawyer was excited about the possibility of the Honorable Olivia Holmes and the Prince of Pruriency himself teaming up against me. If that happened, he told me, we could not lose.

My lawyer, by the way, was Travis Small, former member of The Smalls, the only black barbershop quartet to chart two top 40 songs on the Billboard Miscellaneous Genre rankings. His brother and two cousins, who made up the rest of the group, also became professional men after its demise. One became a mortician, another a horticulturalist, and one, Travis' brother, a producer of Rastafarian Christian music.

I first met Travis when the shit was coming down and I knew I was going to need legal representation. I could not stomach most of the attorneys I knew of from my 3rd District days, so I looked around for someone new and discovered The Small Law Firm.

Travis turned out to be one of the truest dudes I ever met. Unlike virtually every other lawyer in America, he was not a poser. What he lacked in legal training – The Geico School of Law Isn't Rocket Science – he more than made up for with natural wisdom and experience.

The Olivia and Frank alliance did not happen. Apparently Frank made the mistake of threatening to sue her if she did not agree, claiming that she was liable for the professional charges as my wife and for the emotional distress suffered by his girls in her home. Poor Frank – he probably did not know of any other way to negotiate a deal.

So when we could not agree on a resolution without going to court Carmella Brown started two proceedings against me. Frank's lawyer – Tony Fabrizio, of Curly, Fabrizio & Taft – filed a third.

Travis advised me that I could file a counter-suit against Frank and the three women for inciting my buddies and I to act like dumbasses. He said we also could cross-complain against the other nine delinquents who contributed to cause the damage. I said no to both.

I could not dispute that I was responsible. But not having the financial means to pay the inflated amounts both my adversaries demanded, I told Travis to defend as vigorously as he could in hopes that we could reach a reasonable settlement with terms that would allow me time to raise the money.

All three cases were assigned to Judge Goliath, from the 1st District, who was specially appointed because a 3rd District judge was one of the parties to the first two and might have some connection to the third.

The first conference we had with the judge did not bode well for me. Technically there were two conferences in succession, one for Olivia's two matters and one for Frank's. As I was the defendant in all three Travis and I had to be present for both.

Naturally the judge knew Olivia, since they were members of the same judicial community. But the deference he patently bestowed on her was almost shocking. He treated her as if apologizing for the lawsuit she was forced to be involved with. Telling her and Carmella Brown, with an annoyed head nod in my direction: "We'll try to get this unfortunate business taken care of expeditiously. I know you both have better things to do."

I wanted Travis to jump up and object, to roundly castigate the judge for such an exhibition of bias, to ask what about he and his client, we didn't have better things to do? Instead Travis wisely sat quiet and stoical as Goliath finished licking Olivia's heels and ordered that we go through a mediation before anything else happens.

The farce continued when the Frank and Tony show opened. Turned out the judge knew both of them, apparently very well. He waited until the two women had exited the courtroom. Then: "Good morning Frank. How's that bursitis? Think you'll be back swinging that seven iron soon? Tony here can drive the ball, but his approach stuff can't match yours." Now I knew I was going to get screwed. Travis knew too. But there was nothing either of us could do.

Goliath ordered a separate mediation for that case, noting, however, that he did not believe two different mediators were necessary, and that he would be "suggesting" someone. His final travesty was warning Travis and me, but not the other side, that he would be receiving a report from the mediator after the two proceedings were completed.

The mediation was another memorable experience.   Goliath's "suggested" mediator was a woman who called herself Flowering Stone. She ran a center for conflict resolution called Peace Through Blessed Understanding. The center's home was a rustic wood structure that used to be a dance hall, transformed only by the addition of an indoor herb garden, carpets, floor cushions, and a portrait of the Dalai Llama wearing a Nirvana t-shirt.

Flowering Stone greeted me and Travis and led us to one end of a long room that must have been the dance floor. There she told us to remove our shoes, sit on the floor cushions, and remain quiet – no talking or whispering – until she returned. Shortly after I saw her do the same with Olivia and her lawyer when they arrived.

She then instructed each party again to stay quiet and this time to practice breathing exercises that she demonstrated. The purpose of this, she explained, was to dissipate as much anxiety and hostility as possible before discussing the issues and demands and all that. While we were "breathing" wood flute music floated in from somewhere and the scent of rosemary and lavender wafted around us.

When Flowering Stone next came to us she started talking about Judge Goliath: what a nice man he was, how supportive of her work, and how eager to try some of the new methods she had devised to further mutual understanding. I asked her for an example. She thought for a moment, then said that she and the judge had enjoyed their experiences with psilocybin mushrooms. Travis and I simultaneously raised our eyebrows. What did she say?

I asked if she could think of any other enlightening methods she had shared with Goliath. Only slightly embarrassed, and with sincere pride, she said "Best not to mention this outside of this place, but the sex has enabled us to reach some marvelous milestones." You and the judge? Now her face colored pink and she nodded bashfully.

The mediation took on a new light after these revelations. Travis managed to take Carmella Brown aside during a pause in the proceeding and casually spilled the beans. When Brown relayed the information to her Olivia knew the stakes had escalated. Now she could be partially responsible for humiliating a respected senior judge, whose 55-year marriage and popular family were models to the community. Avoiding any part of that was a hell of a good reason to settle for virtually anything I offered.

Which was not that unreasonable. Like I said, I mostly wanted terms that would at least give me a chance to resurrect my life, and God willing, my relationship with Angel. So Travis and Carmella, with little help from the Flowering Stoner, worked things out and we settled both cases. I got the installment agreement I needed, Olivia got Angel, and I at least was awarded supervised visits.

Not having a similar motivation, nor an enlightened view of blessed understanding, Frank and Tony bolted the mediation for their case as soon as they were told to sit on the floor. I'd rather eat a plate of rancid rigatoni, Frank shouted on his way out.

Notwithstanding their links link, Goliath was not happy that Frank abused the Flower. Apparently he let it be known that, unless Frank accepted whatever I could afford, he would toss out the case, close down The Penguin Club for violations of City of Glenn's Penal Code sections 2.108, 109, and 3.201 through 230, and throw Frank's mama in the slammer as an accessory. The deal was done. My legal battles were over. Now I just had to come up with a shitload of cash.

To be in demand for product demonstrations as often as possible I had to elevate my game. Yes, I already was among the best. To squash the competition, however, I needed to constantly improve. One of the means for doing that was to hone my skill as a performer.

So I enrolled in an adult education acting class at El Chapo Community College. Taught by a 70-something woman whose claim to acting fame was an occasional part as a young girl scout on *Three's Company*. She filled a portion of every class with stories about what Suzanne Somers and Joyce Dewitt were really like and how John Ritter was a complete asshole.

At the first meeting we had to stand and deliver a brief statement about why we were taking the class and what we hoped to get from it. There were only eight students: me, another guy, and six excited women. But by the time everyone had delivered this "brief" statement one of the two hours scheduled for the class had passed.

Four of the women went on and on and on. Always wanted to act, but never got the chance. Told many times I would be a good actor. Played Rheba in *You Can't Take It with You* in high school to rave reviews and I should have made something of that, but with one thing and another time goes by and I was not able to let my thespian self emerge. The gentleman was not much briefer. No one in the class was honest enough to say they were taking the class because they loved to hear themselves talk.

When my turn came I wanted to say "I dunno". And sit down. Instead I lied and said I would be auditioning for a home security commercial in a couple of months, so I was hoping to learn something about acting.

The most valuable aspect of the class for me was the improvisation sessions. The teacher would pass around a box containing the names of well-known persons. Each student drew a name and then had to be that person for five minutes. My first: Jack the Ripper. I also got Jimmy Hoffa and Paula Deen.

Jack was the easiest. I simply drew my finger across two of the ladies' necks and told them I would slash deep into their throats, mutilate their faces and abdominal and genital-areas, and remove some organs for my collection. Not necessarily in that order. The other students were horrified by the genuineness of my blood lust. But I was only surrendering to my character.

For Hoffa I repeatedly called out plaintively "here I am". Did not get any laughs. Tough crowd.

Paula Deen was a challenge. I understood that she was once a celebrity cook, whose fifteen minutes of fame expired early when she was discovered to be a rabid white supremacist and matron of the neo-Nazis and that she advocated deporting every African American to Tasmania except those with signed professional sports or recording contracts.

How do you ad lib a person like that? All I could come up with was: "Sure I used to call nig — I mean African Americans -- that n-word. But everybody down south here did back then when them nig — I mean African Americans -- wasn't so proud."

Anyway, the class taught me one very precious skill that would be crucial to my career: How to surrender myself to a product, rather to a person who sincerely believes in the product and is devoted to getting it in hands that can use it.

Many product presenters will attempt to identify themselves with the product merely by saying "I have one just like it at home and I love it!" His audience, however, does not believe him. They assume that if indeed he has one at home it is only because the sponsor provided it and paid the presenter to "love it".

My art became much more refined. I never said I have one at home. Because normally the product was not designed for someone like me. Example: a toilet bowl brush that also dispenses the cleaning fluid. I never came off as a guy who ever in his life has cleaned a toilet, much less loved doing it.

Instead I talked about the researchers and developers at the company that made the product, working folks who knew what a challenge it is for those who must keep the home spaces clean, and how they had labored to create a product that would make the job easier for those who do have to clean toilets. I told the audience that I had talked with these workers, discovered the faith they had in the product they came up with, and how they hoped I could show people how good it is.

Now, ladies and gentlemen, I hope you will understand that demonstrating a product like this requires a pretty disgusting prop. So I know you will forgive me for showing this gross toilet bowl, which you can see reflected by the overhead mirror. We will now see what the Zephyr Home Products TTC109 can do even when used by someone – me -- who has never cleaned a toilet.

I did pretty well. With the toilet and selling the product.

So for a little more than a year I did nothing but work. I took every demonstration offered. When not doing one I studied as much product information as I could get my hands on. If I had not been assigned a specific product I created conceptual categories of products and studied each product in each of the categories. I watched a thousand or more videos, anything that was remotely related to pitching a product or itself pitching a product.

During that year I must have done 300 demonstrations, improving my game with every one. I even developed sort of a following, at least among people who were frequent visitors of the stores I performed in. Many of these people, if they heard that I would be doing my thing in a particular store, would make it a point to be there.

My results, in terms of units sold, consistently improved as well, although that of course depended on the product. Some products were more large ticket and required more investment that did a toilet brush.

Power tools are a good example, especially those that are less portable. When I demonstrated how the Revlon PPX11 Cordless 7-1/4 inch Rear Handle Circular Saw could slice up a pile of 4 x 4s in the time it took to grill a T-bone steak, with only minor loss of finger tissue or blood, I did not expect a flurry of on the spot sales.

Probably the climax of my development as a demonstrator occurred when I had three different grills cooking meat at the same time that I used various power tools to saw, rip, cross-cut, drill, and plane every type of building material my host home improvement store carried. I became a product demonstrating legend, at least within my home region.

Yet after meeting the monthly obligations set by the settlement agreements I had barely enough left to live on. My prospects, however, were about to brighten.

I have been informed that the medical authorities are transferring me to Plankton. Nurse Shapely is here again, stabbing my arm with soothing and delicious chemicals guaranteed to purge fantastic, out-of-control thoughts from my mind, to be replaced only by those that most closely replicate reality as defined by the International Commission on Uniform Standards of Reality.

A blue-skinned lizard is pushing me in a squeaky wheelchair along corridors of undulating linoleum, out through the double service doors to the loading dock where a mechanical whale on wheels waits with its mouth open. The wheelchair accelerates across the dock and stops abruptly. I am launched into the mouth and onto the whale's tongue. He closes his jaw and we are in motion.

10

One afternoon, while I was demonstrating a panini maker, I noticed a woman standing at the back of my audience, apparently watching with admiration. She looked a bit like a young Kathy Gifford – very professionally attired in a dark blue dress. The most noticeable aspect of her presence to me was that she laughed at my jokes.

At the conclusion of my program she came forward to introduce herself. Jill Taylor was her name. Her card indicated that she worked for some kind of talent agency. She had heard about me and came to see if I was for real. And ...? I said. "I am convinced", she responded laughing. She took me for coffee.

Jill Taylor was a talent agent and she wanted to represent me. I did not believe her. Product demonstrators do not have agents. The extraordinary ones do, she said. Then she outlined the plan.

I would be on a short list of superstar demonstrators who are sought after to present products in regional markets around the country. So I might be hired to do a program in, say, Houston. My travel and expenses would be paid and I would receive a much higher fee than I had up until then, plus commission from sales revenue and possibly a discretionary bonus if I generated enough interest in the product regardless of how many units were purchased at the show. Jill also would place me at trade shows, conventions, and fairs. Ultimately, she teased, I could have a chance for television work.

Needless to say for someone clawing his way out of debt hell, I was blown away. I wanted to embrace her, snuggle up into her neck, kiss her ankles and lick her heels. She was a moderately attractive, late 30's early 40's woman, but decidedly not my type. At that moment, however, I would have made ravenous love to her and become her sexual slave.

So I set forth on my new life as a roving product demonstrator. It was not glamorous. The locations I visited initially were not prime destinations. Swayze, Texas; Sparky, South Dakota; Iketown, Kansas.

And the agency did not book me for swanky hotels. Instead of a minibar, HD television, body revitalizing lotions and creams, and room service, the rooms

I stayed in featured complementary packets of powdered Dr. Pepper, black and white mechanical televisions, bottles of all-purpose liquid chemicals, and the number for a local pizza joint that delivered if the credit check came back clean.

But I loved it. For one thing, I was able to escape the constant reminders of what I had lost, which seemed ubiquitous in my home area. Another feature I relished was the challenge of constantly connecting with new and different types of people, not only while live before an audience, but even in the countless casual interactions that fill an itinerant sales person's day.

Some people were exceptionally difficult to reach. During one three-hour flight across the Midwest I was sandwiched between a shriveled old lady on her way to see her grandchildren and a burly chiseled gentleman wearing a dark gray silk suit, a starched white shirt with turquoise cufflinks, and a red and black silk tie. He also had large jeweled rings on three of his fingers.

The lady was easy. I only had to ask for pictures of her ugly grandchildren and she was ready to tell me all about them. Jimmy wanted to be a chimney sweep and had to be regularly rescued by the fire department when he became stuck in the chimney. I asked if anyone had thought about lighting a fire in the fireplace while the kid was in the chimney, to teach him what common sense obviously had not. She admonished me silently for my naughtiness. Her 13-year-old granddaughter Helen was already interested in boys and wanted everyone to call her Lolita.

The gentleman, however, was difficult. Taciturn to the max, he did not utter a word for the first hour. I fell back on the principle that sometimes the best way to make a good impression on someone is to leave them alone.

Finally I told him his cufflinks were extraordinary. He looked like he was going to punch me. Then said "thanks". A few minutes later he told me his daughter made them. Talented, I replied. He nodded in appreciation.

No dialogue for the next 20 minutes or so. I tried again: "Does she make them to sell or just a hobby?" Again he seemed ready to clock me. Instead he fished out his elegant wallet and gave me her card. Angie Donovan – Crafter of Southwestern Jewelry. Keep it, he said.

Fifteen minutes later he offered an enormous hand and said "Roy Donovan". The hand enveloped my relatively puny one like a man shaking a boy's hand. "Business trip?" he said. Which opened the squawk box. I explained my line of work in some detail, relying on another principle: Someone who says nothing in response to a soliloquy may very well be listening with interest. When I finished he nodded that he understood me.

Now I could ask the same of him. More concisely than I ever thought possible, he explained that he headed a private security firm and was on his way to investigate a little incident involving one of his clients. He added that he had been a police officer for ten years and a detective for fifteen.

Keen as I was to inquire about the incident with his client, I kept my mouth shut and asked granny for more family anecdotes. Of course she had overheard my conversation with Roy. So she told me, loudly enough for him to hear, that her grandson Blake was in prison for armed robbery.

It seemed he and a pal had held up an all-night donut shop. They got sixty-five dollars and two dozen assorted glazed, powdered, chocolate, and iced, of which they had consumed only three before they were caught. My response: I suppose the police impounded the rest as evidence that somehow never made it to court. Roy laughed; he did not want to, but he did.

During the remaining minutes of the flight Roy occasionally supplied hints about the nature of the incident he was going to investigate. I had the impression that he would have trusted me with more information, but did not want to share it with granny. The hints included that the incident was similar to a kidnapping, that official law enforcement was not involved, and that no one had been hurt – so far.

After we landed and parted I felt that Roy and I had become friends and that if we met again sometime he would be glad to see me. So I accomplished my goal. I succeeded too well with granny. She invited me to dinner at her son's house and suggested that we could do "something nasty" afterwards. I politely declined.

About a week later I saw a news item about a man named Roy Donovan being arrested for assault and battery. Apparently he was working for an unidentified celebrity whose pet zebra, Zimmy, had been stolen by a brazen gang of animal activists. Donovan found the gang's hideout on a communal farm located near an abandoned grain silo.

When three of them tried to stop him from rescuing Zimmy he beat them with a crowbar, causing multiple fractures and left with Zimmy before the police arrived. Since the police obviously knew where Roy was going with the zebra they apprehended him without incident at the client's residence. To think that I had reached such a man gave me great satisfaction.

The first shows I did outside my home territory were not very successful. One reason is because I was starting from scratch with respect to any following I might have had. Having at least a few fans always helped to get the program rolling; more would inevitably show up just to see what was going on.

Another element that I encountered at this new level was the difference in personalities that tended to characterize some regions of the country. A group of potential customers in Youngstown was not the same as a group in Natchez, Mississippi.

What did I do to deal with this? Nothing. I ignored it. I just did my thing. Because even though one person be a cosmopolitan homosexual atheist who believes that American-style football is not true "futebol" and another person be a God-fearing provincial redneck who believes soccer is not even a real sport, both would judge my product by the same standards: 1. Does it work? 2. Will it be useful to her or someone she knows?

My job was to satisfy the first standard by demonstrating the product live and passing on my own confidence in it. To satisfy the second standard I pointed out as many uses of the product as I could imagine, hoping that each customer would acknowledge at least one as relevant to him or her or an acquaintance. This dynamic was the same wherever I went.

The typical course of an assignment in those days was as follows: Jill Taylor would notify me that the Cronkite Cooking Company wanted someone to demonstrate its Portable Potato Peeler at Hank's Home Helpers in Holbrook. Technically I had the option to decline the assignment, but I never did, so she stopped asking and just provided the details of when, where, etc. Someone else at the agency would then contact me with details of the travel arrangements.

Through the days leading up to the program I would study everything I could get my hands on about the Cronkite peeler, as well as all competing peelers, the techniques of manual peeling, and the history of potato peeling and potato cuisine. In addition, of course, I would acquire every peeler on the market, including Cronkite's, and practice with them until I mastered the art and learned how Cronkite's was superior to the rest.

I never failed to find something my product did better than the others. Then I would try to convince people that this something was the most important something about that type of product.

The program itself I would plan only a day or so beforehand. It was important for it to be fresh and to leave plenty of room for ad libs and for handling unexpected events. The show usually took place on a raised platform of some kind, brightly lit. I would have a wireless microphone pinned to my collar.

For the potato peeler demonstration I might open the presentation standing behind a twenty pound bag of potatoes, holding a manual peeler, and grimacing at the work ahead of me. I might draw attention by such cracks as "Anyone want to watch me peel potatoes? Too much excitement for a Saturday afternoon?"

Then, by attempting to use the manual peeler I would exhibit the toil, the struggle, the frustration of manually peeling potatoes. A nick and a little blood would be helpful. "I have to make mashed potatoes for the entire North Southwest Atlantic Pacific University football team, the Fighting Flea Beetles. My wrists are sore already."

When I judged there to be enough of an audience, I might mimic the demonstrator stereotype and come out with the cliché everyone is expecting: "Gosh, I wish there was a better way". The actual demonstration would then begin.

The trade shows, fairs, and conventions were a different scene. A lot more work for fewer immediate results. Because for one of these events I had to perform multiple times each day. There also were competitors. Whereas normally I had the shopping throng to myself, at one of these monster affairs product demonstrators were everywhere.

Although a bit intimidated at first, in time I held my own and rose above by faithfully following my basic formula of leaving everyone who talked with me, including other demonstrators, glad that they did. A corollary to this was providing a show that the audience would recall with pleasure, whether or not they purchased the product or ever intended to.

Crucial to this objective was to distinguish myself visually, by my livery, if you will. I had a silver silk jacket custom designed to supply prospective customers with extra incentive to gather around my corner of the event. Bright red sequins formed a heart on the back. Along the lapels and down the sleeves were strings of fairy lights, each flashing different and brighter colors until culminating in strings of gold lights around the cuffs. Along with the coat was the dramatic ritual of putting it on, which came to signify that I was about to perform.

The point was to draw attention. So that an attendee who could not care less about whatever product I was pitching nevertheless would saunter over to see what I was going to do. If they enjoyed my presentation, were charmed by my personality, and convinced that I was sincere and genuine, selling them on the product was much easier.

Occasionally I ran into some local jokers who tried to ridicule me. One young would-be cowpoke wearing an "I Came for the Custard Cowpie" T-shirt shouted "that coat is creepy" at me during my demonstration of a device that made bologna from chicken gizzards, adding "and you're creepy .. pervert".

Since the crowd heard him and turned to look, thus interrupting my flow, I had to respond. "Like what ya see, eh big fella? I guess it takes one to know one. Wait until I tell your boy friend." Instead of charging forward to beat the crap out of me, which seemed his initial inclination, he disappeared in the passing crowd, probably intending to assault me later in the parking lot. Must have changed his mind because I never saw him again.

Thus another absolutely essential attribute a person needs if he is going to put himself "out there" like I did is to be fearless. Or, more accurately, to have what it takes to conceal fear – to *act* fearless.

In my case it was easier than in a lot of others. Because I did not care. My circumstances remained desperate. I still owed a bunch of money. And I still did not get to participate in Angel's life in any meaningful way. So what if some clown beat the crap out of me. As long as he killed me anyway, I would be debt free. If he just put me in the hospital or left me disabled that might be more problematic, but I was too fatalistic to worry about that.

I was put to the test a couple of times. Jill contacted me once to see if I would take a job demonstrating a chicken fryer at a hardware store in the heart of a predominantly black section of St. Louis. She said she preferred to send the lone African-American demonstrator she represented since the population might resent a white man coming to sell them a chicken fryer, but he had another engagement. I said yes.

While 99 percent of my audience was interested in the product a heck of a lot more than the white guy selling it, there were two gentlemen who took exception to what they called my privileged, patronizing attitude. I told them I was not too patronizing or too privileged to fight them both for insulting my respect for all peoples of the world.

If it had come to that, I am sure they could have mangled me into an unrecognizable condition. But I meant what I said. Maybe not about fighting necessarily, though certainly about my indignant anger at their utterly unfounded accusation.

Anyway, apparently they believed me, my principles I mean, and afterwards even apologized. Which led into a friendly discussion about The Smalls, Richard Nixon, and, of all things, the potential for developing plant-based alternatives to ground beef.

Some weeks after that episode I experienced one that I was truly lucky to survive. It was in Southern California, an LA suburb I believe. A mall. A platform set up in the common area. The product: Another weight loss gadget. El Suave's Fat Food Processor. Designed to separate out the fat from foods before they are cooked.

I did my usual thing. Donned the coat. Dazzled the gathering spectators. Especially three dark-haired young Latinas. They watched my every move, laughed at my jokes, and seemed to be having a fun time. When I was done they each bought the product.

Then, as I was crossing the parking lot to my rented car, this fellow stepped in front of me to block my way and several others joined him to surround me. This guy had trouble on his mind. Turned out one of the Latinas was his girl friend. He did not like the way I "flirted" with her. He needed to "teach me a lesson".

For a split second I considered attacking first, grabbing the element of surprise, but common sense restrained me. Instead I yammered the following at him, confident, without *showing* my fear: "If you think I was flirting with her, man, you were not paying attention. I don't know which one is your girl friend. It doesn't matter, because I was flirting with the honey behind them, the tall blonde, with big tits and a shirt that said 'These are fake. My real ones are at home'." Some of his posse chuckled at this, so I felt I had a chance.

"You didn't see her? Man, maybe you didn't have the right angle. And I'm up on a little platform, so I can see everybody. In fact, I am pretty sure I saw you, at the back, and I saw those other girls back there looking at you and I was thinking I wish I was that guy to have those babes lusting for me." Now he was embarrassed and his chums were pushing and teasing him. Threat averted. Apology accepted. See ya next time.

I have been sleeping and not sleeping in this vehicle now for some immeasurable time. Sometimes it seems like I just woke up, so that I must have been sleeping, but I do not remember going to sleep or waking up. My body has tuned itself to the myriad of knocking, whining, and grating sounds the ancient transport makes as we clatter over ragged streets at what feels to me like very high speed.

Supposedly we are on the way to Plankton. Yet I have no idea where we are and no way to tell if the driver is not just looking for a deserted spot where he can strangle me and take my cash.

I should escape. Open the door and launch myself into whatever is out there. But this drug .. I cannot even move my hands. I am not sure that I still have hands. Good god, they hacked off my hands! Why would they do that? Did you see that dude's hands? Weirdest hands I ever saw. I gotta take them. I can hang 'em from the mirror in my car. That rubber chicken is done.

We've been hit! A window shatters. I am thrust forward head first into a barrier, then flipped onto the floor to the sound of grinding crunching metal. The van is careening sideways. Hit again. Another car slams into the right side which buckles inward upon me, striking and pinning me between sections of metal and fiberglass.

After one screeching, sickening spin the vehicle stops. Silence. Someone, maybe the driver, calls to me: Am I ok? I cannot answer. The drug and the trauma have paralyzed me. Although I am still conscious, I can do nothing but exist and wait for the pain.

Urgent voices and the echoes of commotion filter through the wreckage. Sharp bursts of pain puncture the profound numbness, mostly my right side. Now other voices are shouting into the cage. Sirens coming up behind it all.

I want to give up, to quit the struggle, to sleep. Now I can hear metal being wrestled. I can feel the cage shudder. They are trying to get to me. I must hold on. But I cannot.

11

Jill Taylor had told me that eventually I might get some television work. It finally happened. A local morning show called something like "Morons in the Morning" or "The Moronic Morning Show" airing on KYKY, a cable station broadcasting out of Shithole, a microdot on the map of Iowa.

The show was the station's only live content. The rest of its 16-hour daily schedule consisted of movies and documentaries it could air for free. These included, during my preview of the lineup, "My Day in Des Moines", "The Gunfighter's Lullaby", and "Corn Dogs", which, incidentally, was about dogs trained to harvest corn, not the deep fried wiener on a stick. The station also aired a syndicated farm report taped in 1962 with only the current weather conditions dubbed in, the same infomercial five times a day, featuring Victoria Principal and a mysterious French doctor she had discovered in Tahiti experimenting with herbal creams that could whiten the natives' skin, and the same commercials for local businesses that had been running for twenty years, long after some of them had closed.

Every minute that did not have programming scheduled was patched with a public service announcement. Viewers of KYKY thus could count on being repeatedly warned not to drink Dichloromethane or listen to any of those rare programs where Lawrence Welk touts the benefits of smoking crack with a glass of champagne.

I was booked for a ten minute segment in which I would appear alongside Mindi Müller, one of the two hosts, to demonstrate a device that could convert almost any fruit or vegetable into a paste suitable for spreading on toast or for use as a dip. Although only a recent graduate of the Danny Bonaduce School of Broadcast Journalism, Mindi was a superb television news and talk show personality. She was articulate, very attractive, and quick thinking. It was plain to me that she would not remain at that back water station for long.

Her co-host, on the other hand, was a complete dufus. Perry Pendleton had played quarterback for the Polk County College Polkers. As a senior he led them to the Division IX Central Iowa Regional Semifinals, where they were trounced by the St. Butkus College Profiteers 38 to 7. The Polkers' only score came on Pendleton's 23-yard pass with 50 seconds to play and the Profiteers' fourth string team on the field. Yet this "glory" seemed to sustain his extraordinarily and ill-disguised vanity.

He was a hunk, I will say that. About six foot three inches, maybe 210 pounds of designer muscle, which he spent hours every day at Krusty's Gym to maintain, his flat-top hair modified for hipness and died yellow, Pendleton was on the air because, after all, television is a visual medium.

I relate this information about Pendleton because, while Mindi hosted my segment, he came to be a part of it, fortunately or not depending on how much one likes to see conceit toyed with. He introduced our segment and the station's lone camera swung over to show Mindi and I behind a counter with the Magic Paste Producer in front of us next to a tray containing an assortment of fruits and vegetables. My role in the bit was reduced from my usual dominance because it was Mindi's show and she sparkled.

So I put the device through its paces, dropping in carrots, apples, strawberries, zucchini. Some of the product I spread on bread so she could taste it and pretend that it was delicious.

During the segment I mentioned a fact that I could not verify, an old wives' tale I suppose: Beet paste is an excellent hair dye. Intrigued, Mindi asked if I had any beets. I did not. So she asked the producer if someone could get some. Five minutes later, after a couple of PSAs, we were back on air with fresh beets. I had no idea what she had in mind, but I duly dropped them into the device and soon had a bowl of beet paste.

Then she asked Pendleton to come for the close of the segment. He swaggered over, smiling indulgently for the camera. Mindi: "Perry, we've got some stuff here that apparently has magic properties. We want to test it to see if it works. You don't mind helping out, do you?" She asked him to bend down, ostensibly to examine the paste. When his head was low enough she took a big gob of the stuff and spread it through his hair.

He lost it. "What are you doing?" he shrieked. Grabbing at his hair like it was on fire, he glared at Mindi and said, live and on air, "You bitch!", before starting to cry and running off the set. She clearly was startled by his action, but kept cool and signed off with a mischievous smirk. That was my television debut.

I did not stick around to see how the drama played out. Later, however, I learned from Mindi herself, when our paths crossed again, that, not surprisingly, she was the one who got fired, while Pendleton remained at KYKY and, the last she knew, was still there. Meanwhile, partially due to the "great TV" she engineered that day, she was offered jobs in larger markets and continued to rise. Yet I was disappointed that she could not answer my most pressing question: Did the beet paste work?

That first taste of television work whet my appetite for more. I created a mock studio in the apartment I was living in by then, a two-bedroom unit in a huge complex, cheap enough so that I could afford it and still make payments to Olivia. Valentino was finally paid up, thanks be to God. Rigging up some bright lights to face, I practiced surrendering myself to the role of TV pitchman.

I continued to live in the same general area as Angel and her mother, close enough that I could have been at her front door within 45 minutes if she had ever asked me to come. In the second year of high school, she had told me during one of our periodic visits that she very much wanted to attend a college as far away as possible.

At the next visit, however, she disclosed that there was a boy in her life, so she was no longer sure about college. The boy played the drums with three of his friends in a band they called The Stink. When I asked what kind of music they played she refused to describe it because there was "no way" I would understand.

How was her mother? The same. You know, Mom is Mom. Still with Heidi? Yes, although they've been fighting more recently. Is that a problem for you? Not really. I got used to Mom's moods a long time ago. Has she met your boyfriend? He's not my boyfriend, Dad. Just a special friend. And no she hasn't.

Towards the end of the visit Angel asked how I was doing. I began an account of my recent experiences before realizing that she really was not interested. It hurt. But, as Ken said, that's the way it is.

The next time I saw her she referred to "the boy" as her boyfriend Odie. I asked what she wanted for her birthday. She said a guitar. Lessons too? Oh Dad, that would be awesome! So I arranged to have the best acoustic guitar I could afford sent to her and for a series of ten lessons to be available from a local teacher. If only I could have been there when the guitar arrived. But I was growing weary of always feeling sorry for myself.

So in addition to six or seven live demonstrations a week, Jill booked me for one or two TV spots. On weeks when there was a fair or convention I would almost pass the limit of what can be done by one man. Once the television work was rolling I hardly ever slept in my own bed. At least the accommodations improved. Real shampoo and conditioner. Mini-bottles of Gordon's gin. Room service offering canned soup and hot dogs.

Since I almost never went out after I got back to the hotel following a show I did not need to pack many extra clothes, so packing was not much of a chore for me. Actually I rarely unpacked. I just fished out a pair of socks and some underwear and with my livery, if you will, in a separate garment bag, I was good to go.

For an afternoon or evening show I could fly in the morning before, kick back briefly in the hotel room before heading out to the venue, kick back some more when I returned, and fly out the next morning. "Kick back" for me after a show mostly meant drinking a beer or sometimes gin or vodka and tonic, eating whatever tempted me from the vending machine or room service – sauerkraut burrito, sea sponge sandwich, deep-fried unidentified food item – and watching television.

Never very selective about the programs I saw, I would change channels until something caught my attention, then leave the TV tuned to that channel until I fell asleep. I recall tuning in to watch halfway through an episode of *Gunsmoke*: Miss Kitty having kicked Doc out of the Long Branch for getting drunk and exposing himself right when the Marshall is shot in the hip by an obsessed ex-lover and needs the bullet removed immediately.

This was followed by the episode of *Gilligan's Island* where Gilligan and the Professor come out as gay lovers and shack up, literally, while the Skipper, unable to come to terms with this development, hangs himself from a palm tree and is found by Ginger and Mary Ann who, it turns out, have been madly in love with him from the beginning and now take their own lives by self-immolation because of their grief.

Next and last was *Star Trek*: Captain Kirk and Uhura are getting it on in sick bay when Bones comes in and shouts "Stop Jim – You'll never satisfy her" followed by McCoy exclaiming "he's giving her all he's got, doctor", which is all secretly videotaped by Spock, whose diabolical scheme to release a sex video is foiled by a Klingon commander who seizes and destroys it to preserve the purity of the universe.

It was a hectic life and continued to grow more so as, gradually but steadily, my reputation spread. For television my appearances at that time were almost exclusively on morning shows, except for an occasional later afternoon talk show. The market was always very small. The format of the shows and my contribution to them were all so similar, and the chances that anyone watching would have seen my appearance at another station so remote, that I could deliver virtually the same performance each time, modified only to suit the product.

Of course, the competence and personalities of the hosts varied tremendously, as KYKY illustrated. Some hosts dominated their shows, exercised tight control and never experienced a moment of uncertainty – or unplanned spontaneity. For their shows I was no more than a temporarily added member of *their* team. Pronounced deference to them was the rule for my bit.

Some hosts, however, were green, lacked the confidence of experience, and generally were just thrilled to have a job on TV. Because these were such small markets this type of host was the most common: Youngsters, fresh out of school, needing to learn the business, and eager to do so. In these situations I was more of an honored guest, someone who had been around and was comfortable bantering under the lights. Deference flowed a different direction. And I could improvise more freely.

Schembechler, Michigan. Station KGOD. "New Day With Bill and Brenda". Two powerhouse rookies three months into their careers, with 5,000 viewers and two hours to fill. "Coming up a little later this morning we are excited to have a man who has demonstrated products all over the country. We are fortunate to have him here to show us the masturbator which will make baking birds a whole lot easier."

Brenda is looking wide-eyed at someone off-camera. Now turning pink. "Oh no. What did I say?" So flustered. Does not know what to do. How to climb out of the hole. She's stuck in a moment and can't get out of it. Bill is not helpful because he does not want to be.

I am in an ante-room, waiting to set up the demonstration. I pick up the product and walk to Brenda's side on camera. "It's all right Brenda. Every time I demonstrate this product the same thing happens. Veteran television hosts have mispronounced the Master Baster the way you did. I can't wait to show everyone how it works." Smile and a wave and I am gone.

Afterwards Brenda was so much in awe and so grateful that she wanted to have sex with me right there in the studio and then to marry me and give me lots of children. I graciously informed her that this would not be necessary and that the wonderful young lady who already was mine was more than I deserved.

Squidward, Washington. Station KBOB. "New World With Amy and Mei". A college town. Stromboli Academy is here. So most of the station's viewers in the morning are college educated women who are staying home with their children for their first two years or so. Perry Pendleton would not be popular here. Amy Dickens and Mei Wong are.

I am here to demonstrate a camp stove and cooler all in one. My visit starts with a meeting: Amy, Mei, Me, and the producer, Mike. Amy wants to be sure that I plan to talk about the environmental aspects of the product, i.e., what effect it will have, if any. Donning my truth hat, I tell her that I do not have any information about that, but I am sure the effect will be minimal, if any.

Treating me like an intern whose screwup she has to make up for, she tells the producer to get some quick research done on the issue so she can comment on it when she introduces the product. And that's how the introduction goes: Today we have a product .. Nothing about ol' Hound Dog.

So I sit in a simple wicker chair facing Amy and Mei, who are also seated, with the product on a stand just below my knees. This Open Lands Stove Cooler is perfect for backpacking, I say. Mei says she assumes I have used it many times on my backpacking trips. I feel disapproval seething into outrage when I say that I have never been backpacking, but if I did this would be the stove cooler for me.

The product uses a new solid fuel cannister to produce both heat and cold. With it I heat a cup of coffee and chill a glass of wine. Amazing, isn't it?

What happens to the cannister after it is spent? Amy asks. Oh, you can either haul it out or toss it for the squirrels to have fun with. I am joking.

She is offended. But isn't it toxic? Yes, but the squirrel will have a wild night before he passes. Amy and Mei are besides themselves with indignant fury. Rightfully so I guess. After all, it is their show.

As was starkly evident when I was escorted out through the frost from their scorn. Although I should have simply rested on the axiom that you cannot please everyone, I regretted that incident and vowed to keep myself more in line when appearing on a show where the hosts are in command like Amy and Mei were. But I had little time to brood about it. Another demonstration, another appearance was always waiting.

I have just awakened in a familiar place. After a nightmare of being sucked from the wreckage, strapped to a flying carpet, inserted into a space ship covered with flashing red lights, where a foot-long needle connected to a fat tube was plunged into my arm so that a hideous monster wearing the name tag "H. Peter" could squeeze fluid into me from bags marked Flintstone Embalming. The ship then seemed to cruise through time backwards, until here I am in the same bed in the same emergency room in the same hospital that spit me out earlier in the day. Nurse Shapely is nowhere in sight.

Medical machines are. They surround me, emitting a gleeful hum through the tentacles they have plunged into ports implanted in my skin. I can hear doctors and nurses and lawyers somewhere near chattering about blunt force, internal bleeding, levels of hemoglobin, leukocytes, Dijon mustard, cost-efficient emergency treatment protocols, costs plus billing, and next of kin. I feel no pain. I feel nothing at all.

Here is an orange-jowled doctor bending over me. "I am Dr. Frankenstein. You are in my laboratory. We are doing everything we can to keep you living, so that my experiments can proceed. First, we must finish stabilizing your critical functions: blood pressure, heartrate, politics, etc. Then we probably will need to call in Arnie, the Bulgarian Butcher, to determine the best operative procedure. Meanwhile, you just lie back, relax, and enjoy the flight."

Next up: Bruno the wildebeest to ask who they should contact to let them know I am here. The queen of Denmark and Axl Rose, I think at him as loud as I can. My mashed up mind can only recall three other names: Angel, Polly, and, that's right, Hound Dog.

The surgeon is here with good news. He will need to remove only four critical organs damaged in the wreck. Afterwards I should be able to live the normal happy life of a disemboweled middle aged man. That is good news, Doc. Maybe I can finally get off this prescription antiacid medication.

Now it's the Wicked Witch of Pre-op. Older than Olivia de Havilland. She has some "end of life documents" for sale. Advanced healthcare directives, she calls them.

Her pitch: All this sophisticated medical equipment costs a lot of money to operate and maintain. Plus the physicians' fees. They have to support their families you know. Add on the legal fees that may be unavoidable and it all comes to a pretty substantial sum. Someone will have to pay for it. Don't let this burden fall on your loved ones. Sign these forms authorizing the surgeon to terminate your life if he does not like the way things are going.

The big boys are here to lift me onto a gurney for a ride to the operating room. Seems like most of the medical robots are coming with me. It's a parade. But I can only see the track lights in the ceiling, so I do not know if the onlookers are cheering or jeering.

They are probably thinking man, I'm glad I'm not that guy. I heard they are going to cut him up in small pieces suitable for storage in Mason jars. I hope they don't wind up on the menu at the cafeteria.

Here we are in the front hall to the OR. Hoisted onto another contraption. Sir, we are going to start another IV with something to relax you, then the anesthesiologist will administer the Pentobarbital. Hopefully he will measure the right dosage; he has been on a drinking binge, no sleep for days, ever since he found his wife in bed with his brother. Did you know that Marilyn Monroe died from an overdose of Pentobarbital? Fun fact. Of course, it also is widely used for euthanasia of pets.

An unshaven, wild eyed and profusely sweating creature is standing over me. Good morning. I am Dr. Death ..er, I mean Kevorkian .. no no .. Dr. Sleep. Yeah, that's right, Dr. Sleep. I am going to fill your circulatory system with Mr. Clean. When I say "motherfucker" you count backward from infinity.

12

One gorgeous spring day, when flowers were opening, birds singing, and the breeze of warmth was wafting across the universe, I received confirmation that my debt to Olivia was fully paid. Oh day of joyous celebration, of exhilarating triumph. I had ventured through the valley of the damned and emerged whole, with a sound mind, decent health, and a robust career as a product moving magician and minor television personality known in many regions of the country.

Demand for my services was increasing every week. I rose to the top of Jill Taylor's list and stayed there. She knew she had a star on her hands. The question for her became for how long? How long before I would be called up to the major leagues? How long before a national network or producer of infomercials would extend a finger down to point and say we want you?

When the call did come, however, it was not from a network or a producer. It was from a sponsor, a manufacturer-distributer that had hired me a number of times to demonstrate its products. And the call came through Jill Taylor.

The company wanted to make an infomercial. The marketing department wanted me to host it. Best of all: The product was a winner.

It was a portable, cordless, soup maker that also did the necessary food processing. The device had four funnels into which the cook could insert, respectively, meat, fruits and vegetables, liquids, and items to be grated or shaved, like cheese. It also featured a sifter for adding spices.

The device would process the ingredients as programmed by the cook, e.g., cube, dice, slice, grind the meat, fruit, and vegetables, before adding them to the liquid, which could be water, juice, wine, milk, etc. With its own solid fuel heat source, it would heat the liquid as the other ingredients were added.

One of its best features was that it could make a single cup of soup or up to ten cups. And it was completely portable; a person could take it camping, to a ball game, even to make soup while taking a long road trip.

It was a huge break for me. I dedicated myself to prepare. Since I was now free from my debt to Olivia I was able to reduce my commitments a bit so that I would have the time I felt I needed. First step was intense study of the product, its market context, and competitors. Then practice and more practice. I would become the supreme master of The Simple Souper.

The contract I signed committed me to work with any format the producers chose. The manufacturer, Convenient Cooking Solutions, a Chinese company operating out of Shenzhen, in the People's Republic of China, and its American distributor, Rolling Triangle, Inc., engaged a production company, Pounding Man Productions, to produce the informercial.

Even though the first shoot would not happen for three months, a representative from Pounding Man contacted me for input on the plan. With no experience in commercial production, or any production for that matter, I did not have much to contribute. When I learned about some of Pounding Man's crazy ideas, however, I had to react, notwithstanding how lucky I felt just to be participating.

The lead producer, a snobby, overly vibrant Latino named Sergio, declared that I would be outfitted like a maître d': a fancy tuxedo with tails, a white cloth draped over my arm, a device inserted into my nose to keep it in the air. In response I suggested a Souperman costume. Sergio, after refusing to discuss it, said he would consider the standard chef's uniform – tall white hat, knee-length white apron over a double-breasted jacket, black bowtie.

Partly out of fear from the thought of wearing such a thing while demonstrating the Simple Souper and flapping my jowls, I said Chef Boyardee would not be caught dead using this product. The whole point of it was to take the "cook" out of the picture. The Simple Souper was a tool anyone could use and should be marketed to people who never cook.

I got my way: Light, loose, comfortable sweater, burgundy with a yellow soup cup embroidered on the front, complete with rising whisps of steam.

Another issue was whether I would present before an audience or only to the camera alongside one or two assistants. Naturally I preferred an audience since that was what I was used to, but it did not really matter much to me.

I knew that the "audience" for an infomercial is not real in the sense of people who will genuinely judge the presenter and the product. No member of such an artificial, paid, audience is likely to shout "that's bogus" or "there ain't any such thing as a walnut fish" or "try it with a true exploding pressure cap, not that fake one". So handling an infomercial audience seemed like a piece of cake compared to what I had experienced. The decision was made by someone to try it with an audience, then re-shoot it without one if necessary.

As part of my preparation I watched as many infomercials as I could stomach, looking for the do's and don'ts. I saw Barry White selling the Miracle Shoe, one size fits all adjustable footwear, to a group of ten individuals who each were able to wear the same pair of shoes.

One of the don'ts I found in this one was the failure even once to show the same shoes on the different size feet. Each person received the shoes from his neighbor, then bent down to put them on, supposedly after adjusting the size, then stood up and talked about how amazingly comfortable the shoes were. There was no visual evidence that he was even wearing the actual shoes. As a result, the informercial was not believable.

I saw Perry Como selling a boxed, five-CD collection of recordings by him, Pat Boone, Mel Torme, and Andy Williams of classic Berber political protest songs. My principal critique of this one was that Perry never explained how the term "classic" was interpreted, what criteria they used to decide what to include, which would have been helpful to avoid triggering controversy. Especially since the collection was not available in stores, Perry himself likely would have been the target of the public's wrath. I certainly did not want to put myself in a similar predicament.

Of course, I watched Victoria Principal lead the women assembled to worship her along on her journey through the Tahitian jungles in search of the mad Dr. LaFarge and his miracle skin care cream. Besides the fact that this infomercial was aired about four hundred thousand more times than it should have been, until long after Victoria's skin had turned purple with skin poisoning, the production could have benefited from one or two J.R. Ewing cameos.

There was Brock Buckner demonstrating his amazing Fool's Gold fishing lures. Purporting to be live wading into a vigorous river, Buckner hooked a trout within seconds each time he cast. This one had some editing flaws: A couple of times it looked like the lure did not even reach the water before the fish snagged it.

This extensive viewing was very educational for me. Yes, I found faults. But I was pretty much just a talking head; who was I to say that Pounding Man and I would make something any better. Nevertheless, it is the aspiration that counts. If you set your sights on becoming number one, and work accordingly, you are sure to reach the top five at least, and you will never regret that you did not try harder.

The final infomercial as aired would be 58.5 minutes, so I needed to plan the demonstration sequence carefully. Because I also intended to demonstrate how easily and quickly the Soupers could be cleaned, I had to factor in the time required for that as well.

I planned to work with three Soupers. The show thus would unfold as follows: Start a soup in Souper no. 1 that would be ready quickly, another in no. 2 that needed a little more time, and a soup that required the most cooking time in no. 3. Pour out the first soup in small cups to be sampled by the audience, clean the device, and start another soup. Repeat the process for Souper no. 2. Pour out the soup from Souper no. 3 for sampling, followed by the second soups from numbers 1 and 2.

Compiling a master list of possible soup candidates, I practiced making some to determine the best five for the demonstration. This master list included vegetable beef, clam chowder, cream of mushroom, cream of chicken, cream of beetle, lobster bisque, tomato bisque, turnip bisque, miyeok guk, Amish preaching soup, split pea, and Communist corn chowder.

While I was in the midst of preparing for this momentous experience I was blessed by a visit from my angel, Angel. It was in August before she started her senior year in high school. What a gorgeous young lady. To me anyway. She hugged and kissed me more enthusiastically than she had for a long long time.

We talked about her plans for post-high school. College? Unsure. You mean where or if? Both. Odie? Just friends now. After some minutes of hesitancy, fidgeting, her feet crossing and uncrossing, she finally told me that she had been composing songs with the guitar I gave her, that she thought they were pretty good, that she planned to perform some of them at a coffee shop that held an open mic night, and would I like to come and listen? I tried hard to stay cool, but I could not. I was so thrilled. Of course I would be there.

When she asked how I was doing I told her about the infomercial. She was pretty excited for me at first. But as I went more and more into the details her attention faded. As she was leaving she "warned" me that her mother might be there. No problem.

Saturday afternoon at Coffee, Tea & Tunes. Intimate place – capacity of maybe 30. When I arrived it was about two-thirds full. Until Olivia and Heidi showed up I was by far the oldest person there. I judged most of the patrons to be contemporaries, probably friends, of Angel, with some exuding the college vibe.

Hoping to be as inconspicuous as possible, I hunkered down at a one-person table in a dark corner and ordered a root beer float. Barista thought I was trying to be funny. Okay, bottle of sparkling water.

Across the tables between me and the small platform they used for a stage I saw Angel sitting with two other girls, a guitar case propped against the wall beside her. Right when she saw me and started to come over the open mic host started the program. So I gave her a thumbs up and she sat back down. Olivia and Heidi then arrived, but did not see me.

The first performer who grabbed the mic that was unfortunately left open was there to spout his shitty poetry: "The coral reefs dying alone and forgotten .. plastic bags strangling their existence .. the hibiscus flower weeps in soulful sorrow .. humanity hovers over the abyss .." Polite, subdued clapping interspersed with "very moving", "extraordinary word choice", and "lovely". I kept my mouth shut and sipped sparkling water.

Next up was a duo: a sickly pale chic stroking a guitar and a dude with red hair blowing the crap out of a harmonica, then both purporting to sing but actually sounding like alley cats trash screeching over a discarded sardine. I shuddered and wished for ear plugs, which probably would not have blocked out the cacophony anyway. Another round of soft applause, along with "interesting", "innovative", and "speaks to the angst of modern life".

Finally Angel stepped up and sat on the stool before the mic. The ten or so minutes that followed were – are – timeless. Moments so incredibly sublime, so exhilarating and euphoric. I was transported to a supernatural scene where only Angel and I existed and she was singing to me with an almost unbearably exquisite voice. Not hearing her words, I was simply dazzled by her melodies.

Those minutes would have been the most exulting of my life .. if it were not for what happened next.

As Angel was finishing her last song, I overheard some punk shithead college boy talking over the music and saying things like "so not relevant" and "thinks she's Joan Baez .. she's not" in that tone of false arrogance common to his kind. Before a single rational thought entered my mind to restrain me, I had slapped the side of his head, shoved him out of his chair onto the floor, and was standing over him breathing fast, pulsing with rage.

Now bewildered, with every face turned and fixed on mine, I looked for Angel and saw her still on the stool staring at me with a look of horror as if I had just killed someone. Then she was sobbing violently and holding her hands over her eyes.

Shooting me a damning glare of shame, Olivia rushed to her. Then it was that I realized what I had done, what catastrophic injury I had caused to the most precious being that ever lived.

I tried to speak, but only choked. Oblivious to the gang of boys that had surrounded me to defend my victim, I noticed only an overwhelming misery sickening my stomach and head. Fixed to the spot for hours, it seemed, finally I pushed through the ring of young bodies, staggered to the door and into the street, praying for a car to run me down at stop speed. I was not to be so lucky.

Eventually I found a bar. Ordered a double scotch on rocks and told the bartender to keep 'em coming. He cut me off after four and sent me home in a taxi. There I finished off the four beers I had left from a sixpack and the gin left in a bottle I had bought a long time before, fought a grim battle with myself over my drunken notion to call and apologize, and passed out.

For many days thereafter I lived in a foul fog of disgrace and hopelessness. I desperately wished I could erase the incident and start over from the moment Angel began to sing. I was afraid of myself, of what I might be capable of doing without ever intending to. Although wanting so much to contact Angel, to crawl to her, to prostrate myself on the ground by her feet and beg her to forgive me, I was afraid even to be any place where I might see her.

I never would have survived those heartbreaking days and weeks if I had not had work to cling to. By the time I was able to focus on it again the day for the informercial shoot was barely ten days off. Somehow I packed the pain into a remote recess of my being, where it continued to fester, and redoubled my preparations.

This robotic effort was interrupted by a letter I received from Olivia. Her message was harsh. She first advised me that Angel was doing as well as could be expected, which acerbity pierced my heart like she knew it would. Then she informed me that she intended to prevent me from having any contact with Angel unless and until I sought and received some form of behavioral or psychiatric evaluation and treatment. Furthermore, if I did not voluntarily agree to the restraint, she would petition the court for an order.

Ignoring the letter's command as best I could, I proceeded to make soup and think Simple Souper, wondering the while if I would be able to publicly celebrate, with enthusiasm and joy, the virtues of my product, even as my tormented soul writhed in anguish. I resolved to sign up with every mental health care provider in the county once I had accomplished this mission.

The day for departure to the shooting location finally arrived. Canseco, Florida, home to the studios of Pounding Man Productions. Once I boarded the flight and we were taxiing I immediately felt a tremendous release, like some heavy weight had been cut from my shoulders. The cold Prairie Dog Lager I consumed after take off helped as well. Feeling so relatively mellow for the first time in weeks, I actually struck up a conversation with the middle-aged woman next to me.

She needed to talk and I was glad to listen. Very nervous about the flight and the upcoming wedding for which she would be a bridesmaid, she chattered almost non-stop in a squeaky voice once I got her started. The brief interjections I made concerning all my flying experience seemed to calm her on that score. The wedding, however, was another thing.

The bride to be was her younger sister. The groom to be was a convicted felon and ex-convict, who had been caught smuggling bogus designer neck ties into Sarasota. She was worried that he had other illegal operations going that might bring the "feds" to the festivities to round up conspirators. A law-abiding mother of two, she claimed no involvement in any of this "trouble", but did not know about her sister.

What other operations do you think he might have going? Money laundering. Drug trafficking. Counterfeit Monopoly and other board games. Unpasteurized dairy products. He's actually a very nice young man, she said. Although she had not seen him since he was released from the penitentiary.

She asked and I told her what I was traveling for. "I thought you looked familiar," she exclaimed. She had seen one of my morning show appearances and even bought the product. This was the first time anyone ever told me they saw me on TV. It gave a timely boost to my self-esteem.

We also talked about our respective children: Her 13-year-old boy and 15-year-old girl and my Angel. The boy dreamed of becoming a professional bowling commentator. He was fascinated by the sport, knew the names and stats of all the pros, and subscribed to every bowling magazine published, including some in languages he could not read. For more than a year the girl had planned to become a nun. They were a good catholic family. However, during the past month she had reconsidered and was now looking at either massage therapy or law enforcement.

She listened sympathetically to what I told her of Angel and my screwing up our relationship. I did not go into too much detail. Her advice lifted me up: Do not give up. So I arrived in Canseco feeling good and strong again, ready to sell the Simple Souper.

And I did. Exceeded my expectations. So did Pounding Man. They had the set ready to go, a cozy room with a platform raised just a foot or so to maintain intimacy with the ten paid audience members. Three Simple Soupers were waiting on a table with all the ingredients I had requested either lining trays beside each Souper or in cabinets under the table. I had prepared so intensely that it felt like I was about to do my forty-seventh infomercial, not my first.

I was in a groove right when I needed to be. My five-soup procedure worked brilliantly, and I was able to make each one, dish it into two-ounce cups that my lovely assistant, Gretchen, passed around to the audience, clean the Souper and load it up again, all while expressing my personal and sincere reverence for that amazing device.

It was a wonderous boon to people who did not have a chef and all his equipment tagging along on a road trip. I told the story of Alphonse, the Duke of Cummerbund, who loved soup so much that when he traveled about the kingdom he had three or four accompanying knaves whose sole job was to transport ingredients for fifty different kinds of soup and to make a certain one on the spot at the whim of the Duke. The hard-working, creative minds who developed the Simple Souper did not do it for the likes of the Duke. They did it to make preparing healthy soup easy for people like you and me.

Yes, before I started using the Simple Souper the only soup I ever made came out of a can. Yes, I am being paid to be here. But trust me, no amount of money could make me recommend the Simple Souper if I did not believe it to be a super product and well worth the price, especially because there is nothing else like it.

Despite my meticulous planning, however, I found it harder to manage the time than I had expected. The main issue was that describing each ingredient deliberately enough for someone watching on TV to comprehend took longer before an audience and live cameras than it had in my apartment. Nevertheless I was efficient enough in the initial run through to get everything necessary recorded, leaving the time problem to the wizards of post-production, and precluding the need for a second session.

So I returned home, exhausted, fulfilled professionally, but my personal life still achingly empty. With no energy to resume a hectic demonstration schedule, I told Jill Taylor I needed a month to recuperate. She reluctantly agreed. I then set about finding a shrink or therapist or medicine man, whatever would work to fix me up enough to satisfy Olivia.

Mules! All twenty. Rumbling across a desert wasteland, churning up clouds of boron dust, headed for a precipice looming over raging river rapids. Stop! Stop! They will all plunge to death in the water and their corpses will course downstream, upsetting tourists, fouling the water supply, scaring the fish. I am helpless watching here from this hovercraft at 3,000 feet.

And it's all my fault. If I had not chartered the team they would still be in the corral, blithely munching on alfalfa casserole and braying approval for the *Death Valley Days* Reunion show. Instead they are about to become a ghost team pulling a load of borax for the Devil.

Oh my God, I cannot watch.

But wait. It's a mule miracle! God himself has appeared, resplendent in a golden tunic, fifty-foot beard, clouds of gilded hair, Birkenstock sandals, floating from nowhere on a silver surfboard. He raises his staff and commands the herd to stop.

Crap! The leading mules obey, but the trailing ones do not see and crash into the others, so that the herd becomes a rolling chaos sweeping even God into its maelstrom.

The Devil is about to triumph. The operation is done, he says to me, breathing hot whiskey breath. We took a lot, but left the minimum you need to continue living. It is only then that I realize I am emerging from the catacombs of unconsciousness. I am lying in a transparent sphere with my dear friends the faithful medical machines standing by. Slowly I am starting to comprehend what the Devil is saying.

He claims to be a doctor, a surgeon even. He asks me if I would like to eat the organs they removed. They can pack them in ice for me. Any of them will be very tasty whether grilled with a dusting of turmeric, catnip, and sulfur or sauteed in myrrh with garlic, mushrooms, and bat phlegm. He's no wine expert, he says, but suggests a 13th century Hurdy Gurdy white.

13

"How can I help you?" A distinguished-looking, gray-bearded gentleman, burnished, trimmed to perfection, dark wool suit. Dr. Komengoing, psychiatrist.

"I don't know. Some psych stuff I guess."

"Well, let me ask you this: Why did you come to see me?"

"I need some psych work before I can see my daughter."

"What kind of psych work?"

"I don't know. I figured you could tell me." The doctor smiled condescendingly at what he saw as me trying to be funny. I had no idea what was supposed to happen. The only psychiatrist I had ever known was Gregory Peck in *Captain Newman, M.D.* I expected questions like when I was a boy did I want to have sex with my mother or my father.

"Did someone tell you to see a psychiatrist before you csee your daughter?"

"Yeah. My ex-wife put it in some kind of order. Not from a court. Not yet. I agreed to it." He wondered if I had a copy of the order with me. I did not.

"Do you know what prompted your ex-wife to do this?" I told him. "I see," he said, stroking his beard. He flipped through his mental catalog of approved behavioral science terms until he stopped at the one he was looking for. "So you need anger management therapy." Sounds good.

However, it turned out that anger management was not on his menu. He would be happy to prescribe some medication: a mood stabilizer, anti-depressant, anxiety lifter, anti-psychotic, boner pill, tic tac, life saver. There was also flackatrol or sentendizine. He did not know what conditions these were effective for, nor what they did to a person taking them, but suggested that I could try one and see what happens. We would both learn something.

But he did not provide therapy for anger management. Referring me to Dr. Angie Pickacock, PhD, LMFT, LCP, Y2K, LOL, EZE, Dr Komengoing showed me the door and sent his bill after me as a paper airplane he had just folded up.

Psychologist, psychotherapist, and fortune teller, Dr. Pickacock was an extraordinarily thin woman. Hip-length straight gray hair, giant glasses with lenses so thick her magnified eyeballs seemed ready to roll out, wearing an angle-length canvas sack purporting to be a dress, she extended a skeletal hand and said, "How can I help you?"

Opting for a different approach this time, I went straight to the ex-wife, psych stuff, daughter thing. "I sense hostility," she said, her years in the Tertullian Temple paying off. I wanted to say "duh?" Instead I said "not to you".

"I mean that you have hostility dwelling inside you that surfaces at certain convergences of circumstances. It is something you cannot control. It is like a beast. A powerful beast. When it is aroused your good nature is no match for it."

Floored, I looked at her in awe, unable to say a single word. She smiled the smile of serene omniscience. "What can I do about it, Dr. P—". "Angie".

Within two minutes Angie had discovered the presence of the monster. Unfortunately, she was no match for it either. Her methods – talking, meditation, breathing exercises, drawing fields of sunflowers, reciting James Taylor lyrics – were calming in the moment and for five minutes after I left the office. But they could not destroy the Thing or convince it to leave me alone.

My final hope was a therapist named Bronco Bobby. His methods were the antithesis to Pickacock's. From the moment I entered his empty waiting room, where he hid behind a coat rack before jumping out and putting me in a headlock, I knew Double B, as he like to be called, was different.

He performed all his "therapy" wearing a nylon warmup suit. He yelled at me like a football coach would, or a drill sergeant, telling me to quit the whining and the feeling sorry for myself and to buck up and be a man. The little prick at the coffee house got what he deserved, Double B said. Too bad I did not finish him off.

Not surprisingly, his favorite expressions included the words "namby pamby", "wuss", "pantywaist", and "get over it". If I did not stand up for myself, he warned, no one would pay me any respect. The stag party sounded awesome and he wished he could have been there. Nothing for me to be ashamed about. Fuck the ex-wife! In the courtroom and out she never stops judging people, especially me.

After taking this punishment for an hour once a week for three weeks, I began to feel that it was doing something, but I could not say what, or whether it was good or bad. It seemed perhaps that he was instilling in me a new, thicker skin, a more callous temperament, which might enable me to function better even if the subconscious guilt still harbored the beast. Unfortunately, I was not to find out what continued work with Bronco Bobby would have accomplished, because my month off passed and Jill Taylor loaded me with appearances.

The informercial was still in post-production and had not aired anywhere. The honchos at the manufacturer and distributer let me know they were very pleased with my work; they were most eager to release the production on the world and had already purchased lots of media time.

So for the next year I demonstrated the heck out of product after product, in places all over the United States, and a few in Canada as well. And I regularly made the scene on local talk shows.

Meanwhile, Angel graduated from high school. I was not allowed to attend the ceremony. Apparently, they were afraid that I would assault the principal if he mispronounced her name. Maybe they were right.

Shrugging it off as best I could, rationalizing that my schedule probably would not have permitted it anyway, I sent her a gold bracelet and a note telling her congratulations and that I loved her very much. A thank you card arrived a couple of weeks later with this inscription: "I love you too, Dad".

The informercial began to air on various cable networks. I had no idea if anyone saw it, but sales of the Simple Souper increased significantly. Or so I was informed by an account executive for the distributor. This news provided a strong boost for my confidence and inspired my ambition to greater levels. Maybe another of the same type of opportunity was in the works.

Not the same. Better. One morning Jill woke me from a sweet slumber I was enjoying at the Dead Man's Lodge in Bleak, California, which is located somewhere between Saltville and Salt Valley in the Southern California desert. I had been dreaming that I was standing naked on a salt bed blanched by a sun five times bigger than normal, demonstrating to an audience of Leopard Lizards a machine that made water from salt. Pissed that what came out was salt water, I stomped on the machine and cut my foot.

Jill had good news. Great news. Fantastic news. An appearance on a nationally televised morning show: Morning Glory with Mary and Mark. As I excitedly demanded more information, she cut me off, saying she had another call coming in, that the appearance would happen in fifteen days, and that she would send the details to my home.

Once again in my apartment, I eagerly perused the materials Jill had sent. Only to be disappointed by the nature of the "nationally televised morning show". Morning Glory was indeed broadcast nationally -- on a cable channel called Your Christian Life ("YCL"). The show was billed as "A mix of news, information, and inspiring words designed to start your day with gusto."

Not exactly NBC or The Today Show. Some of the air that had puffed me up drained out. I told Jill that I was uncomfortable with the religious emphasis of the network and the show. However, she assured me that my segment would have none of those aspects; it would be strictly about the product. I would not have to tell the good people watching that God himself had one at home and loved it.

The best news, and the detail that convinced me to go for it, was that the product would be the one and only Simple Souper, the same product that was the subject of the infomercial and that I knew in and out and top to bottom. As I learned later, someone at YCL had seen the infomercial and liked both the product and the demonstrator.

The network headquarters and studios were in Greendevil, North Carolina, so that is where I headed the day before my scheduled appearance. Booked to stay at the Greendevil Holiday Inn, I was met at the Charlotte airport by John Anderson, one of the show's producers, who then drove me to Greendevil and along the way convinced me to stay in his home instead.

When we arrived he introduced me to his beautiful wife Polly and his two children whose names escape me now. Very fit and energetic, with blonde hair curling to her shoulders, framing bright green eyes and a fresh, unblemished, sometimes pinkish face, Polly easily could have passed for twenty-two, when she was actually thirty-something. She welcomed me to her home as if I was visiting royalty. Never had a Hound Dog received a warmer, more embracing welcome..

Since she was cooking dinner, which filled the house with sumptuous aromas of garlic, mint, and lemon, John guided me to their guest room and left me to settle a bit before dinner. I lay on the bed for a while, shamefully contemplating how Christian dudes, especially southern ones, snagged the hottest wives.

Dinner was extraordinary. Multiple dishes of freshly made goodies. Once everyone was seated, John asked if I would like to say the blessing. I declined, remembering that as far as I knew, Burlap and Barbed Wire did not have any words for such an occasion. So John did the honors. He thanked the lord for providing the delicious food, for keeping he and his family safe and healthy, for bringing me into their home and to their television ministry, and for the Heels' defense, which had held the Gators to ten points on Saturday. Amen.

After dinner Polly demonstrated, wittingly or not I did not know, how she could overpower a man without a single sign of sexual intent. She did not flirt. She just came real close to me, like she was taking me into her deepest confidence, her body and face exerting a stunning force, and asked me personal questions.

Was I married? Children? Did I do anything professionally before I became a demonstrator? Was I a member of any church? At my answer in the negative to the last one her lips, colored with dark red lipstick, parted into a dazzling smile. She winked and said "Well, I guess we'll have to do something about that."

The questions were presumptuous, but that seemed to be immaterial for some reason. Her marvelous being allowed her license. John did not even seem to notice; no doubt he had seen her do the same thing many times before.

Morning Glory was very similar to all other morning shows. Mary and Mark both were polished broadcasters and they worked from a carefully crafted script with a well-defined theme. They introduced themselves to me beforehand, but did not engage in any chit chat, other than to welcome me to their television ministry.

Their introduction to my segment: "Some of you may have seen an informercial that has been airing on some channels around the country promoting a device for making soup without having to chop or grate or slice any of the ingredients. We are blessed today to have the charming man who hosts that informercial here to show us the Simple Souper".

"Thank you so much, Mary. I feel blessed too to be here." Blessed by the god of money that is. "It is a pleasure for me every chance I have to show what this marvelous product can do. Anyone who likes soup, but doesn't cook, will love this thing. Anyone who, like me, normally eats soup that came from a can, will love the Simple Souper."

They allotted me only ten minutes, time for one soup. I chose cream of celery with chicken. In went the water, milk, and cream, followed by a pre-cooked chicken breast, celery, and a few spices. While the machine was whirring and steaming up the soup I mentioned some of the cool things it was good for.

Suddenly, about seven minutes into the segment, the Souper began to shudder violently and emit a loud hissing sound like a pressure cooker pushed to the limit. This had not happened before. Now, during my first appearance on national television, something had gone wrong. The Souper was about to explode and kill me with sharp shards of stainless steel and thirty-two ounces of boiling cream of celery soup. Time to panic.

I did not. Looking defiantly into the camera and lifting my arms towards the ceiling, I said "Ladies and gentlemen, a demon has entered this Souper. It is working evil in there even as we speak." Then laying my hands over the top and calling for the will of righteousness to be served, I surreptitiously flipped the power switch. The Souper shut down.

I smiled beatifically at the camera before they switched to the hosts. Who were agonizing between concern for the integrity of the program and a powerful urge to laugh. Mary coolly wrapped up the segment with "thank you for demonstrating the power of righteousness so dramatically."

It was the first spontaneous event ever on YCL and was received almost jubilantly. After we discovered that someone had tinkered with the machine the producers praised my response to the crisis. Viewers contacted the network to say that it was the most entertaining segment they had ever seen on the network.

Even the makers and distributors of the Souper accepted the event as my making something memorable out of a potential disaster. I never learned if the widely-seen video clips of the segment boosted sales of the Souper or broadcast the impression that it was dangerous.

About two weeks after I returned home I received a call from John Anderson. We reminisced about the increasingly famous incident. Then he invited me back for a second appearance on Morning Glory, to try again with the Simple Souper, or to demonstrate any other product I wanted, subject to the network's approval, of course. I assumed this meant no sex toys. I happily accepted.

This call was followed a few days later by another. Angel. She had seen the video clip. Thought it was so funny. Did not know I had that in me. Barely restraining my excitement at hearing her voice, I told her how thrilled I was to talk with her after so long.

Neither of us wished to discuss any part of what had happened between us. But I managed to elicit a quick update on her life: Taking classes at the community college, playing music with friends, and still writing songs.

My second visit to Greendevil, North Carolina and the Anderson home was even more pleasant than the previous one. John and Polly obviously had planned a grand welcome for me. They again treated me like a visiting potentate, only this time with warmth normally reserved for close family. Polly, especially, paid me such special attention that I worried John might get the wrong idea, stupid as that was to suppose.

She radiated the charm of a wholesome southern belle who happened to be ruthlessly attractive. Apparently no one saw anything out of the ordinary when she hugged me upon my arrival, making sure I felt the press of her ample breasts, or when she looked up into my eyes like I was the man of her dreams. This was the way of southern Christian women who knew they had men in their power. Nothing intended beyond capturing their platonic devotion, which would energize the magnet of religious belonging.

There were additional guests for dinner both of the nights I was there. All executives and other producers at YCL. Some I had met during my first visit. Wearing incredibly sexy, but conservative, dresses, Polly was absolutely the center of attention, which she tried to deflect onto me.

The evening after my successful demonstration of a breakfast sandwich maker that cooked bacon or sausage on one mini-grill swiveled out from the base, an egg with cheese on another, then slapped both together between a split biscuit, roll, or croissant, the topic of conversation at dinner became my plans for the future. At that point I figured out the reason for all the fuss in my favor.

Although he was a producer, not an executive, John spoke for the network. They wanted me to join the team. They wanted to hire me to work full-time for the network, appearing on Morning Glory and other programs, primarily focusing on selling products, but also on developing new programs that would inform viewers about a variety of ways to enhance their everyday Christian lives.

Needless to say, I was stunned. And grateful. Mentally processing John's words, I happen to look at Polly. She was staring at me, smiling mischievously, and appeared to physically project the suggestion that she would be the reward if I said yes.

But a disciple of Burlap and Barbed Wire appearing regularly on a Christian network? I explained that I was not much of a religious man. Which prompted Polly to flash those alluring eyes around the table and back to me and say "Well, we're working on that".

One of the executives told me that they all thought I was extraordinarily charismatic and persuasive, without the big head that many such people have, and that they believed I could liven up the network. He said that as long as my mind was open and that I had not declared my faith in a non-Christian religion they predicted that I would "come around to Christ" in the long run. No one could be certain of it, but that was a risk they were willing to take.

The offer included a salary higher than any I had ever had, reimbursement of my expenses for moving to Greendevil, or whichever local community I chose to live in, and benefits for health care and retirement. After emphasizing repeatedly how grateful I was, I pleaded for and received two weeks to think it over.

With one exception, every person I consulted with about the offer advised me to reject it. You will not be happy working for people who have a direct phone line to God, one said. Another cautioned me to think of what will happen after I am discovered frequenting the Greendevil franchise of The Penguin Club. Jill Taylor warned that the move could end up short-circuiting my career as a professional product pitchman.

Olivia was the only one who thought I should take the offer. For her it was a matter of me finally having a stable occupation and a chance to "straighten myself out". I was unable to communicate with Angel about it. Just as well, because I was sure she would say "Are you crazy?"

However, Angel unwittingly helped me decide to accept by announcing, as I heard from her mother, that she was moving to California, at least temporarily, to see if she could get anywhere in the music business. So I no longer had any personal reason to remain. I called John to give my formal acceptance and planned my move to Greendevil, North Carolina, or thereabouts.

The mules have organized. They have gathered their angry faces before me. Their spokesmule has delivered a list of demands. But I cannot read it. It's written in Mule, a language with which I am not the least familiar. I have asked for a translation, but their only response has been frenzied braying and snorting. We are at an impasse.

Yet even now there is a glimmer of hope. Because God is again descending through the clouds on his silver surfboard. He who can command the sun, the moon, and the stars surely also can command a herd of recalcitrant beasts.

He arrives with a slick 360 and offers a high five. How ya doing? man, he says. What's up with this confrontation thing? I explain to him that the only stumbling block is lack of communication. I am not literate in Mule. Apparently none of them are versed in anything else.

Is that all? he says. No problem. He turns to them and begins to bray and snort just like they do. They are quiet now, listening to him. When he finishes and they have brayed a response, he turns to me. Well, that was easy. What do they want? I ask. They want to see Nicholas Cage movies.

No way, I tell him. I draw the line there. I will not be cajoled by a band of terrorist mules into showing even one of his films. Not even one of the early ones. They have to be joking.

He shrugs his divine shoulders, adjusts his tunic, puts out the Marlboro cigarette he was smoking, and, in a whisp of golden vapor that turns orange, transforms into a wholly different being.

This one is blindingly bright red. Instead of hair there are purple flames around his head. He wears a full-length crimson cloak. He is grinning and nodding like he knows something I don't. I know who it is, but I cannot say his name. The mules are suddenly quiet and motionless.

"I saw your daughter singing the other day. Not bad," he says. I start to thank him and he laughs. "Not her singing, fool. That was ghastly, even to my degenerate taste. I mean what a hot looking babe. And as the Devil, I know hot babes. Maybe you can set me up with her, so she can fan my flames?"

I leap to grab him by the balls and throw him into the pit of non-existence. Except that he doesn't have any, so all I get is a handful of steaming, rotten blueberries that burn my hand. He laughs more and strikes my balls with a flaming rod. Curled on the ground in agony, I watch as he summons a shimmering image of Angel alone and afraid in a stone quarry. "I'm coming, my dear," he shouts, stepping on my head to jump toward the image and out of sight.

And here I remain. A vegetable that can see and occasionally think and nothing else. Living at the pleasure of technology, not God's or the Devil's or the Next of Kin's. I am doomed to suffer for eternity the horror of remembering.

14

W hile I looked for a place to live I was welcomed once more into the Anderson residence. John and Polly continued their warm, almost nurturing treatment. Even the children cheered me on.

Polly's coquettishness had tempered somewhat. But to a certain extent it was not something she could just turn off and on. So I remained very attracted to her and very much in orbit around her.

This was not problematic in the least, as far as I could tell, because I was hardly the only one in thrall to her. Not problematic, that is, for the family, the network, or the community. It was problematic for me because of her mysteriously powerful influence on almost everything I did, said, or thought.

John was a good man. Kind, generous, and forthright. He had been an athlete in college, Maddux Baptist Institute, the Fighting Anenomes, which is where he and Polly met. His best sport had been basketball, but he excelled at swimming, golf, and fly fishing as well. Apparently, Maddux boasted one of the few fly fishing teams among American colleges, before competitive team fly fishing became the spectator sports phenomenon it is today.

John took me under his wing. He introduced me to members of the team I had not met previously, showed me the lunchroom, the refrigerator that videotaped anyone who opened it, a measure adopted after a host of sack lunches were pilfered, and the walk-in pantry converted to a small chapel where employees could ask God to bless their lunches or snacks or cups of coffee. While I stayed with his family I rode to work with him in his Chevrolet Impala.

As part of my dogged effort to fit in, I also accompanied the family to Sunday services at the Weaselville Baptist Church, located in the neighboring town of Weaselville. The only pleasant part of this experience for me was sitting next to Polly in a crowded pew.

The pastor, Rufus Jefferson Davis, ran a most intense operation. He had been a fixture there for more than two decades. The congregation filled the pews every Sunday. So he had the confidence and authority of long tenure and popular devotion in addition to that transmitted along the power cables from God.

The pastor found sin everywhere he looked. Virtually all of his sermons, all the ones I heard at least, were litanies of where he had found sin during the previous week, since he had provided the last report the previous Sunday. He found sin in the produce aisle at the supermarket, where he spied two young mothers laughing over a phallus-shaped zucchini. He found sin at Jiffy Lube, where some "colored fellows" were listening to blasphemous "raping .. excuse me .. rapping" about disciples of the Devil "doing it" with "hoes" of Christ.

He found lots of sin on television, a medium he denounced as encouraging worship of the flesh in place of the holy spirit. He grandly excepted from this indictment the stalwart brothers and sisters who brought Your Christian Life into our homes, some of whom were members of his congregation.

As the only one present who was not a fervent Christian, and not accustomed to such a somber view of the world and humanity, I was not comfortable listening to the pastor's sermons. This kind of solemn certainty was alien to me. I kept hoping the pastor would hedge his bets by telling a joke once in a while.

John was an avid golfer. He played at least three times a week. One of his more remarkable achievements was convincing me to join him on the links, usually with some associates from YCL or Weaselville Baptist.

I knew about golf. I had even been on a course a few times. But never happily. I did not have enough of the attribute golf most demanded: concentration.

Still, since I never seemed to mind making a fool of myself, when John said he needed me to complete a foursome I obliged. The result was high potency frustration, relieved only rarely by a miraculously decent shot.

Our playing companions generally were patient and tolerant of my ineptitude and aggravation. They surely would have responded differently if I had carried out any of my frequent impulses to smash my club over a bench or hurl it into the water. Nevertheless, they unwittingly added to my exasperation by repeatedly broaching the subject of the Christian faith and how it could be of great benefit to me.

Those who had come to Jesus as adults were eager to share their stories. One, a CPA, told of how he had deposited a big client's tax return in a mailbox that he later saw did not have a scheduled pickup until the following day. Postmarked then the return would be late.

He agonized about it all night, contemplated turning to alcohol, even considered suicide. Instead, he chose to pray as he never had before, promising God that he would devote the rest of his life to Christ if only He would help.

The next day he lamented the tragedy to his regular mail carrier, who explained that an extra pickup had been scheduled for that box because it was tax day. So the return would have been postmarked on time after all.

While he told the story we were walking to my ball, which I had hit all of forty feet into a patch of weeds. After swinging twice without contacting the ball, I kicked it onto the fairway, intending thereafter to smack the guy in the head with my seven iron. Fortunately he had moved along the fairway, so I took it out on the ball and hit my best shot of the round.

At some point a month or so after I joined YCL some genius decided to have a golf tournament with two-person teams, a male and a female, but no husbands and wives on the same team. Decidedly averse to participating, I avoided any talk of it around the office.

However, John came to me one afternoon to say that Polly wanted to play but did not have a partner. Would I do it? Horrified at the thought of displaying my pathetic skill and sour temperament to one whom I still regarded as a supernatural goddess, I reminded him of my sad game and asked him to find someone else. Later that evening my phone rang. It was Polly.

"What's this I hear about you not wanting to team up with me for the tournament?" she said.

"Polly, I stink at golf. You don't want me on your team."

"Yes I do."

"Why?"

"Never mind that. Will you do it? For me? Please."

Melting like butter in a flame, I said ok.

I expected disaster. My feet barely wet with the new work, I would be peremptorily dismissed because my most enthusiastic supporter finally saw what a foul-tempered loser I was. If only I could bear the humiliation with dignity.

It was chilly and breezy when I arrived at the Mayberry Golf and Tennis

Club just after dawn on the day of the tournament. I had planned to get in a little practice before the ordeal began. However, many of the participants were already there, so I was obliged to socialize and eat pancakes instead.

John and Polly arrived shortly after. Wearing a long wool jacket because of the weather, she greeted me with her usual dazzling smile and said "howdy partner – ready to tear up the place?" Sure, I said sarcastically.

By start time the sun had dissolved the cool mist into warm muggy steam. Just before Polly and I went to the first tee she removed her jacket to reveal a sleeveless Carolina blue golf dress that immediately accelerated my heart rate. The powerful lust did not bode well for my golf game.

Luckily for us the tournament was played under best ball rules. This meant that after our tee shots we would play from wherever the best shot wound up. I teed off into an alligator den outside the course. Polly hit hers straight and true a hundred yards. Then we hopped on the cart and headed for her ball.

I somehow managed to hit my second shot back again to the alligators, who probably were growing irritated at my assault on their quarters. Polly again put us a hundred or so yards straight down the fairway. My third shot shattered a window in a condominium adjacent to the course. Polly's shot landed thirty yards from the green. From there I chipped into a waste basket beside the second tee. Polly left us a ten-foot putt.

This pattern then repeated for pretty much every hole For me it was golf at its absolutely most wretched, a round that will live in the annals of the sport as a model of golfing incompetence. A cow would have played better. If we had been keeping score as solo players my final total would have been 447 over par. Because of Polly's fair but steady game, however, we finished 17th out of 25.

Yet the astonishing aspect of that day was that it was the most fun I had experienced in many many years. For the first couple of holes my frustration dominated. I swore right and left, disregarding the sensitivities of my partner. I even considered wading among the alligators to retrieve my balls and crack some gator heads.

How did Polly react to this surliness? She laughed at me. Entertained actually by my foolish antics, she offered no sympathy and no encouragement. At first I was quite offended and hurt by her seemingly callous treatment of my intense aggravation. I let her know by clamming up and refusing to converse. Yet she persisted in enjoying the show.

After the second hole, having finally given up any hope of impressing her with my manly golf game, I accepted my fate and took her ribbing in a more resigned stride. From that point on we talked like gossiping housewives. About a myriad of subjects. Naturally she too prattled about how uplifting it was being part of the Christian community. This theme was easier to stomach when Polly addressed it.

She pointed out to me that the biggest hindrance to my golf game was my ego. One immediate benefit of surrendering to Christ, she said, was the tempering of the ego. Believing in something greater than yourself disarms the negative influence of the ego and frees a person to enjoy something just for its own sake.

I played golf, she said, like the I in me demanded. Every bad shot was a personal blow to this I. If I could rise above this influence I would improve my game. While scoffing at this nonsense, I told her that I appreciated her opinion.

We talked about our children, mine mostly. I was defenseless to Polly's skill in drawing information from me. Her interest was so genuine. I found myself blabbering about events in my life that I had never discussed with anyone.

She asked if I thought I would marry again. Doubtful, I said. A Hound Dog like me was not compatible with marriage. Her response: That's what all hound dogs say about themselves. Which she said with such a tender expression I wanted to hug her right there, on whatever fairway it was, in view of whoever might be watching.

Instead I remarked that married life seemed to be charming for her. She answered that the Christian faith they shared so fervently had everything to do with that. This profession should have shamed my mesmeric attention to every tee shot, approach, chip, and putt she made in that fetching golf dress. But it didn't.

I lost at least two balls on each hole. We did not bother to look for any of them. Polly hit her tee shot on the 15th hole into a grove of pine trees where some viney plant covered the ground. I said we should just play from the edge of the rough, but she wanted to look for the ball.

As we stepped through the vines she tripped on one, leaned into me for support, and remained in that position longer than necessary. Her perfume was incredibly sweet. I was paralyzed with delight. Finally, she pulled away, looked guiltily up into my eyes and said "sorry".

Three and a half hours after we started we finished the 18th and turned in the cart. I was exhausted and euphoric and ready to join the after party. However, after only a few minutes of watching Polly and John make the rounds as a happy couple, my joy evaporated. I left without notice. Went home and drank a tumbler of rum.

By the time of the tournament I had moved into an apartment in a large complex located in Pin Pointe, yet another of the small towns adjacent to Greendevil. This was a major step for me, because living with the Anderson's afforded me no relief from the sanctimonious and righteous ambience that pervaded the YCL facility and any gathering of people associated with it.

Everyone I encountered at YCL treated me like a member of the family. They were kind and generous and always seemed to genuinely care for my well-being. Yet it was not difficult for me to notice an ever present undercurrent of anxiety for my spiritual welfare.

I never sensed it when in conversation with one or two individuals. But it was eerily evident whenever I was with a group of YCL people. They seemed to share a concern for the presence of a deviant member whose lost soul must be rescued to restore the unanimous purity of the whole.

When I returned home to my pagan apartment, however, I could cast off the anointing oil I had been sprayed with all day. I could drop onto my couch with a Devil's Draft Lager and watch licentious and lascivious television programming, like *Baywatch* or *Desperate Housewives* or Lifetime movies.

The work itself was not challenging at all at first. I appeared on Morning Glory twice a week with new products, and on the late afternoon show, Your Christian Day, usually once a week. Otherwise I spent my time "developing" new programming. This entailed researching what other religious broadcasters were doing, imagining what products or services or activities would enhance a

Christian's lifestyle, and dreaming up innovative ways of presenting them.

The brass and I early on decided to produce a special one-hour experimental program to see how the concepts I came up with would fly. Naturally I would host it. So it would be a test for me as well.

I wanted a live audience. YCL programs were not taped before a live audience. Hence this would be a big leap for the network if I had my way. My main argument was that presenting products or services to a group of real people would enhance the show's authenticity and lessen its commercialism.

Instead of rigging the audience with paid actors, or network employees and their families, I wanted to announce that anyone could participate, even non-Christians. The show thus would exhibit a realism that might attract a wider audience and would demonstrate that YCL people were not closed minded puritans who wanted everyone to worship exactly the way they do. I was brought there to enliven YCL. This was the best way for me to do that.

After much debate, and with probably merited trepidation, the board in charge voted narrowly to go ahead with my plan. From that moment to the opening of the show I focused every active cell in my being on preparing the event. The stakes were pretty high for me. I knew that the format I insisted on could backfire big time, the show could slap a black eye on the network, and I could be run out of Greendevil on a rail.

First, we needed a venue. Some place large enough to accommodate the 25 to 30 audience members I had in mind and yet still be conducive to the intimate setting I believed was essential. YCL did not have any such facility, so I scouted around the area until I found what I was looking for at a local hotel.

Another new aspect of the program for me was that I would host but not do any demonstrations and I would not advocate for any of the products or services we featured. Essentially we would offer a forum for anyone who wanted to present something he or she believed would be of interest to our viewers. My job would be to keep the program entertaining.

The program would not have any deliberately planned religious elements. I did not yet feel comfortable working such a feature into the concept. Plus we hoped to attract a more general audience which we could steer to YCL's other programs.

Once the date, time, and location was set I began the search for guests. I mentioned the upcoming show during my appearances on Morning Glory and Your Christian Day and encouraged anyone who wanted to participate to contact me. I published notices in some of the small circulation weekly newspapers in the area. I even asked Pastor Davis to announce it. He refused, but said I could ask Deacon Pinkney, who then mentioned it during one of the services.

My efforts succeeded too well. I then had to select from all those who submitted the ten I deemed most appealing and appropriate for the program. Then came the challenge of disappointing the rest without losing their support for the show and YCL.

To come up with the live audience I posted a notice at the community college offering twenty bucks and a can of soda for anyone who attended, provided they called in beforehand to get on the list. Only a few days passed before we had our twenty-five names and fifteen backups.

The big event was scheduled for right about the six month anniversary of my joining YCL. As the day grew near the fear and anxiety of management became evident. They preferred to have more control. My maverick ways disturbed them. However, much to their credit, they did not interfere. The taping would not air live; so they could cancel the actual broadcast if things got out of hand.

John Anderson did approach me casually now and then to inquire how things were going. One time he was with Polly and I sensed with her an enthusiasm for the project that she was keeping to herself.

I bought a new suit for the occasion. White with very thin blue and red pin stripes. Enough flash to draw attention. Not enough to offend my conservative bosses.

The production would be raw. No music or fancy graphics. Just me, the presenters, and twenty-five citizens of the world.

Actually, by the time the camera started rolling and I started my introduction there were more than twenty-five people in the audience. Some members of the YCL family showed up, including the one and only Mrs. Anderson, whose smiling and encouraging presence motivated me immensely.

"Hello my friends here before me and out there wherever you may be watching. Welcome to the premier of Your Christian Life's newest program, *Your Inspired Lifestyle*, featuring folks who have new products or ideas they want to share to make your life better. Before we get started let me just say that I know how excited you all will be with our featured guests, but I ask that you hold your applause until they finish their presentation."

First guests: Jim and Kathy Fox, from Fox Fitness. Two wax people looking like they were just carved from a block. Their expertise is helping seniors stay fit. Both 60 plus, wearing skin tight body leotards.

I ask for an example of the regimen they might advise for someone like me: Run fifteen miles every day, swim for one hour, lift weights for two hours. That's all? I say, to laughter from the audience.

Also I should eat the Fox Formula, their own mix of alfalfa, platycodon, lima beans, plankton, goat liver, lizard eggs, and magic milk, a blend of extra fatty milk, creatine, ashwagandha, and magnesium. They have some of the Formula; would I like to try it? Sure. It is awful. I share my aghast expression with the audience and viewers. Needs a couple shots of whiskey.

Pearl Jenkins. 82 years. Shuffles up like she's afraid to be late. Could be Granny from the *Beverly Hillbillies*, but with much less situational awareness. She has designed a plant grower, four bowls connected consecutively to a watering tube fed from a bulb at the end. In the sample she brought there are four apparently healthy parsley plants. She demonstrates the watering process.

Some dude in the audience shouts "Perfect for growing weed". Nervous laughter among his fellow onlookers.

She says "Sure dear, but why would you want to grow weeds?" Giggling in the audience. I say "Pearl, I think the gentleman is referring to marijuana, which, as we all know, is not legal here".

Pearl responds: "Oh, that weed. I haven't tried to grow that. Only the poppies I use to make opium".

"While we're on the subject of plants and smoke," I introduce Perry Wilkinson, an earnest, middle-aged looking fellow, who is here to promote his discovery of a foolproof method to quit smoking. "Tobacco, that is, right Perry?"

Perry does not understand the question, ignores it, and pulls from his pocket a pouch containing leaves. He fishes out a leaf, pops it into his mouth, and chews it like gum. Does not say anything.

"What's that you're chewing on, Perry?"

"Sure enough" he responds.

I walk over to him and pick up the pouch. "What's in this pouch, Perry?"

"Leaves", he says.

"I can see that". He does not realize people are laughing at him. Gently squeezing his shoulder, I say "What kind of leaves are they?"

"Persimmon", he says indignantly, like I should know.

"And so you chew on these persimmon leaves to keep from smoking tobacco?"

"Yep".

"How long has it been since you had your last one?"

"Just now. You all saw me."

"I mean cigarette".

"Oh, I don't know, maybe a week."

"A week without smoking and you owe it all to the persimmon leaf. Thank you for coming and letting us know about your marvelous discovery. Perry Wilkinson ladies and gentlemen."

Next up: A young lady by the name of Kelly, and her dog Joe. Ten-year-old Kelly comes out nervously, but not as much so as might be expected for the age. Joe is a happy cocker spaniel who smells persimmon.

"Now Kelly, I understand that you have created a new food for dogs. Is that right?" She nods. "How did you do that?"

"Well, I just mixed up some stuff and tried it and he loved it." She is looking down at Joe while talking and cannot be heard.

"So you just mixed up some stuff, fed it to him, and he loved it?" Nods. "And you're going to show us how it's done?" Nods, hands Joe's leash to me, goes off and comes back with a tray she can barely hold, but does.

I can hear the repeated rounds of "aahh" and "so cute" coming from the audience. Kelly sets the tray on the counter we have set up. In a bowl she pours cheerios, chicken broth, tuna fish, and pancake syrup, mixes it with a wooden spoon, and sets the bowl on the floor before Joe.

He is not interested. Still trying to find the persimmon. Kelly is ready to cry. I say "maybe if I try it first" and kneel down to sniff the bowl. Joe is curious, comes to see what I'm doing, and, since he is there already, decides to wolf down the concoction. Success! Kelly is ecstatic. The audience is cheering. And I am back on my feet raising Kelly's hand in triumph.

The rest of the show proceeded smoothly, but unremarkably. A juicer of course. A talking coffee pot that reminded the user to do such things as take medications, etc. A magazine dedicated to helping people simplify their lives.

A woman who self-published about a new way to lose weight: Eat the same thing every day. To lose weight successfully people need to make food less important in their lives, not more. Eating the same thing every day will help them do that. Her book contained 160 pages. I was about to ask her why she needed that many pages to explain what she just did in five minutes when I got the signal that our hour was almost finished.

I thanked everyone for participating, YCL for their willingness to brave new trails in broadcasting, and the Lord Jesus Christ for having a sense of humor.

It was a memorable event. For me especially, not the least because of the extended hug I got from Polly after we finished. Although I ascribed the affection she communicated to my shamefully lustful imagination.

She thought the program had been "awesome", but could not say whether the YCL brass would feel that way. John did not come with you? No he stayed with the kids. Want to go somewhere and have a drink or some tea? She would love to, she said, but she had to get home. Rain check? Rain check.

The YCL management was not entirely pleased with the program. However, they did not prevent it from airing, which happened two days later, and three times more over the following week. They did not fire me. But they did insist on having more input for future shows.

One day, while debate over the program's future continued, I came home to find an envelope from Angel. In it was a CD and a short note explaining that she had recorded a demo of some of her music. I listened to it more than 100 times.

I am in a pathetic situation, what with all these tubes and wires and cables servicing what is left of my body. And this fiberglass dome sitting on my head rooting shafts that are plumbing the depths of my parietal lobe.

And this catheter like tube that has swallowed my penis. Is that to extract sperm to impregnate women with my mutating DNA? Maybe there are women even now hooked up at the other ends, receiving lunatic sperm cells that will insure the survival of inherent insanity, even when the Commission is dictating regulations that would conform all chaotic theories to one smooth standard coated with tree sap to steady the feet.

But we're coming for you doctors. Monty has fired up the men. He has General Halftrack commanding a tank battalion. They are driving the new Kia KL25, which pushes 22 knots and fires a ten-inch shell loaded with explosive bacon grease.

15

The YCL executives decided to adopt a modified version of the program for a weekly broadcast. Specifically they wanted it to have more of a Christian emphasis. No ideas were offered on what that meant or how to do it. I was to come up with a proposal for revising the format accordingly and they would review it.

Disappointed, but hardly surprised, I began to wrestle with the concept. Right away I realized that I did not have the proper perspective on the matter and that I needed help from someone who would know what they intended by the term "Christian emphasis". Also someone who would have influence at YCL.

I immediately knew who I wanted. But there was a heap of politics involved. And personal complexities. I started with John.

I invited him to have lunch with me at Diddley's Dog Palace. Over his Heel Dog and my Demon Deacon Dog I explained what I had in mind, the type of person, without mentioning any names, hoping he would figure it out himself. He thought it was a good idea, but did not mention any candidates. So I let it drop until we were driving back.

I asked him if Polly ever talked about going to work outside the home. He said no. They were a traditional family, he explained, which meant that she believed it was important for her to stay home for the sake of the children. That was that. Time to search for other possibilities.

The problem I had, however, was that the idea of having an assistant and the idea of Polly being the one had occurred to me almost simultaneously. So I was not motivated to look for someone else.

About a week after my lunch with John I had a visitor. Polly. Made up to kill. Thigh length red dress, tight on top. She said John had told her about my inquiry and they had talked about it a few times since. The more she thought about it, she explained, the more excited she became about the idea. Finally, she convinced John that she should at least go talk to me about it.

In my mind there was nothing to talk about. She would not need to work full-time, just whatever hours she could spare. Much of what I needed her for she could do at home anyway. So there did not need to be much disruption for the family. I got the impression that she did not believe there was much to talk about as well, but also that the situation with John required delicate handling.

Another week passed before she called to say that if I still wanted her she was ready to accept and get started. And John? I asked. He's on board. Not enthusiastic, but ok.

A week later and there she was. Looking gorgeous as usual and reporting for work. We met in my glass-walled office, she in a guest chair, me behind my desk, and talked about ideas for the show. Members of the YCL family came by to welcome her and a group that included John and I took her for lunch at Chez Lafarge.

Our task was challenging: To take a show like I had designed, featuring products and services in a loose, popular, homespun format and give it a religious, specifically Christian, orientation. What do we do? Quote some bible verses in between presentations? Have Pastor Davis appear each week with a new list of sinners? Offer mini-sermons on the spiritual benefits of persimmon leaf chewing?

Our show was intended to promote living a good Christian life beyond the weekly attendance at Sunday services. So Polly suggested that she could search for passages from the New Testament that concerned living a good life in ways that did not constitute worship. Examples? She would find some.

"Paul's first letter to the Corinthians has a few good ones," she said at our next meeting. Wait a minute, I responded. I never liked his music. I did not know he had any religious significance. She thought I was joking. "Saint Paul the apostle, not Paul Macartney." Sorry, that was the only Paul I knew not associated with a last name.

"Chapter 6, verses 18, 19, and 20: Every other sin a person commits is outside the body, but the immoral person sins against his own body ... Do you not know that your body is a temple of the holy Spirit within you, whom you have from God, and that you are not your own? ... For you have been purchased at a price. Therefore, glorify God in your body."

That's good. That should work nicely. I thanked her and asked about lunch. No, she was already engaged for a church meeting.

And that typified most of our work days. We would meet in the morning and talk over the progress we had made. Then every day I would mention lunch and every day she would decline, except when John or other YCL people were going too.

I did not view us having lunch as being anything other than two colleagues having lunch together. It was not like I had ulterior motives, at least not consciously. My feelings for the woman certainly were not diminishing the more she sat in my office. But I also respected her and I respected John and believed that it would be truly horrible and tragic if I ever did anything to come between them. As to Polly's motives for consistently declining lunch alone with me, I did not know anything and tried not to think about it.

So the YCL executives approved our idea to include references to New Testament passages as a predicate for the rest of the program. We scheduled another premier. 30 minutes this time. A much smaller, more carefully selected audience.

"Good afternoon ladies and gentlemen, both here and out there watching. Welcome to what we might call the second premier of *Your Inspired Lifestyle*. We have some very interesting and inspiring guests here with products and ideas to enhance your Christian life. Before we welcome our first presenter, I would like us to hear and consider the words of Paul the Apostle, in his first letter to the Corinthians. This is found in Chapter 6, verses 18, 19, and 20.

"Every other sin a person commits is outside the body, but the immoral person sins against his own body ... Do you not know that your body is a temple of the holy Spirit within you, whom you have from God, and that you are not your own? ... For you have been purchased at a price. Therefore, glorify God in your body.

"Now what is Paul telling the Corinthians, and us? I think he is saying that our bodies, our lives really, are not ours alone, to do with as we please, to abuse and disrespect. No our lives belong to God as much as to ourselves. So if we maltreat ourselves we maltreat God. That is really what this program is all about: Exploring ways to help us thrive as individuals, so God can thrive."

This little talk blew Polly and the YCL honchos away. They were astonished that I had in me this religious eloquence. They finally got excited about airing the show in a regular weekly spot. Little did they know how ridiculous I thought my talk was. Crafty, but hardly sincere.

With more subterfuge like that I was able to keep the show going, all the way disguising superbly the fact that I was faking it. Every week Polly came up with new bible quotes and I weaved them into my introduction with similar gloss.

There was never a shortage of presenters. Once the program was going out across the nation every week we were deluged with inquiries and submissions. YCL even had to hire a second assistant for me to process them. This was partly due to Polly's reticence in devoting the time needed. Her family came first.

Except that she continued to dress so as to maximize her sex appeal. I concluded that she was unconsciously trying to attract me, sexually and otherwise, while at the same time maintaining an impassable wall preventing me from doing anything about it. Increasingly frustrated, I struggled to stifle the desire she was stimulating and concentrated on my friendship with John, in hopes that it would keep me out of trouble.

Like we did on the golf course, Polly and I treated each other almost like buddies. Whenever I got upset and complained about some stupid thing she teased me mercilessly. She liked to remind me of her little sermon about ego.

Now and then, with a mischievous deadpan, she told me I needed a wife. I usually responded that a wife was the last thing I needed, but that I would "work on it". She would then stare at me somberly for a moment, before brightening and changing the subject.

When we talked during the tournament about our families she told me she had three sisters, one older and married and two younger, one engaged. One day I responded to her "wife" comment by asking playfully if her sister was still available. She reacted with rare anger that surprised both of us. She did not mention the subject again.

Pretending to be horrified by my account of the stripper party, Polly nevertheless asked for more details, as if she were indulging in a perverse thrill. Similarly incredulous at other stories from my past, she exuded awe for the mystery man I appeared to be. She always concluded these conversations by assuring me that she would pray for my salvation.

It was inevitable that eventually the magnetic force Polly exerted on me would become irresistible. Unable even to contemplate what would happened then, I repressed all thoughts about it and consequently grew steadily more bitter and resentful, which poisoned my attitude towards the work.

Nonetheless, I managed to keep up appearances, both in the YCL offices and on the show. Firmly believing that no one knew what was going on beneath my charismatic façade, I labored on and rode the show's success. I developed a national image and even accepted offers to speak at various functions around the country.

There were extreme challenges in purporting to be a real Christian broadcaster. It required me to learn and keep up with matters that a Christian television personality should know about. Faking religious knowledge and faith was not easy.

Not that I, or anyone at the network, ever represented that I was a Christian, or that I was not. The YCL management continued in their hopeful assumption that I was on the road to Jesus and that it was only a matter of time before they could celebrate my grand baptism. Those stalwarts outside the network who met me or listened to me took it for granted that I was one of the flock. I do not believe it ever even occurred to them to question it.

However, this unquestioning acceptance would have been sorely tested if I had displayed ignorance on topics with which most Christians would be familiar. When I first arrived at YCL I knew very little about such topics. With help from the Andersons, other YCL people, and even Pastor Davis, I scaled enough of the learning curve to survive longer than I should have.

It was not like I completed some exhaustive survey of Christian theology. My hunch was that I only needed enough education to enable me to convince people that I knew what I was talking about. For me accidentally to assert an unacceptable viewpoint would not be too problematic. But were I to state as a fact something the Christian world regarded as untrue, however dogmatically, trouble would ensue, especially if anyone suspected that my statement was a product of ignorance.

For example, I could contend that the apocryphal writings of the Second and Third Centuries, which were left out of the New Testament, more fully and accurately described the general reception of the Sermon on the Mount than did the gospels that were included. No one would accuse me of being a fake Christian.

On the other hand, if I referred to Jesus laboring for days to scratch out one hundred copies of the sermon for distribution among the curious who were not present, plenty of the Christian faithful would at least wonder whether I was on the level.

Sometimes I had to improvise and come up with my own spin. During one episode of our show a lady was demonstrating how to make sweet deviled eggs. An audience member stood up and loudly declared: "The apostle Polybius warned us that nothing of the Devil be sweet."

I responded that he must be referring to the apostle Polobicus and what he actually said, "if I recall correctly, is that the Lord is so mighty He can make even the Devil taste sweet." The guy's consternation was touching. But he had no answer, and no one else called me on it.

The conferences were especially nerve-wracking. I would speak to more than a hundred zealous Christian soldiers, each with knowledge that dwarfed mine and possessed of a powerful secret weapon: Certainty. For my disingenuousness to remain undetected and unsuspected I had to pick through a minefield of potentially troublesome topics. Generally I stayed safely in secular subjects, only tangentially related to religion.

Yet whenever I got rolling on a subject that aroused the passions of my audience the danger of exposure vanished. "Brothers and Sisters: As I was traveling here to this great blessed conference I happened to see an article in some slick big city magazine – I forget which one – where the author stated as his opinion that most people in today's society deny that our Lord and Savior Jesus Christ actually lived and died. He called this fact of faith a myth. As a television broadcaster disseminating the word of Christ throughout this nation, I can tell you categorically that this author is mistaken, misinformed, and misguided!"

After the session I was besieged by excited champions of the cross wanting to shake my hand and praise my commentary on the sorry state of the world. Fortunately, no one asked for more information about the magazine, the article, or the author, which were wholly the product of my imagination.

At one conference I attended I came dangerously close to blowing it. Lucky for me it was a smaller, regional event, in Big Drum, Montana, so the ripples were geographically limited. In responding to a comment about arbitrary Roman justice, I noted the example of John the Baptist, "the Apostle", who was beheaded at the whim of the "Empress Salome".

A palpable stir spread through the assembly. My fellow panelists looked at me with stern puzzlement. The scene was tense for me because I had no idea what error I had made. So I sat down and kept silent for the remainder of the session.

Afterwards a couple of Methodist ministers questioned me about the "apostle" John the Baptist and "Empress" Salome. Before they finished the interrogatory, however, I figured out my mistake. So I was able to escape by claiming that I had misspoken. They were not convinced, and they may have passed their suspicions around their little village in Nowhere, Montana. But that would mark the furthest extent of the damage.

These speaking trips provided great relief for me from the tension I increasingly felt at the YCL offices. Once again I was able to relax in a hotel room – full mini-bar now, luxury liquids for cleansing and revitalizing, the finest gourmet meals brought to me at my summons. I could watch ordinary television. Like *Jeopardy*: What are the ingredients for an ANFO bomb? Or *60 Minutes*: So chemical analysis of the traces of feces on these slips of toilet paper prove that George Bush ate Kentucky Fried Chicken at the time he claimed to be having chicken carbonara at the Olive Garden?

One day I was scanning radio stations while waiting in a rental car return line at an airport when a song caught my ear and grabbed my attention. It was a song I had heard before. The singer was someone I knew: Angel.

My Angel on the radio! One of the tunes on the CD she sent me, a piece I had listened to, like I did the entire CD, over and over and over again. "Back in the Alley" it was called. A blues ballad. Beautiful. Almost drowned out by the horns honking behind me as I waited for the song to finish before driving into the garage. When I was back in Pin Pointe I sent her a congratulations card and pleaded for details about how her song came to be on the radio.

So for many months I lived a daily routine of false behavior. Essentially I was an actor playing two roles, or two angles of the same role: A sincere promoter of a creed I actually did not accept and the *friend* and mere *colleague* of a woman for whom I had a burning, barely controllable desire. I endured a long slow slide into abject bitterness.

Somewhere along this painful path my will finally began to weaken. I continued to keep a professional distance from Polly and refrained from any statement or act that would have blown up our relationship. But my commitment to YCL faltered. I grew apathetic. I no longer cared what the executives might do with me.

This attitude affected my performance on our show. At first I merely displayed less enthusiasm, and truncated my religious commentaries. After a few weeks had passed, however, I became downright mischievous. In place of an epistle from the apostle Paul, I recited from Yogi's epistle to the Yankees:

"Though I be not among you as I would wish, do not forsake the struggle, but double or triple your progress, and steal the base left open and the next, until you shall come to home. As the bat strikes the ball it will fly and be coveted by those who would glove it, but beyond the confines of the heavenly park it shall pass and all shall come together at home. Then must you guard the fields of green against the self-same ball and thrust your welcoming glove to stay its path and keep thine enemies from mounting onto their desired bases."

The storm broke more slowly than I anticipated, probably because the brass had stopped watching the show. The response registered by viewers over the following day, both positive (humorous some said) and virulently negative (blasphemy some called it), alerted everyone in the "family" to the anomaly. I shrugged off the complaints, saying I was only trying to inject some levity, so I survived for one more show.

"What is going on?" Polly, almost in tears, finally confronted me.

"You tell me," I said petulantly. We were in my office as usual, standing this time, my desk between us.

"That stunt you pulled. Why?" I did not want her to cry.

"I don't know. I just felt like it. Just trying to goof things up a bit." Her moist eyes burned my conscience.

"Are you going to keep it up?"

"No. I don't know. Probably not."

"*Probably* not!" she stammered. "Don't you know they will fire you?"

With as sympathetic an expression as I could muster, I said "Polly, I really don't care". Our eyes locked. She started to sob. "I'm sorry," I continued. "I wish things were different. Oh how I wish things were different." She appeared to understand, to recognize something she had for so long refused to acknowledge.

"Is it because of me?" With intense sadness I nodded yes. Suddenly still, eyes downcast, she seemed overcome by profound melancholy and despair, where she had always exhibited brightness and exalted joy. "Ok, I understand," she whimpered, and, with a longing gaze at me, left the office.

Now even more dispirited, I avoided contact with anyone at YCL, except the handful who were necessary to produce the show. John in particular I did not wish to see, much less talk to. He made no effort that I knew of to counsel me. Perhaps he knew that it would be pointless given the circumstances and what I guessed was a significant change in Polly's demeanor that would not have been difficult for a perceptive man like him to explain.

So we did one more show. Polly, who had attended every one we did, was not there. "Today I have a very recently discovered missive from Clyde of Beryllium to the Millipedians. Beware of this dude calling himself Paul the Apostle. He is a fake and regularly wets his robes. He sucks the camels' genitalia. He leavens his bread with the sperm of lambs. His doctrines are like the gum produced by the pyracantha bush, which pierces the flesh of those who would take it, while the gum itself sticks permanently to them, not to be removed even upon their inevitable remorse at disturbing it. Tis better to inhale the back wind from a cat than to set foot in his den of iniquity."

The set suddenly went dark and the standard lights came on, indicating that the taping had stopped. Two uniformed men approached me and said they had been asked to escort me from the premises. My career in Christian broadcasting was over.

One final heartbreaking scene would cap my time living in North Carolina. I resolved to leave as soon as possible, but I had nowhere to go and the landlord required thirty days notice, so I was stuck there for at least a couple of weeks.

Most of that time I spent just feeling crappy, sorry for myself, lovesick, and wondering what the hell I was going to do. I left a phone message for Jill Taylor asking if she might have any work for me. She responded that she would put me back on the list.

A week after I was dismissed from the show and YCL I was taking an afternoon nap on the couch. Someone knocked on the door. It was Polly.

She was buttoned up in a drab raincoat and wore a very old and faded baseball cap. I invited her in, but she would not sit down. She told me in a somewhat hoarse voice that she had come to say good bye. I did not answer. I could not speak. I could only stare helplessly into her eyes, now filling with tears.

I stretched out my arms to hug her. At first she shook her head and drew back. Then she lunged forward to hug me, sobbing.

We remained together for a few minutes. I lifted her head gently. Tears were glistening on her face. Her lips parted, inviting me to kiss them. I did.

The dam that had contained the passion burst open. At that instant we became lovers, our mouths locked, our hands grasping for each other. For those moments of ecstasy I was transported to a paradise I never knew existed. Overwhelmingly powerful joy.

She pulled slightly away and said through wretched weeping "I love you. I have loved you for months. I am delirious with it. But I can't. I can't! Please understand. I can't do this to my family. I can't! I can't!"

What could I say, except "I love you too, Polly. I think I have since the first day we met." This brought a courageous, but weak smile. And resolve.

One more look. One more "I can't". She bolted through the door, ran to her car, and rocketed out of the parking lot.

Three wretched days later I returned to my old stomping grounds.

I am awake, lonely, and miserable, existing here among mechanically throbbing medical devices, the only light glowing blue and green off their digital display panels. I imagine the committee meeting erupting in a melee over some trivial issue, like Oppenheimer passing around doodles of Teller as a bilious bull frog.

The committee was mine and I have lost it. Now all I have are bitter memories and despair. The devices keep me living. Why?

16

The only glimmer of joy that appeared amidst my profound gloom was a letter from Angel:

"Dear Father. Thank you for the card. That's pretty wild how you happened to hear the song. Not much to say about how it happened. I have been sending that demo CD I sent you around to so many places. With no response. Then one day a guy invited me to audition at a club where recording people hang out. I did. One of the producers liked my stuff and signed me to a tentative contract. We recorded a couple of the songs again and one of them got picked up by a radio music service. A few people have told me they heard it. But so far nothing else has happened. I do shows at small clubs, etc. now and then, but otherwise I still have my waitress job to pay the bills. I hope you are well. Love, Angel".

At least she had not forgotten me. That was something. Otherwise my life felt as empty as an abandoned house.

Jill Taylor set me up to demonstrate a fish cleaning gadget at a sporting goods store. The more fish guts I pulled out the more despondent and apathetic I became. Until no one was watching or listening and the store owner angrily shut me down.

After that I did not hear from Jill. I called to ask my status and she told me I was still on the list but that nothing "suitable" had come up. It did not take a rocket science demonstrator to read between those lines. I needed to find some other way to earn a living before the money I had saved ran out.

I had no hope whatsoever of ever getting over Polly and certainly no hope of ever seeing her again. My memory of her dominated my thoughts, festered like a boil in the pit of my stomach, and secreted toxic chemicals into my brain. How was I going to find work in such a condition?

Yet I had to try. Banking on my sales experience, I applied for a number of retail positions. I colored the gray out of my hair, hipped my wardrobe, and tuned up my swagger to disguise my age. But:

"Have you ever sold herbal teas and extracts?" Well, maybe not *herbal* teas. I have enjoyed a few Long Island ice teas. What do you mean by 'extracts'?

"It's a bit unusual for a man like you to want to sell women's lingerie. Do you have experience in this line?" No, I have never worn women's lingerie. I have handled some. I know how to unfasten a bra strap. And I did try some edibles one time.

"Selling pharmaceuticals requires some affinity for chemistry. Would you qualify with respect to that?" I know the difference between a beaker, a test tube, and a Bunsen burner. I know that AUH_2O is Goldwater and that hydrogen is number one. Is that affinity enough?

So I tried substitute teaching. Which lasted only until I had sent the entire class to the office because one of the students had called me a goat and the rest refused to identify the culprit.

A funeral home gave me a chance to work as a program assistant. Unfortunately, during my first viewing I saw one of the elderly visitors sleeping in a chair, mistook him for the deceased, and was about to put him back in the casket when I realized my mistake. Too late.

It was beginning to look like I would have to turn to a life of crime. Knock off a couple of banks or something. Or do some check kiting, whatever that is. I even thought about looking up Frank Valentino to see if he needed me to take care of anything.

Finally I landed some sales work: telemarketing. Did not even have to leave my apartment. Got a list of names and phone numbers, sat down at the kitchen table and dialed the first one.

"Good afternoon sir, how are you?"

"Fine. What do you want?"

"Well I'm with a company called Phenomenal Floors. We do expert installations, refurbishing, and cleaning. Our estimator will be in your neighborhood in the next few days and I was hoping to schedule an appointment for him to show you what we can do. How does that sound?"

"No thanks."

"Sir, it would only take a few minutes of your time, depending on how many rooms you have. Even if you don't take us up on the incredible offers we have going right now the estimator will give you some valuable information about your floors and how to maintain them. May I put you down for Thursday in the afternoon, say about 2:30?"

"No I really don't want it."

"Well, sir, let me just ask you when was the last time your floors were done? Re-laid or refurbished or cleaned?"

"I don't remember."

"So it must have been a while if you don't remember. You know that well-maintained floors are one of the most important considerations in determining the value of a home. And if you leave them in that condition for too long it takes a lot more work and a lot more expense to restore them if you or your heirs ever decide to sell. How about Friday morning at 10:30?"

"Oh all right." Victory. At least some commission, more if the estimator hooks him for a job. But this employment required far too much work for the pitiful compensation I received. I only lasted two weeks.

Hoping, praying, fantasizing that Polly would try to contact me, and wallowing in idleness, I began to center my day around the arrival of the mail. When I looked from my living room window at an extreme angle I could see the bank of mailboxes. So each day I stationed myself there for a couple of hours hoping to see the mail carrier distributing the mail. Then I would stroll over to see if I received anything, my heart pounding harder with every step. If I did not see the carrier I would make multiple trips. Fully aware of what a pathetic life it was, I felt powerless to change it.

Time and time again I decided to solve my dilemma by writing to Polly. I would carefully compose what I considered a courageous letter that did not beg for sympathy and then tear it to shreds in a fit of anguished rage. Sometimes I stared at the telephone fantasizing that it was about to ring with her call. or that I would summon the will to dial her number and fuck the consequences.

Months passed with no job and no word from Polly. My savings dwindled below what I needed to live, although I still had unused credit card credit. I paid the rent late and only after threats from the landlord. Food I bought with a credit card. Alcohol too. Yes lots of alcohol.

Screwdriver for breakfast. If I had orange juice. Bloody Mary if I had tomato juice. Otherwise plain old vodka and coffee. Breakfast usually continued for at least two hours, while I watched one morning show or another. Had to know what the princesses of England were wearing to Ascot. Or whether director Albert Pujols regretted casting Whoopi Goldberg as the villainous professional bowler Madam Blackball in his movie about the infamous Gutteral Ball Scandal that shattered the once polished wholesome image of the sport.

For lunch, which started right after breakfast, it was Mike Ditka Malt Liquor or Duesenberg Ale or Houdini's Hard Cider. Sometimes all three. Sometimes all three mixed together.

By Noon I was preoccupied with the mail delivery, so I took in only snatches of the mid-day TV offerings. Soap operas mostly. One in particular, because it had a character, Sophie Christensen, who looked a lot like Polly. If Sophie was not on screen I was not interested.

If she was I masochistically stared at her teaching remedial quantum mechanics to a class of jocks who were not shy about asking for some "private tutoring". That is until her husband, Sammy "The Greaser" Botanski, showed up flashing the .45 he concealed inside his jacket. "If any a yous wants tutoring I got the perfect pedagogical tool right here."

If the mail had not yet arrived by the end of lunch I limited myself to a few Budweisers. From the time the mail did arrive until I passed out I enjoyed one whiskey and soda after another. I will not try to describe any of what I watched on television during this period because it likely would not be accurate.

I gave up trying to find work or a way to earn a living. I stopped paying rent and waited to be evicted. I expected to spend the rest of my life, what little was left of it, homeless, on the street, eating what I could find in the trash or discarded in the gutter, and sleeping wherever there was room and a decent chance of not being disturbed.

Someday some bloodthirsty loser would cut my throat and that would be that. Just had to hope he knew how to do it. A botched slashing would be horrendous.

The weird thing was, however, that I did not get evicted. Two or three months passed without me paying any rent; yet I heard nothing from the landlord, who previously had been so eager to pry the money from me one day after it was due. I could not figure it out. Not that I tried very hard; I was too drunk most of the time to even think about it.

One day I even passed by the landlord on my way back from the mailbox. He just said hello and went about his business. What the fuck, I thought, afraid to mention it in case he had come down with dementia or something and would demand all that back rent if I triggered his memory of it.

Finally I could not stand it any more. The mystery was likely to be blown open at any time, with horrible consequences for me. I saw the landlord trimming some bushes and went down to confront him.

"What's going on?" I said.

"With what?" he answered pleasantly.

"With my rent. I haven't paid you any rent for months. Why haven't you evicted me?" He did not suddenly realize how behind I was and come at me with his trimmer. He just looked at me placidly and said "Somebody's been paying it."

"Who?" Sworn to secrecy, he would not say. "Come on, don't I have a right to know who is doing this wonderful thing for me?" Maybe, but not from him.

"It's not my daughter, Angel, is it?" Nope. Might as well throw out some long shots. Someone at the Your Christian Life network? Nope. Travis Small, Salty Pete, El Greco, Del Baxter? Nope. One more try. My ex-wife Olivia? No answer.

Oh my God. That blessed woman. Saving her despised ex from the streets. I was stunned to the core. And grateful beyond measuring. I could not imagine what had motivated her to do such a thing. And to do it without taking credit. Furthermore, how did she know anything about my situation?

I ran back to my unit and called the court, asking to be put through to Judge Holmes, but her courtroom was in session. I was offered voicemail, but I was afraid I might start blubbering and screw up any message I tried to leave. So I poured up a whiskey and soda. But I could not drink it. It was disgusting to me all of a sudden.

With less than $200 left in credit on my card, I used a chunk of it to buy flowers and have them delivered to her at the Third District. I had the florist inscribe "I will never forget this" on the card attached, with a postscript explaining that I had wrangled the truth from the landlord; he did not blow the secret.

That done, I stared myself down in the mirror. Poured cold water over my head. Slapped myself several times with a spatula. Poured every drop of alcohol in the house down the drain. Walked five miles. Read a few chapters from *The Wealth of Nations*. Took a long hot and cold shower. Wrote a letter to my congressman complaining about the capital gains tax structures, the underfunding of infrastructure improvements, and lax enforcement of the Endangered Species Act. Took another shower, cold then hot. Ate a plate of flaming hot chicken wings and a raw garlic salad. Which resulted in yet another shower. Read one chapter from *Wildflowers of North America*. Drank four cups of chamomile tea. And fell asleep.

In the morning a new man woke up in my bed.

The wound named Polly still festered, but it did not hurt quite so much.

I resolved to do whatever was required for me to crawl out from this hole I had dug for myself, starting with adopting the right attitude for turning my skills into a profitable occupation, to stop drinking, and to repay Olivia. Who called to thank me for the flowers and invite me to have lunch with her.

It was a delightful meeting. Gone was any trace of the animosity that had so clouded our relationship in recent years. She listened raptly to the tale of my adventure in Christian broadcasting, although for the moment I said nothing about falling in love with Polly.

Nothing much had changed at the court, she said, except that she was getting weary of the daily grind, the daily parade of knuckleheads that came before her, which sometimes included the parties themselves, she added with a wry chuckle.

My story of hearing Angel on the radio amazed her. She had not heard from Angel for a few months, which she supposed was good, since it should mean Angel was at least making a living.

When I had finished enough of my Rueben sandwich to talk without spitting food I started a lengthy speech I had rehearsed about how grateful I was for what she did and how it already has dramatically changed my life. She did not want to hear it and interrupted me with "I heard you had been hurt and I wanted to help. No big thing."

From whom had she heard that I had been hurt? Evasive, clearly not wishing to disclose anything, she just said a little bird had told her and immediately proceeded to reveal her real purpose. "One of my reasons for doing it was a selfish one". I must have looked painfully perplexed, because she wasted no more time.

"I am considering a run for public office. State legislature or maybe even higher." This was tremendously exciting news for me.

"That's great! A great idea! About time I would say. Please let me know how I can help." Calling her rent payments on my behalf so far "an advance", she asked me to manage her campaign.

She explained that while she knew I had no experience in politics, what I did have, however, and what she needed most, was media savvy. I was just the kind of suave, charismatic, smooth talking dude who could really excel managing a campaign. After all, it would not be much different from selling products. Or convincing people of what was good for a Christian life, even though I was not Christian, and not even a religious person at all for that matter. Finally, she said she had seen some of my YCL programs, and that I was as good on my feet as anyone she had ever seen on TV.

It was a no-brainer. Although I had no interest in politics, and needed some education on the subject, I knew how to work the media and people in general. The day before I was a pitiful drunk, expecting to die at the hands of a vagrant with a switchblade. Now I had what seemed like a real sweet job.

Olivia explained further that campaigning as a sitting judge would cramp the manner in which she could stump. She had to maintain the dignified aura expected of her. So she needed me to work the muck and to promote her views and experience, etc. by means that would be foreclosed to her personally.

So just like that I started a new life. There was a lot to do. A lot to learn. Sinking myself into it forced the memory of Polly into a pocket that remained closed as long as I was busy enough.

I wanted her to run for president. Governor? Congress? But no. Olivia decided she wanted to win. So, twelve months before election day, she filed as a candidate for the State Senate representing District 35. The incumbent republican, Orville Roundtop, would be trying for his second term. We had no idea at that time who else would sign up for the democratic primary.

There was one thing we desperately needed before we could even do anything besides fill out the registration forms: Money. We had to amass a modest war chest to launch the campaign and hope that it would grow once Olivia's candidacy gained some traction.

Fortunately she had some fans with a little cash to spare. Principal among them was her partner, Heidi, and her family. When they first learned that Heidi was homosexual they were not pleased. After she met Olivia and entered into an enduring relationship, however, they became more accepting and grew to love Olivia as a member of the family.

Heidi's father had been a Major League Baseball player, a pitcher. Even though he had enjoyed only a modicum of success with four different teams, he had saved his earnings and invested it in a chain of sports bars called The Relief Pitcher.

Heidi's mother inherited a substantial estate acquired in the funeral home industry. Apparently she wrestled with lingering emotional issues resulting from having to eat and do homework on a coffin with a dead person inside.

Olivia's own family was always supportive, but, with one exception, did not live prosperous lives. The one exception was her cousin Buddy. Buddy was "in real estate" as he called his profession. It seemed that he was associated with a great number of deals, some legitimate, some not so much, involving property in Southern California and the Las Vegas area of Nevada. Out of Olivia's jurisdiction, the family often said thankfully.

One of my early assignments was to travel west in search of Buddy and some of his money. I found him living at the Bellagio Hotel in Las Vegas. Never having met the guy, and knowing of him only his reputation, I expected a garrulous and unctuous smooth talker, wearing a loud silk suit with no tie. No doubt he would be constantly at meetings, anticipating a phone call, or waiting for a messenger.

Buddy, however, turned out to be a fat slob. He answered the door in his underwear, offered me a Coors and some of the Chinese food he was eating out of a box, and lowered the volume of the TV, which was showing a *My Three Sons* marathon. He did not stop chewing while he talked, so particles of food projected onto his enormous belly.

A warm and affable man. Flattered by a visit from someone representing the family back home, especially his cousin the judge. Grateful to be asked for a donation to the campaign and eager to come up with more should we need it. Not likely that he would be going back there any time soon, but I should take his regards for everyone.

Financial support also came from the legal community: law firms, like Blizzard, Gizzard & Wizard (having taken on William Wizard as a new named partner) and Lizard, Brown & Brinkerhoff (having taken on Brenda Brinkerhoff as a new named partner), and some solo attorneys. They figured it was wise to help the judge, at least until she resigned or lost. A couple of her judicial colleagues tossed in a few bucks as well.

Some successful small business owners also kicked in. These included Carolyn Miller, owner of The Greenland Grill, the first restaurant in the area to feature grilled Greenland cuisine. Another was Jerry Bottompumper, who operated four locations of The Water Store. Offering containers of water, each specially treated with a different array of chemicals and minerals, it was the only store east of the Great Divide that sold salted sulfur water in a bottle, primarily for use as a mouth rinse, but also to induce vomiting.

A final, but important, source of campaign cash was the Elect Lesbians Fund or ELF. This was the product of a group who wanted to support lesbian candidates in a discreet manner so as to prevent a candidate's sexual orientation becoming *the* issue in her campaign.

We anticipated that Olivia's orientation would help and also hurt her campaign where it should not have made any difference at all. It would help to the extent that lesbians themselves, and liberal minded voters in general, all other factors being even, might favor her for that fact alone.

It would hurt, of course, because ignorance and pre-conceived prejudices typically engender a negative reaction to such candidates, even if on the most subliminal level. I knew also that I would harm Olivia's chances if I handled any oral expressions of this prejudice in the manner that I was inclined to, i.e., with my fists or whatever other weapon I had at hand.

So we were able to collect enough to get past the first threshold. The next task was to draw the public's attention to a veteran 3rd District judge who was little known outside the court and its associated community. What we needed, I believed, was a newsworthy event involving Olivia that would expose the world to her unique qualities.

The most likely prospect for such an event was a controversial matter coming before her. But if we were forced to wait until the right one developed we might still be waiting on election day. I needed to get crafty.

I contacted the local office of Rent-A-Lawyer to hire an attorney for an appearance before the judge. Must be someone, I told them, who projected exquisite professionalism in manner and dress; some impudence would be helpful, but neither skills nor brains were required. They satisfied my need with a chump named Lucas Smart, a silky moron with all the style and arrogance I had ordered.

The papers I prepared applied ex parte for a preliminary injunction preventing the *Diller Tattler* from publishing the names of players cut from the Diller Terriers semi-pro baseball team. Such exposure would cause irreparable harm to the team, the papers argued, because two of the players had threatened to let skunks loose in the clubhouse if anyone found out they had been cut.

On the appointed day I visited one of the local television stations, where I was known from my product pitching days, and convinced a producer to send a video technician to Olivia's courtroom that afternoon. Might be some drama, I said. So that she would not question his presence, I told her that someone from the station would be coming to do a brief interview of the new candidate.

I met Smart outside the courtroom before the ex parte calendar began. He looked like a more elegant Dan Fielding, the prosecutor on *Night Court*. I gave him the papers, which he submitted to Betty the clerk for the judge to review before she took the bench. Apparently he did not notice that the papers were in his name and contained a forgery of his signature. At that point my work was complete pending the outcome of the proceeding, so I escaped to Starbucks to await developments.

I did not know what happened until I called the video guy over as he was leaving. He seemed confident that he had captured something they could use and let me see it. Smart did not get to say a word. The judge was incensed, as I knew she would be.

"Let me get this straight, Mr. Smart," Judge Holmes declared very contemptuously before he had even identified himself. "You want me to toss aside the First Amendment, and the venerable proscription of prior restraints, to order the sports section of a weekly newspaper not to disclose who a baseball team cut because someone on the team is afraid of skunks! You don't think judges have anything better to do than sit here and listen to such preposterous sniveling?

"This morning I did my duty as a judge and sentenced a poor man to five years in prison for robbing a bank to pay rent. And then you present this garbage – yes, that's what it is, garbage – to me and ask me for manifestly illegal relief? I don't know if I have ever been so insulted in my years on the bench. No, your insult extends to all the judges of this court, indeed of this state, and to the people whose welfare we are sworn to protect and for whom we are honored to do justice.

"Mr. Smart, I find you in utter contempt of the court. I order you to pay $20,000 in sanctions to the Legal Aid Fund. And consider yourself lucky that I do not order you arrested and imprisoned. Which I will if you utter one word."

The video then caught Smart's shocked, pale face as he made his way, ghostlike, to the door. The technician observed him afterwards sitting on a bench staring at a wall as if comatose.

The station aired a brief segment that evening. It ostensibly concerned the request for a preliminary injunction, but played up Olivia's blistering rebuke of Smart and impassioned vindication of the critical role judges play in our society: an eloquent small time judge giving an attorney what he deserved. With my facilitation, a few other stations in the area picked up the segment. And the legend of Judge Olivia Holmes was born.

I thought my scheme was brilliant. Olivia, who at the time had no idea that I was behind it, was pleased with the publicity. I had to tell her eventually, however, to save Smart from jail for not paying the $20K.

By the end of January three other candidates had joined the democratic field. Paul Shapiro was a dentist. I called him "Wiggly" because he never sat still, but was always squirming like he had ants crawling round inside his shirt.

Abigail O'Donnell was an economics professor and administrator at the Warren G. Harding Institute for Advanced Sociopolitical Strategies. I called her "Abbie" because everyone else did.

Robert "Jumpy" Jackson was a lawyer and member of the Diller City Council. I called him Jumpy because he had a tendency during the council meetings, and during the first senate debate we had, to jump up from his seat whenever he had a point to make, which was virtually every time someone else had finished speaking.

As I had in the only campaign I had participated in previously – for class Dad – I did what Olivia hired me to do: mercilessly undermine her opponents. Wiggly was taking questions informally from the lone two reporters occasionally covering his campaign when I happened to appear behind them. I said "Dr. Shapiro, is it true what I've heard that you are opposed to sterilizing your instruments and that a few of your patients have been infected as a result?"

He wiggled violently with anger and used multi-syllable words, like preposterous, contemptuous, mendacious, and ludicrous, to deny the charge. But the reporters followed up. "Have you ever stated publicly your support or opposition to sterilizing instruments? Are you saying none of your patients have ever been infected? Or that it was not your unsterilized instruments that caused the infections?"

I authored an anonymous letter to the editor for all the newspapers in the district asking why a school named after one of the great early enemies of Communism had not investigated professor O'Donnell's relations with the party and advocacy of policies similar to those espoused by the Kremlin over the years. At her next public appearance Abbie had to respond to questions concerning whether she had ever advocated any policies that any Communist leader had ever also supported.

Jumpy, with already some political experience, should have deflected these misinformation missiles better than the other two. But I used a more insidious tactic with him. Shortly after the first debate I called him at his office, pretended to be a reporter, and asked him if he knew why so many people called him "Jumpy". He claimed not to know about the nickname nor why it would apply to him.

Nevertheless, as I expected, he figured it out, as evidenced by his behavior at the next council meeting and the next debate. He was so self-conscious and reluctant to speak that people thought there was something wrong with him. Or that he was bi-polar and the depressive phase had kicked in.

I did not claim that these tactics pivoted the primary election. One thing I learned quickly in my crash course on politics was that an election almost never hinges on one factor. Each voter may have a slightly different reason from another for voting the way he or she does, so one event or development will not influence a majority.

My actions affected the candidates more than the voters. Once I planted a disturbing seed in each of the candidates' minds their struggle with the seed and what grew from it hampered their effectiveness as confident campaigners. And if a candidate displays so much as a hint that his or her confidence has weakened he might as well give up.

My contributions to Olivia's campaign were not all underhanded, however. I extolled her virtues to many different groups in a variety of contexts, as well as to viewers of the local morning and talk shows I had appeared on in my product demonstrating days.

Olivia was correct when she said plugging her candidacy would not be much different from what I had been doing since my first day at Del Baxter's New and Used. The principle I relied on to sell cars, the Simple Souper, and Your Christian Life was the same one I relied on to sell Olivia Holmes as a State Senator: If I could convince the viewers and listeners that *I* fervently and sincerely believed in her as the right person for the job I would give her something no other candidate had. No person supported a candidate as rabidly as I did Judge Holmes. That alone set Olivia apart and inspired voters at least to consider her more seriously than they did the other candidates.

Of course, whenever someone is willing to put it out there like I was he automatically becomes a target for all the anonymous haters that pollute our world. My method of dealing with such people probably was not the best. I was neither suave nor defusing. I had no wish to placate or "win them over".

One afternoon I appeared on a radio talk show that had a call-in segment, which followed my colloquy with the host concerning why I believed Olivia to be a most exceptional candidate. A male caller: "We all know Holmes is a deviant lesbo out to screw everyone with her homosexual agenda .." and more of the same.

Waiting until he finished, I said: "Tell you what. After this program I am going to stay here at this radio station. Here is the address ... I am going to wait for you. To see if you, or any other cowards like you who might be listening, have the guts to come here and say this garbage to my face. I will wait for you in the lobby here for one hour. Call if you need more time. Bring as many of your pathetic friends as you wish. Ok?" Caller: "You're asking for it." Me: "Yes I am. I'll be waiting."

The only people who showed up in the lobby were members of a TV news camera crew there to see what happened. Nothing did.

Olivia told me I was "nuts".

Naturally we did all the customary things campaigns do: Distribute flyers, door-to-door visits by volunteers, before the primary some small ads in the cheaper weekly papers. Also the two pre-primary debates were carried live on a local cable channel and replayed a couple of times.

However, the debates were not very helpful for Olivia. She did an excellent job in a technical sense, destroyed her opponents with eloquence and logic. But not in appeal to the hearts of the voters. Fortunately, very few watched the debates and we managed to reach them in other ways.

So Olivia won the primary by a solid, though not overwhelming, majority. Abbie and Jumpy virtually tied for second place. Poor Wiggly.

Now we moved on to face Little Roundtop. An incumbent state senator, former state representative, and former director of the county's clandestine overdue library books operation, Roundtop was a formidable obstacle. Yet I found a weakness.

He wore suits that were custom made in Sicily. Not normally a weakness for a politician, in my hands it was. First, I convinced a local haberdasher to question why Roundtop bypassed all the fine men's clothing retailers we had. Did he consider himself so special and important that only custom *foreign*-made suits would do for him?

Roundtop ignored this jibe. So I initiated step two: Answering the haberdasher's question by suggesting the only possible reason there could be.

Roundtop must have, or want to have, connections to the Mafia. Or maybe he just wanted his wardrobe modeled after mobsters. I started calling him "Vito".

Vito's response again was to issue a terse denial and otherwise ignore the issue. Whenever he was asked anything about it he simply said that he had addressed it previously and would not speak about it again. I felt that I should not pursue it any further and Olivia certainly was not going to touch it.

As the general election season progressed I became well-known – infamous in some quarters – for my brash style, labeled uncouth or even vulgar by the republican nitwits. My image contrasted sharply with Olivia's, who increasingly was seen as the opposite of her campaign manager. I believe that she benefited from this comparison, although the opposition tried very hard to tag her with my lack of refinement. When asked about me in this context she said something to the effect of my way is not her way, but that no one could doubt my belief in and passion for the campaign.

She debated twice with Vito. Did very well, but the debates convinced no one on either side to change his or her vote.

One incredibly delightful event occurred about a month before election day. Angel came for a visit and to help in the final weeks of her mother's campaign. It was truly euphoric for me to be with her and Olivia and Heidi and the rest of the crew without the tension and hostility that had previously ruined such reunions.

She had adopted a modified 1960s look – more designed and sophisticated, less homemade. For example, she only wore jeans, but they were embroidered with turquoise and other colorful stones. Her long golden hair tapered to bangs in the front. A white or blue denim shirt, again with stones in the collar, cuffs, and replacing buttons in the front. Olivia and I were most happy to see that she was healthy and reasonably fit, if a bit on the plump side.

Unfortunately, we could not also see happiness. Angel continued the close to impossible struggle to become a professional recording artist. Having sold a few songs for other artists to record, landed some higher profile live gigs, and with "Back in the Alley" still playing on the radio once in a while, she was not about to give up. Not about to give up her waitress job either, however.

Election day finally arrived and we had no idea how it would turn out.

Olivia was certain that she would be returning to the court, from which she had taken a leave of absence after she won the primary. I, on the other hand, never one to take reality for real, was ready to celebrate. The whole gang gathered at Olivia and Heidi's home, the same one I had occupied and trashed not that many years before, to wait for the results.

Which were not final until past midnight. Then we popped the champagne, broke out the noisemakers, and paraded through the streets. Olivia had won by a single percentage point! Not that I deserved any of the credit, but I have to say that was the most triumphant night of my life. I felt that I had finally done something right and good, and that benefited more than just me.

More gross, veiny eyeballs hovering over mine trying to see through to my ego to see if the boiled monkey blood is having any effect. Better try the pancake mix. Be sure to use enough water. Otherwise it will clog his arteries.

Oh my god. This one has a booger balancing precariously on the edge of a nostril, about to fall. Haul in that thing before .... it .. falls .. into my eye. And I cannot scream. I cannot shout for someone to pull it out. He doesn't even know. He sees my eye watering, but he doesn't even know why. I am filled with pressurized fury. Yet I am utterly helpless.

17

Olivia did not see a role for me in her senate office and neither did I. So once again I was unemployed. Jill Taylor said she would put me back on her list, but I did not hear anything further from her. Grateful for my work, Olivia told me she would help me out for a while. I accepted two months worth of support, figuring I could get by on my own after that.

My spirit was so much more positive than it had been the last time I was in this predicament that I remained optimistic through the series of rejections I experienced over the first two weeks or so. Weary of selling, products and candidates, I steered myself in other directions – hospitality, transportation, office administration, floral, illegal drugs, off-brand shoe smuggling, resident amusement park lecher. I even applied to the Post Office, in hopes of fulfilling my life-long dream of being a mail carrier. Did not pan out.

In hindsight I guess I should have just waited. Because three weeks into my two-month dependence I was contacted by a man who was about to launch a campaign for mayor of a modest sized city in Southern California. He knew of my work and wanted to hire me to manage his campaign.

His name was Carl Strong. I have intentionally forgotten the actual name of the city of roughly 75,000. For after living there for seven months, I chose a more fitting name: Trashtown.

Carl told me he expected a rough campaign. If only because he was a black immigrant from the Ivory Coast and much of Trashtown made Andy Taylor's Mayberry seem cosmopolitan by comparison. Despite my inclination to do something different, I could not resist the challenge. Or the money. So I relocated, temporarily thank God, to Trashtown, USA.

My first taste of the city was sitting down at a table in a small diner and looking up to see a large photograph of Rush Limbaugh mounted to a prominent spot on the wall. It was even signed: "Kev—Thanks for helping the cause of American purity. Rush." I asked the lacquered walrus who waited on me if she could direct me to a public library. She had no idea whether the city even had one and did not offer to find out.

Driving from there to the KKK Hotel I tried unsuccessfully to find a radio station that was not carrying a conservative talk program. There was even a local show, Dave Redd, The Liberals' Worst Nightmare. Dave's broadcast that day was about organizing militia to protect the border and "the American way of life".

He noted that he was not promoting any privately sponsored paramilitary groups, since that would violate laws that leftist operators had put on the books. Rather, according to Dave, he was only reporting and commenting on specific units that already were "patriotically" patrolling areas near the border.

"Apparently", he explained, these units had orders to make citizens' arrests of anyone they suspected of being undocumented or of being an accessory to the presence of undocumented persons in this country. He also "announced" that there would be a meeting Thursday night at the American Legion Hall, where Colonel Blake Sharpe would explain more about what his volunteers are doing to protect America.

As I checked into the hotel I asked the clerk about the hotel name. She looked defiantly at me and said "It ain't what you think". I asked how she would know what I think, which brought a look of hostility that probably mirrored mine. KKK, she said, were the initials of the hotel founder, the late Kevin K. Kirkham.

The next day I met Carl Strong at his business, a dry cleaning and tailoring shop at the very edge of town called Strong Cleaners. He told me that his mother was native to the Ivory Coast and his father had moved there from Australia, hence the decidedly English name Strong.

My main question was why in hell did he want to be mayor of a city like that. He explained that its large community of immigrants, and minorities mistaken for immigrants, was being egregiously mistreated by certain other portions of the city's population. The bulk of its citizens were tolerant, but also apathetic and/or afraid of the white trash bullies. He wanted to do something about the situation and running for mayor seemed the only way.

Yes, he had a family: wife and two children, five and three. Yes, he feared for their safety and his own, which could be jeopardized by his candidacy. But he would fear for their safety even if he did not run and he believed that somebody had to do it. I wanted a challenge, I told myself, and boy did I find one.

Money was not a problem, as he had family resources in California and back in Africa. No, he did not own a gun and no, he would not buy one. He was confident it would not be necessary. I was not so sure, so early on I bought a compact Smith & Wesson .38 revolver, took a crash training course for it, and obtained a concealed carry permit.

Carl was more widely known in the community than Olivia had been at the start of her campaign, so the initial hurdle was not so much name recognition as it was convincing people that his candidacy was for real. Most of those whose votes he could count on thought he had lost his mind when they heard about it. I knew that without some preliminary buildup the citizens of Trashtown would ridicule the idea of a "colored" foreigner having the audacity to declare himself for mayor.

We needed a dramatic event to shake these status quo habits of thought. I came up with another ingenious idea. A big, blockbuster extravaganza, the largest party ever thrown in Trashtown. Prizes, including a year of free dry cleaning and anything else we could convince Carl's small business friends to pitch in. Balloons, face painting, petting zoo. Plenty of beer and soft drinks. Massive barbeque, with twenty grills cooking hot dogs, hamburgers, ribs, chops, chicken, sausages. All free.

And pictures of Carl Strong everywhere. On posters. On a giant billboard. His smiling face watching over every concession stand. Thousands of Carl Strong T-shirts, displaying his name and photograph on the front and back, thrust into people's hands before they could even consider whether they wanted one.

As I expected, Carl hated the idea. He was a serious man. The problems he would undertake to resolve were serious problems. The frivolity I proposed was anathema to his ideals.

Your ideals are not going to win this election, I told him. And you will not be able to effect any change if you do not win. To have any chance you must demonstrate right away that you are serious about the election and that you are a wonderful, likeable, generous, friendly guy who loves children and puppies and ice cream on a hot day. And that you are not an arrogant, self-important, supercilious, self-righteous warrior for justice who thinks he is better than the white trash he must convince to vote for him.

Furthermore, I added, since we anticipated trouble from the ignorant assholes who hated immigrants and, because they assumed that Carl was Muslim, hated him in particular for that reason, if he could reach enough hearts beforehand their tactics would backfire. The community's sympathy would be with him and his family, who were Catholic, not Muslim.

Winning is all that matters to me, I said. I understood that I was hired for that purpose. If I was mistaken, better it be made clear now, so I can move on.

When he still was not convinced, I pointed out that all he had to do for the project was smile when we took his picture. He did not have to participate in the frivolity at all, except to make an appearance. At some point afterward he could even disavow responsibility for the party and declare that it was a product of the out of control campaign manager he hired. With additional prodding from his wife, he finally agreed.

Carl's wife, Christina, who handled the customer service side of their business, took charge of organizing the extravaganza according to my instructions. She enlisted the help of friends and a couple of cousins who had followed her and Carl to Trashtown.

Possibly because no one else knew the event was related to the election, the response was tremendous. More than twenty small business owners stepped up to offer prizes and free stuff.

However, some of this largess was less generous than first appeared. The White Dove Martial Arts Studio, for example, provided 30 minutes of taekwondo instruction weekly for four weeks. The student only had to pay for the rest of the 60 minute lesson, as well as for the remaining six weeks of the ten-week course.

The Galloping Geezers seniors dating service offered to cover the cost of one first date -- to be enjoyed watching *The Love Boat* reruns at the owner's home with a home cooked spaghetti and meatballs dinner. There would be a forty percent refund if either party died before the date.

Addie May Bender, the 130-year-old proprietor of Aunt Addie's Antiques, put up a set of copper serving dishes she claimed were used by General Custer's widow in the brothel she established after his death. The prize award would be canceled if she died before the winner redeemed.

Not even mentioning the election or that Carl would be a candidate, we spread the word through the network of minority residents, modest advertisements in the weekly newspaper, the junior college and high school newspapers, and posters placed around the city. Both the daily newspaper and the two radio stations were off-limits because they were so right-wing and I preferred not to tip them off too soon about our real motive.

Oddly, one of the most difficult obstacles we had to surmount was getting our impresario to smile for his photo portrait. He tried, but it was so forced it looked like he was trying to push one out his ass. We told jokes, tickled him, asked him to think of his wonderful family. Nothing would bring a natural smile.

So I had the photographer sneak into Carl's home while I was there and, with Christina's help, stay hidden to see if we could work the unsuspecting curmudgeon into letting his guard down. We tuned the TV to a rerun of what I had declared the pinnacle of television: *The Tonight Show* when Johnny Carson was still hosting. Don Rickles was the guest. Ed McMahon was chortling at something Johnny said. Don turned to him and said "Ed, how much do you get paid for braying like a drunk jackass?" Carl grinned and laughed and the photographer's flash went off. We had the photo.

By event day we had a thousand copies posted all over the grounds where it was to take place, the giant parking lot for a closed K-Mart. Another five hundred on T-shirts, worn by everyone on the team, except Carl, and ready to be forced on all who attended.

We had music. A DJ playing popular country and pop songs. Technically in violation of copyright laws. Something to worry about later. And live performances from artists who had no idea they were supporting Carl for mayor.

The Patriot Posse, a country-rock band from Lubbock, Texas, made up of the meanest looking red necks that ever drove a moonshine-laden semi-truck across state lines. A bit uncomfortable seeing Carl's grinning face everywhere they looked, they nonetheless gave us a good show.

A marching band from one of the two high schools. I asked them to play the Washington Post March for old times sake, but they had no clue what I was talking about. The Desert Twisters, a group of local middle-aged guys reviving their heyday playing 50s and 60s rock 'n roll favorites, including their mashed medley of Blue Velvet, White Rabbit, The 59th Street Bridge Song, and War .

Carl gave the only speech. I told him what to say. A very brief one merely welcoming everyone and urging them to have a good time.

About an hour into the festivities I noticed a gentleman walking about shaking hands and handing out some kind of flyer. Carl identified him to me as one of his likely opponents in the election.

Apparently there was no "likely" involved; the guy had already started his campaign. On our grounds. I arranged to have someone spill a beer on him, while I accidentally knocked him over and scattered his flyers. Then we had a paramedic crew take him off for a precautionary exam. He said he was fine and did not want to go. But I told him it's just like the NFL: he must be evaluated for a concussion.

The weather was perfect. More people came than I expected. Most appeared surprised to see Carl's face plastered all over the grounds and on the giant billboard we set up. Those who knew him or had patronized Strong Cleaners were probably more surprised to see his gleeful grin.

I worked my way through the crowd dropping casual remarks like "about time we had an event like this here", "those knuckleheads we have now in City Hall would never come up with something like this", and "do you think it's true that the mayor leaves town every few days to visit his mistress in Los Angeles?"

Of course, the mayor himself stopped by later in the day. A chiropractor by trade, Dr. Ward Spindler was tall and lean, wiry I guess is the term, bristle brush military hair, and an aura of command. Not leadership – command. He did not lead, he did not inspire others to do things. He commanded them. He also was fiercely religious, what others call a Christian fundamentalist, what he would call righteous.

I strolled over to where he was contemplating a picture of Carl and asking someone who that was. When I was about ten feet away he looked over and recognized me. From my appearances on YCL. He came forward, shook my hand, and said "I am very pleased to meet you in person, brother."

Since he had not seen me on the network recently, he wondered if I was still "doing the good work" of Your Christian Life. Nope, working for someone else now. He wondered if I knew who this guy was, pointing to Carl's picture.

One of your constituents. And my boss.

Looking keenly at the picture and back to me, he said "yeah I thought I recognized him. He's the cleaners guy, the foreign guy. Shows up at our council meetings once in a while. Always bellyaching about something. You say he's your boss? Surely you don't mean at the cleaners." No, another project.

As he moved on he invited me to say a few words during the Sunday services at Church of Redemption and Glory, where he was a deacon. Twisting the ends of my mustache, I said I would be happy to do that.

I believed the event was a great success. It could hardly have failed to make the citizens of Trashtown conscious of Carl Strong and associate good times with his name and face.

The TV and radio stations and every newspaper featured the event that day and the next, even though they might have condemned it instead if they had known what it was really all about. So they were surprised and chagrined when I delivered a press release Sunday afternoon two weeks later announcing that Carl Strong was running for mayor.

They could not very well refuse to do anything with the announcement. Especially when telephone calls started coming in about four times each hour from people asking about it, calls that I had arranged for, and many that I did not. However, the coverage they provided was patently hostile.

"Foreign Dry Cleaner Running for Mayor", ran one headline. The TV and radio reports went something like this: "Carl Strong, a dry cleaner, owner of Strong Cleaners, a recent immigrant from Africa, and a man believed to be Islamic or associated with Islamic groups, announced yesterday that he is a candidate for mayor. Strong, known for his disruptions of city council meetings with complaints about the treatment of hoodlum minorities, put on an extravagant celebration of himself just two weeks ago, without disclosing his intentions. Mayor Ward Spindler remarked to this reporter that this seems to have been a grand deception by Mr. Strong."

Before delivering the release I had showed up at the Church of Redemption and Glory to redeem Dr. Spindler's invitation to speak. He had forgotten about it, but, given my former work for a national Christian broadcasting network, he prevailed on the pastor to let me address the congregation.

After thanking Dr. Spindler and the pastor for the opportunity, I explained that I had come to Trashtown on a mission of peace. I noted that it had been reported to me that the city was suffering division and contentiousness, and that I came hoping to heal the wounds that had rent the peaceful fabric of the great community.

"In his first epistle to the Corinthians, at chapter 3, verse 3, the Apostle Paul asked rhetorically, 'While there is jealousy and rivalry among you, are you not of the flesh, and behaving in an ordinary human way?' I hope that you can cast aside that which divides you and embrace that which would unite you in love of Jesus Christ. That is my hope.

"That is also the hope of the man who brought me here, Mr. Carl Strong, a man of strong faith. Although of the Catholic faith, so not exactly the same as you, he is a righteous man, devoted to doing good for all of us, for all of the people of this wonderful town. I believe he is truly walking as God wills and I pray that you will join him. Thank you."

For about 24 hours the mayor, the pastor, and the congregation were exceedingly puzzled by my encomium about Carl. The mystery was dispelled when the news broke that he would be a candidate for Spindler's job.

I was certain that he and the pastor were sore for having been used. However, I hoped that at least some other individuals among the congregation would react positively and judge Carl's merits independently from the church leadership.

Having leveled the playing field somewhat, the rest of the campaign was a battle, sometimes vicious. We bought time from the radio station to host a call-in program with me as the host and Carl as the featured guest. Not surprisingly, I had to repeat the stunt I pulled for Olivia, inviting abusive callers to appear at the station in person. Carl was horrified at my audacity. He wanted to clear out the instant the program was finished. But I made him stay.

Three mangy looking dudes showed up in sleeveless T-shirts. They swaggered into the lobby where Carl and I and a video crew I had hired were waiting.

"Don't think you two know what's good fer ya", one of the them said.

"You're probably right," I responded. "But what are you going to do about it?" The video camera was blinking a light into their faces.

"I don't know. Maybe knock your asses back where they came from." He wanted to stare me down but could not help glancing at the camera.

"I tell you what," I said. "Since this transaction will be recorded, I will give you the opportunity to explain why you are going to beat us, so the viewers will know and understand. How does that sound?"

Infuriated, he did not answer. So his buddy did. "Ok. Tell 'em Sim." But Sim was having difficult thinking of anything to say. So the buddy said "We don't want any of you terrorists running this city."

"So if I understand you correctly, you want to beat us up so my friend here won't get elected mayor?"

"That's right", Sim confirmed, moving closer to my face.

"And this act of beating us up – you will do this to keep Dr. Spindler as mayor?"

"You're learning."

"And what do you suppose he thinks of your doing this?"

"Oh, I know he's all for it. He doesn't want this African Muslim running the city either."

"So you are going to beat us up on behalf of Mayor Spindler. Is that about it?"

"Yeah. That's about it."

At that point I sensed that one of them had figured out my trap and began backing towards the door. He tugged on Sim's arm, trying to get his friend to accompany him. I stood my ground and even inched forward a little, determined to demonstrate that I was ready to fight. After a tense one-minute standoff, Sim hissed "next time" at me, and the gentlemen departed. Carl gazed at me like he was in the presence of Superman.

I was not Superman, but I had what we needed to cut off Ward Spindler's political legs. No amount of damage control could save him after we launched the video – via larger market media that quickly disseminated the story into Trashtown, forcing the TV station there to play the video.

Spindler then announced that he would not seek reelection. None of the other candidates could match Carl's momentum. So on election day he was elected mayor by a comfortable margin. And once again I was unemployed.

I just awoke from a very bizarre dream. I was hired to manage a campaign. For an orange, twenty-foot praying mantis that was running for Master Predator. If he won he would be entitled to eat all other creatures, including humans.

I tried to explain that for him to win he must convince the voters that he was a kind creature who cared about the same things they did and that if they gave him power he would use it to do good. So he had to project a different image.

The candidate listened, then ate a trio of folk singers who were trying to entertain him. No no no, I said. That will not do. Whereupon he regurgitated the sloppy, partially digested mess that was left of the trio.

As I was pondering how I could make this disgusting – and terrifying – insect palatable to the electorate, I remembered what I had done for Carl Strong and resolved to tease the thing into laughter so I could take a photograph. I would moon him. I turned my back to him and dropped my pants. His mouth closed around me. And I woke up.

18

Again I was not unemployed for long. In fact, I received multiple requests for my services. Some of these would-be clients, however, were just too long of a shot, even for me.

Like the newly elected member of the Doodleville Unified Board of Education who figured the next step in his career should be to run for president of the United States. An incarcerated methamphetamine smuggler serving five to ten years who wanted to "lay the groundwork" while locked up for a shot at becoming the state controller. A woman who wrote to me from her cottage deep in the woods, asking if I could publicize her abandoned "plump" child rescue home.

The request I responded to also was a bit unusual. It did not involve politics or selling in the customary sense of those terms. I responded because the work would be quite different from what I done with Olivia and Carl and might lead me into fields of life I had not yet experienced. It did, although in a manner far from what I expected and with consequences that, had I foreseen them, probably would have convinced me to pass on taking the job.

The first contact I had was with a young lady named Ethel. She wrote explaining that she represented an embryonic collection of individuals with certain shared convictions and passions about human life. They were not a religious cult or sect. She vaguely supposed that their beliefs did not constitute religious ones, but was not sure about that.

According to Ethel, the group wanted to cohere as some kind of spiritual entity, some organized body of believers, with a name to identify it, and then to spread their "'gospel', for lack of a better term". Again, she reiterated that they did not imagine this body as a new religion, but that they were unsure how to categorize it.

They knew of my eclectic experience in product demonstration, television hosting, religious broadcasting and unconventional management of political campaigns. They did not know if what they had in mind was something I could help them with or if I would want to try, but they hoped I could at least come and talk about it. It would not be a lucrative prospect for me; however, there would be a steady salary and a place to live.

The group all resided in a small Northern California town called Squash. So, with nothing to lose except a few days that I would have wasted anyway, I traveled to Squash and checked into the Squash Inn. The clerk there did not know of anyone named Ethel. By return mail I had let her know where I would be staying, so I kicked back in the quaint room and watched out the window for the Abominable Snowman.

A couple of hours later someone knocked hesitantly on the door. On opening it I found a sprite, a wisp of a woman barely taller than my belly button and so slight I could easily imagine her floating away before my eyes. It was Ethel, come to lead me to the place she and the others regularly met: an anteroom in an abandoned Baptist church.

Waiting for me were seven eager souls sitting on benches that lined the walls of the room. When I entered they immediately jumped up and greeted me one by one with such forthright enthusiasm I felt like a long lost son returning to his family.

A fairly diverse group, there were six women including Ethel, and two young men no older than thirty. One of the women was obviously older than the rest. Her shoulder-length dark hair was tinged with traces of gray and age spots showed here and there on a leathery face. Her green eyes, however, were very bright and clear and she appeared to be in remarkable shape physically.

Our meeting commenced with each person saying whatever he or she wanted to without interruption by anyone else, including me. Although some of the terms and expressions used in these monologues were corny and cliched, the emotions fueling them were powerful and genuine and fresh to my experience. I cannot mock what was said to me.

The older woman – Grace – who seemed to be sort of a principal for the group, spoke last. She surprised me with my own words. She had seen a video clip of the first regular episode of Your Inspired Lifestyle. What I said in the introduction to that show, she explained, encapsulated what the group believed, although they would interpret my reference to "God" differently than perhaps I or my employers then intended. She had even memorized the words.

"You were referring to a statement by the Apostle Paul in one of his letters to the Corinthians. You were explaining what you thought he meant. 'I think he is saying that our bodies, our lives really, are not ours alone, to do with as we please, to abuse and disrespect. No our lives belong to God as much as to ourselves. So if we maltreat ourselves we maltreat God. That is really what this program is all about: Exploring ways to help us thrive as individuals, so God can thrive.'"

"I need to be more careful with what I say", I cracked, which drew some laughter. Grace smiled and said she thought it was beautiful.

Not accustomed to praise like that, and recalling how insincere I was when I spoke those words, I was acutely embarrassed and unsure what to say. The group appreciated my apparent humility.

We then grappled with the practical matter of what they wanted me to do. Never in my long experience with products and politics had I encountered such a nebulous assignment – as difficult to define for my would-be clients as it was for me.

Each of them had tried to express a belief that, while roughly common to all, could only be described in hopelessly vague terms. Now they wanted me to make sense of it, to articulate some cohesive and understandable concept incorporating their varied notions. Then I was to create an entity the members of which would share a commitment to the concept. Ultimately I would attempt to sell the concept and the entity to the world.

No problem. Piece of cake. Too easy. I was churning in sarcasm that I dared not reveal. And already feeling guilty for the fraudulent scheme I probably would foist upon the chumps, taking full advantage of their gross naivety and purity of spirit. Except that all I would get out of it was meager compensation and a place to live for a couple of months.

Two factors combined to convince me. Number one was just to see if I could do it. The assignment genuinely was as intriguing as it was challenging. In effect I was to be like a latter day apostle Paul: articulating a kind of gospel or doctrine or creed, then persuading people to buy it.

The second factor was that I did not have anything better to do at the time.

Clearly I was not qualified for the task. But then, I was never qualified to be a judge or religious broadcaster or a campaign manager for that matter. The group knew what I had done. They admitted that they had no idea whether I could do what they wanted, whatever that was. If they were willing to risk failure so was I.

We agreed on a monthly salary and reimbursement of my expenses. The salary was nothing close to what I had been making recently, but they also rented a small two-bedroom house for me, tucked back in a wooded ravine that fronted the foothills thresholding the Sierra Nevada mountains.

There I would work for as many months as I needed putting together whatever written work I deemed appropriate and planning our proselytizing campaign. Although they did not want to formalize any reporting requirement, the group did ask if I could let them know informally every month or so how I was progressing.

Squash being a rural community of about 2,500 residents, there was not much in the way of dining. There were but two restaurants, Uncle Billy's Forty-Niner Diner and Stump Grill. The Forty-Niner offered just about every food item ever found in any all day eatery west of the Great Divide. Two of my favorites were the goat liver frittata with butterscotch sauce and chiclets and the roast badger stuffed with deep fried okra.

The Stump was started by a sheriff's deputy whose right arm was bitten off to the elbow by a mysterious lake monster chasing after a fish the deputy was reeling in. The monster, believed to be some type of shark-type fish that had been transplanted into the lake when young or descended from a transplanted fish, had never been seen again. The restaurant served hamburgers, ribs, sides, and beer. I could get a quarter pound burger, a basket of fried zucchini, and a pitcher of Coors for twelve bucks.

Both places were within easy walking distance of my Squash house. Pretty much everything in Squash was. I walked along a rough dirt path through knee-high Algerian snodgrass, past a ramshackle chicken coop holding five insane hens that clucked hysterically at me – like there was anything I could do about it - - to Rigor Mortis Road, which a quarter mile further on met Main Street, the Squash thoroughfare along which all its businesses were located.

There were no other houses behind mine in the other direction, only bushes of oak, elm and aspen trees, and a stone's throw from my porch a small pond about fifteen feet in diameter, fed by a tiny rivulet trickling down from the foothills. By August the stream was dry and did not come to life again until April.

The pond was visited by a great variety of creatures. I could see only one side of it from my porch because bushes blocked my view of the rest. However, sometimes I would walk over and sit on a rock about fifteen feet back from the pond, so I could observe the action. A family of deer were the first and most frequent visitors I saw: A buck with four-point antlers, a doe, and two fawns.

The family showed up so often I gave them names. The parents were Chuckwagon and Ingrid, the fawns Thirty-Eight and Forty-Five. Occasionally one of them would see me, freeze, and, if I did not move, continue the scene. Once I threw a big rock into the middle of the pond to see what they would do. Nothing. Probably because vegetation under the surface muffled the splash.

A pair of sickly coyotes appeared once in a while. Their drill was to saunter to the edge, sip some of the muddy water, then squat in the wet sand and have a discussion. I was never close enough to hear them distinctly, and I don't understand coyote.

But once at dusk it was so quiet that I thought I heard them talking about another coyote they both knew. Apparently, he had infiltrated an aviary somewhere in the habitat, and come away with a fat juicy pigeon that he enjoyed afterward and pronounced extraordinarily delicious. Their envy was pathetic.

One night I woke up to the horrible shrieking of some terrorized animal. I went out on the porch and shined a flashlight toward the pond. All I saw were two glowing orbs that I took to be eyes reflecting the light. They fixed on me for a few moments, then rose into the air and disappeared. In the morning I found Thirty-Eight's still bloody carcass ripped open, his guts spilling out into the shallow pond water. Creepy.

Creepier still was what I discovered at the other end of Rigor Mortis Road: A cemetery. It appeared abandoned; there had been no new occupants for some time. Plus I saw no signs of maintenance. Weeds grew where there were no headstones, of which I counted twenty-four. Most of the inscriptions were obscured by moss and mold. The most recent date that I could read was 1937.

For some reason I became a regular visitor to this graveyard, maybe the only one in years, besides rodents and rabbits, lizards and ants. I even went there after dark, tempting the long dead to emerge and torment me. None did. That I knew of.

However, one evening as the daylight was fading, I was walking home along Rigor Mortis, my stomach full of Stump's beef ribs, mashed potatoes, and Budweiser, and just about to turn into the path to my house, when I saw a figure, human shaped, emerging from the cemetery. The figure continued in my direction for a minute or so. Then, apparently seeing me, it turned abruptly, ran back in the direction it had come, and disappeared. Needless to say, I was spooked.

The following morning, after inspecting the graveyard for any signs of new activity and finding none, I went to the Forty-Niner for breakfast. I asked the employees and patrons who were there if anyone ever hung out at the cemetery. No one there had been near the place since they occasionally had as children to prove they were not afraid. So I attributed the vision to the pitcher of Bud and moved on.

The work I was supposed to be doing was turning out to be more difficult than I expected. Every day I sat at the kitchen table, a notebook open before me, on which I intended to write notes on the ideas that came to me. But after a couple of hours the only marks I had made were elaborate drawings of space ships hovering over a golf course and faces with hair growing out from the nostrils.

It seemed that I understood the task well enough. And I had no problem envisioning the essentials of the ultimate product. My trouble concerned the initial steps toward that product, the nuts and bolts, the getting there from here. Putting it most succinctly, I did not know where to start.

Start with a name, I finally decided. If I could come up with a name – for the concept, the group of believers, the principle, whatever – it would give me a handle. Label the entity, then figure out what the entity is.

The specific details of a doctrine have never been as powerful as the name they were associated with or identified by. How various have been the particular points of doctrine all associated with the label Christian or Muslim?

I could have called it The Jackass Club or The Squashers -- followers of Squashism, students of The Squash Scrolls -- or the League of Livers, the Lust for

Life Lodge, the Living Large Alliance.   How about the Society of People Who Believe That We Are Not Our Own.   The We Are Not Our Own Society – WANOOS. Catchy. We are the WANOOS. I could picture the T-shirts.

We are not just we. We are also God's. Or the Supreme Being's. Or the Higher Power's. Or Zeus's. Odin's. Allah's. The Martians'. The Klingons'. The We Are Not Our Own -- We Are Also God's, Allah's, The Supreme Being's, Some Higher Power Or Other's, Take Your Pick -- Society.

Or, I thought, we could use the term "God" as referring to something greater than ourselves that we cannot specifically identify, We can say "we are not our own because we are also God's" without meaning specifically the Christian God or the Islamic God. The We Are God's Society? We can also go further and say that God exists in and through us, that this is the ultimate meaning of belonging to God. God is us and we are God. The We Are God Society.

It was time for another meeting. I called the number I had for Ethel and left a message requesting a meeting at the same place the following morning at ten. She was to call back if it was not possible. Not hearing from her, I walked to the old church and entered promptly at ten.

There were a few more people there this time. Strangely, however, the only one I recognized was Ethel, who looked exactly the same as when I first saw her. An elderly lady with short white hair introduced herself to me as Grace, but she was not the same Grace I had met before. I asked if there were any other people named Grace in the group. She replied "Oh, I'm sure there are. I don't see any here today though."

Those who were present at that second meeting were eager to learn how the project was progressing. I tried to explain the crooked course of my ruminations and how I had come to some absurdly nebulous concepts. We are God's. We are God.

Expecting skepticism at best, if not ridicule and demands to know why that was all I had done, I was astonished to hear the most enthusiastic praise and congratulations coming from everyone there. That's it, they declared. That's exactly what we were all trying to say. I am God. You are God. We, all of us, are God. Some even wiped away tears of joy.

Then someone called out "What about the C-141?" We all looked around to see who said it in hopes of finding out what the heck he or she was talking about. But no one acknowledged having spoken. As if the Invisible Man was attending the meeting and throwing out random nonsense just to confound us.

I moved on, noting that the group could call itself the We Are God Society. This proposal also drew excited and unanimous agreement, all heads nodding and repeating the words multiple times. That's just one idea, I said, so if anyone has additional suggestions ... No no, they responded in chorus. And they chanted "We are God" and "this is the We Are God Society".

The group's uncritical, unquestioning acquiescence disturbed me. I did not know why.

Suggesting that the next step should be to compose a statement of beliefs, I asked if anyone would volunteer to do that. No one did. Ok, I said, I guess I will give it a try. Hooray, they shouted. And we adjourned. I went straight to the Stump for a pitcher of something strong.

That afternoon, before I collapsed on the couch to sleep off two pitchers of a locally brewed IPA called Skunk Piss Pale Ale, I received a card from Angel announcing that she had a new recording contract and was going on tour. I was delighted and sat down to write her congratulations, but quickly realized I was in no condition for that and staggered to the couch.

I woke up to a loud whirring sound above the house, like a huge hawk or eagle passing low and vigorously working its wings. Whatever it was made three passes. With great effort I stood up to go outside, hoping I could see it. At that moment someone knocked on the door. Whoever it was would be my first visitor.

However, when I opened the door no one was there, either on the porch or anywhere else I looked in the vicinity. Yet as I walked back to the house a powerful sense that someone or something was following me rattled my nerves. Looking behind me apprehensively a couple of times, I then panicked, ran to the house, burst in and locked the door. It was not until almost midnight, after waiting and pacing for hours, that I decided the incident was over and lay down for a night of rocky sleep.

During which I dreamt that I was visited by Paul the Apostle. He looked ghastly. Basically just a skeleton encased in transparent gray skin through which

I could see thousands of maggots churning in his abdomen and chest. The skin on his face was peeling. His one eyeball peered from deep inside the socket. Inside his skull, where his brain should have been, was a muddy green liquid that bubbled like soda.

He did not speak. He just floated into the kitchen, directed his eye at the notepad I had left open on the table, at the page containing space ships and nostril hair and the words "we are god" scribbled along the edge. He nodded what remained of his head, and floated back out the door.

The dream left me in a state of extreme uncertainty. That is, the dream coupled with the events of the previous day. I felt as if I was being played with, like a rat caught in a science experiment. The cheese is right there for the taking, but the rat knows from his experience so far that it is not that simple. Something is trying to convince him that the cheese is not worth the pain he must suffer to get it.

Yet there was no choice for me but to persevere. I ate one of the Pop-Tarts I had bought when I first arrived, sat down at the kitchen table again, wrote a brief note to Angel about how proud I was of her and asking where the tour would take her, then tried to concentrate on composing a statement of beliefs for the We Are God Society.

The task was not exactly within my skill set. Any good pithy phrases I had ever come up with were spontaneous and adlibbed. I probably had never uttered anything that was premeditated. Even my masterpiece about Johnny Carson and *The Tonight Show* was composed off-the-cuff: random musings to embroider excerpts from the show transcript.

The announcements and press releases I had prepared to promote my YCL programs and Olivia's and Carl's campaigns were transient blurbs that required minimal thought. I had no experience creating something intended to have meaning beyond the temporal event it concerned. The only lasting writing I had ever produced was the list of rules I was asked to put together for posting on the door of Del Baxter's lunchroom.

So I tried scribbling whatever my stream of consciousness generated, hoping that something usable would appear accidentally.

We are God. We are God. We are not fancy three-toed sloths in spats and spacesuits. God backwards is Dog. We are Dog. I am Dog. I am Hound Dog.

I cannot say that one of my fingers or my heart or my brain is not me. Hound Dog is not one thing and they another. My parts and I are one. Likewise Hound Dog and God are one. Just as my heart is Hound Dog, so I am God.

Obviously my heart is not the whole me. Likewise I am not the whole God. But it is not possible to know the whole God. I can only know me.

Humans fantasize about God. We fantasize about God having properties we are familiar with, that are merely supernatural versions of human ones. Because we want to know God we do not fantasize about a God that has unknown properties.

We want a God we can talk to, pray to, one that will help us. Thus God must be separate from us and there must be a subject-object relationship between us. I (subject) know (verb) God (object).

Like I could meet God on the street walking to the barber shop. "Howdy God. How ya doin'?"

"Not bad Hound Dog. How 'bout yourself?"

"I'm ok. Kinda confused. Trying to figure you out. I mean my relationship to you."

"I'll give you a hint: It's much more simple than you're trying to make it. And your talking to me shows that you are on the wrong track. You cannot talk to God."

"But I am talking to you."

"It's not my fault that you think I am some being you can meet on the street and talk to. A lizard relishing a tasty cricket knows more about God than you do."

I needed a break. So I went over to see what was happening at the pond. My friends the deer family had been there very recently. I found their fresh tracks. Scavengers had picked clean Thirty-Eight's bones, which were still half buried in silt at the edge of the pond.

As I was looking down at them, pondering whether I should dispose of those still visible, I felt a strange sensation of something passing close by me, as if a large bird had swept by almost touching me. But I saw nothing.

However, walking back to the house I saw someone out of the corner of my eye on Rigor Mortis Road looking down the path past the chicken coop. The person was in view just for a moment, before hurriedly moving out of sight. I ran along the path and called to whoever it was. There was no one on the road when I reached it. So I proceeded towards the cemetery, thinking it might have been the figure I had seen there before.

The sky was overcast with heavy dark clouds and the wind was picking up, signaling a storm. The cemetery appeared particularly eerie in the crepuscular light. I saw no one.

Unsettled by the creepy scene, and feeling the sprinkles of rain that precede the real thing, I hurried back towards the house, barely hopping onto the porch just as a vigorous downpour commenced. With it came lightning that struck close by, followed almost immediately by bone-rattling thunder.

Stepping into the kitchen from the porch I received a tremendous shock. Someone had been there. Just in the few minutes I was gone. One of the kitchen chairs had been tipped over and my notebook had been moved and was closed.

I opened it to the pages containing my notes and gasped. The notes had been scribbled over by a powerful but unsteady hand writing these words three times: "THIS WICKEDNESS CONDEMNS YOU TO ETERNAL HELL!"

Instead of quivering with fright as I should have. Instead of quaking in awe at the occurrence of such a bizarre supernatural event. Instead of cowering before a power obviously beyond my own, one bent on shriveling my pretenses, and perhaps my destruction. Instead of dropping on my knees to beg forgiveness. I was pissed.

I was no philosopher or theologian. Thinking in terms of human existence and God and all that was not something I practiced on a regular basis. But I had been making an effort, an effort that was costing my peace of mind, and while I was not ready to brag about the results, I was proud to even come up with what I did. And for some shiftless ghost cast about by the wind to infiltrate my personal zone and deface my private musings with exaggerated threats was infuriating.

I stepped back onto the porch, the rain and lightning and thunder still at full force. And with as much lung compression as I could muster, I howled into the storm: "Fuck you, you worthless incorporeal piece of supernatural shit. You can't intimidate me with your fairy-tale threats. Your silly antics have inspired me to see this assignment through. If it means eternal hell, I say fan the flames!"

I would not leave the house again until I had finished a draft of the statement.

Realizing that neither substance nor consistency actually mattered very much and that interest in the Society would not depend on the statement's wording, I gave up my quest for the extraordinary and composed something that would do. Something that would help me sell the Society, which, after all, was what they hired me for.

I finished the draft in half an hour:

We are not our own. We are God.
We can know about God only what we know about ourselves.
What we do for ourselves we do for God.
What we think, God thinks. What we feel, God feels.
What we create, God creates. What we learn, God learns.
If we are healthy, God is healthy. If we are strong, God is strong.

I left another message for Ethel, telling her that in the morning I would post the statement on the front door of the church where we had met. Below it would be sheets of blank paper on which anyone could leave comments. I would respond as needed to any comments by revising and reposting the statement.

That night I slept the deep sleep of the accomplished and first thing in the morning I posted the handwritten statement. I spent the better part of the rest of the day walking around Squash, daring the spirits to hassle me. None did. That I knew of.

The next day I went to the church expecting to see comments that I would need to address. What I found were two pages filled with fulsome praise: "This is wonderful!" "Best statement of its kind ever written". "Puts Saint Paul to shame." "Thank you so much for this excellent statement." "The We Are God Society is on its way!"

No names were associated with these "comments". They might have all been written by the same person. They gave me no gratification -- only relief that this part of the job was done.

The next step was to incorporate as some form of non-profit. For that I needed some professional help, as I did not feel confident that I could do it properly myself. The very existence of the enterprise was tenuous enough; its prospects for success were slim and the potential causes of failure already evident. I was not going to doom it simply by screwing up the routine preparation and filing of papers.

No lawyers graced the town of Squash with their practices. However, thirty miles from Squash was a larger municipality called Sanyeti, which was fortunate enough to have two law offices.

Beautifying the highway into this community were multiple billboards advertising the services of these distinguished professionals. "Injured? Forget the doctor. Call me instead: Attorney Jerry 'Mad Dog' Braddock. You pay nothing!" In tiny print at the bottom: "Except for the huge chunk of money I keep for my services."

The other law office was slightly more subtle. They used four different boards, spaced a few hundred feet apart. The first one displayed pictures of a sophisticated gray-haired man and a young blonde woman wearing glasses. "Dickinson & Dick" announced the name of the firm. The next board: "Experienced ... Dedicated ...". The third board: "... Millions Paid In Compensation". The final board repeated the name with a phone number and address.

I dropped in on Dickinson & Dick to see if one of them could prepare and file the papers. The receptionist asked me to sit while she checked to see if "Ima" could see me. Soon a stout woman of about thirty-five years appeared and introduced herself as Ima. We proceeded into her office where I told her about the Society and what I needed her for.

She said she could take care of the papers and the filing, but wanted me to know how complicated – and time-consuming -- the process was, so I would not be surprised by her bill. At my request she estimated twenty hours at $350 per hour. I choked on the water the receptionist had given me.

$7,000 just to prepare and file a few papers? Ima acted like I was getting a bargain. Then she added: "And I will need an advance retainer of $5,000, plus an extra $1,000 for me to participate in a blasphemous project."

I told her I would go see if Mad Dog could do better. Good luck with that, she sneered as I left.

Mad Dog had an assistant who would do the whole thing for $500. In fact, I did not even need to speak with the great man, only the assistant.

The assistant needed the names of the president, secretary, and the board of directors. That would be me, me, and me. Principal address: My house in Squash. Statement of belief? In my pocket – here you go. Bylaws? Bylaws? Do you have any we could use and just change the details. She would look in the files to see if they had any that might work.

Do we plan to accept donations? Decide later. Will we need to apply for tax exemption? Decide later. What about a house of worship? We were not going to worship anything. So we needed no house for it.

Meetings? The Society should have meetings. Otherwise it's not a society. Does not matter what happens at the meetings. Maybe just recite the statement, followed by silent meditation on its meaning, etc. Then the members can say whatever they want. They can talk about what the statement means to them and how they have followed it. Recitation, meditation, and testimonials. That is what the meetings would be about.

While I was in Mad Dog's office I witnessed a poignant scene involving a young man in a grimy work jumpsuit and his father, an elderly gentleman whose guidance system seemed to be malfunctioning. The son told the receptionist that chemicals released from a smelter upwind had damaged his father's brain. Which his father then demonstrated by ordering the Viet Cong guerillas in the next room to throw out their weapons and come out with their hands behind their heads.

Afterwards a passing thought troubled me for seventy-five seconds: Would the We Are God Society be able to help this man? Probably not.

I let Ethel know that we would hold the first ever meeting of the We Are God Society the following Thursday evening at 7:00 p.m. at our usual venue.

Meanwhile I heard back from Angel: A very short note saying that she and the group she would be opening for, Alligator, were scheduled for a series of small venues, colleges mostly, in Arizona, New Mexico, Colorado, and Utah.

She included a promotional card with the itinerary, which listed the first show in three weeks at a place in Flagstaff, Arizona called The Big Basement. Who knows, I thought, maybe I can cross paths with the tour somewhere.

The meeting would be a free-wheeling affair. Not much planning. I would announce the incorporation, explain that I was only a temporary officer, until the members elected the real president, etc., ask for volunteers to work up the newsletter and maintain the membership roll, and then recitation, meditation, testimony.

Twelve people showed up for the meeting. Once again, Ethel was the only one I recognized, and she looked exactly the same as she had on the two previous occasions. Before starting I asked everyone to write their names on a piece of paper I circulated. When it came back to me I was surprised to see no last names and the name "Grace" written three times in different handwriting.

Thank you all for coming to the first ever meeting of the We Are God Society. I assume all of you have read our statement of beliefs, which was posted on the door here for a few days. If not, I have copies here.

I am pleased to let you know that the process for incorporating the Society as a religious non-profit organization is underway and should be completed shortly. I am listed as president and the only director, but that is only until you choose other persons for those positions.

"I nominate you", someone called out. This was followed by clamorous approbation of the proposal. I opted to ignore it and move on.

We are going to have a newsletter, monthly or quarterly. I expect that it will mostly contain stories about members, what they are doing, how they are using our principles in their lives, that sort of thing. So we will need some volunteers to put this newsletter together –

"I volunteer you", someone else called out, which again was followed by general acclamation. We can work these matters out later, I concluded.

Now my idea for how these meetings should proceed is for someone to recite the statement of beliefs. Maybe eventually everyone can join in this recital. The assembly then would spend ten minutes or so in silent meditation and reflection on the meaning of the statement and introspective confirmation of its truth. What do you think?

"Fantastic. Perfect. Exactly what is needed. You are a great leader."

I wanted to tell them that the next item would be for everyone to strip naked and stick their noses in their neighbor's asses. To see if they would lap that up too. But I just wanted to get the thing done.

So I recited the statement as solemnly as possible and led the meditation segment by sitting on a bench and closing my eyes. Furtive glances around the gathering confirmed that they were following the directions. Apparently at least. Some of them could have been thinking about the rear end of a mule for all I knew.

Okay. I hope that was beneficial for everyone. Now the floor will be open for anyone who wants to talk. Please do not feel like you must speak. But if anyone desires to say something now is the time.

An uncomfortable wave of group shyness passed over the group and at first no one was courageous enough to expose her inner soul to the public. Then one man, about thirty, shaved head, white t-shirt, an algebraic equation tattooed on each arm, rose and began to speak.

"I appreciate this chance to talk. Don't get many opportunities to do that. My name is Matthew. But in prison everybody called me The Goat, so I pretty much got used to it. Not sure why they called me that, except that I had a picture of me and my girl friend when I had a little scraggily beard. Maybe that was it. Anyway, I just got out a couple of weeks ago. After four years. All I did was borrow a car once in a while to run some coke up from Galveston. I was gonna return the cars, but I guess they think borrowing without permission is like stealing. Anyway, like I said, I just got out and came here to Squash where my mom lives, when she's not traveling to Zinac 23. She only goes like three times a year, when the call comes from Mozzy. He's the leader of the Zinacon Cadaver Council, so when he puts out a call mom has to go. Not as bad as it used to be, though, because the transport is way quicker now. Anyway the public defender told me they were going to have me checked out by a psych doctor to see if I could be tried. I guess they thought I was nuts because I told them about my mom being away on Zinac 23. They asked me where it is and I said I don't know the exact coordinates, but it's somewhere in the fringes of the Peanut Galaxy. They asked me how she got there. I said I didn't know that exactly either. She used some kind of space saver device. Anyway, I went for a plea bargain to keep the shrink out of my head. The prison doctor prescribed me some kind of medication – I think it's called Hydropissamine – and he thought it helped me, but I didn't see how. So like I said when I got out I came here to stay with my mom for a bit and she told me about you guys and then about this meeting. She said I should come. So I did. I like it so far. I am going to give it a try. Sorry for talking your ears off. Thank you for listening to me."

The Goat did not want to be touched, so he had to fend off the Graces who wanted to hug him. I rescued him by pointing out that no one, not even God, should touch God without being invited to. And then, since no one wished to follow his act, we adjourned the historic meeting.

Afterwards I asked The Goat if he might be willing to help out, maybe with the newsletter. I told him that we probably would invite members to submit commentaries or testimonies of 100 words or less about themselves as God. Anything they wanted to say basically. He eagerly agreed to do it.

We needed to come up with a name for the newsletter, I told him, so he should think about that. His supercharged brain commenced and completed the task immediately. "How about The Voices of God?" So that was it.

THE VOICES OF GOD

A QUARTERLY NEWSLETTER FROM THE WE ARE GOD SOCIETY
COMPOSED ENTIRELY BY MEMBERS OF THE SOCIETY

WHAT WE BELIEVE

We are not our own. We are God.
We can know about God only what we know about ourselves.
What we do for ourselves we do for God.
What we think, God thinks. What we feel, God feels.
What we create, God creates. What we learn, God learns.
If we are healthy, God is healthy. If we are strong, God is strong.

Following this masthead would be the collection of statements composed by members. Simple format. Easy to put together. Even an editorial novice with family connections to Zinac 23 would have no problem.

For the time being, my house on Rigor Mortis Road would be the Society's home, where we would maintain the membership records and produce the newsletter. However, when I told The Goat where I lived he refused to come and asked if he could do the work at his mother's house. The guy who had run coke and spent four years in prison was afraid to go near the graveyard by my house, even in daylight.

He then told me the story no one else would. The locals called it the Scarecrows Graveyard. The Scarecrows were an early twentieth century Christian cult who believed that Jesus would be coming back soon in the form of a scarecrow. They were led by a tyrant who called himself Holy Peter, a polygamist said to have five wives and numerous children.

A fanatic fundamentalist, Holy Peter enforced a mercilessly strict code of scarecrow worship. Anyone, even his children, caught disrespecting the sacred scarecrow they erected as a shrine would be whipped and, if caught again, buried alive.

Most of the members were buried in the graveyard. Holy Peter was the last one alive. No one knew what happened to him. But now and then over the years someone reported seeing a creepy ghost-like figure near the entrance.

Ok, work at your mother's house. As for me, I was for getting the hell out of there. As soon as The Goat was set up to administrate the Society and we printed the first issue of The Voices Of God I did. Driving a 30-year-old Mercury Villager with an odometer showing 374,000 miles, which had been parked unused in a field behind the feed store before the owner donated it to the Society, and which was brought to life by a mechanic friend of The Goat, and after loading 5,000 copies of The Voices Of God and a single-size mattress to sleep on, I set off to spread the We Are God word wherever it might take root.

They so neglect me now that the flies finally have found something in this semi-sterile chamber to hang out and shit on: My face. One is perched on the bridge of my nose analyzing my eye. I can see the scores of photoreception units that make up his compound eye, his antennae twitching quizzically, his fly butt swiveling sensually from the excitement of discovering a helpless host.

You think you and your buddies have me where you want me, don't ya? I will not surrender to your insidious intentions without a fight. Sure I have no physical capability to resist. But, you see, my winged adversary, my mind is more powerful than any merely physical force. If you dare to test me I will contemplate you and your entire species out of existence.

He acknowledges the truth of my thrust by taking to the air. The toxic saliva bubbling over my lips also may have helped to convince him. And the long legged spider moving in to protect me with a web connecting my nostril to my left ear and on to a bolt in the holy machinery that is sustaining my life. If the spiders are on my side maybe I can still hope.

19

God started the day with a delicious breakfast: Mushroom and Havarti cheese omelet in a garlic cream cheese sauce, a bowl of peaches, pears, and strawberries, and coffee, of course. Then I went walking and saw red and pink roses in full bloom, brilliant purple and white lilies, young poppies, mourning doves (saw and heard), hummingbirds, and even a California condor. Comforted my sister whose husband died recently. Ate yummy broccoli soup for lunch. Read a letter from my son in Ecuador. Listened to some beautiful Chinese music. Ate a Caesar salad with shrimp and anchovies for dinner. Watched a very funny TV show.

104 words. But The Goat wisely printed the whole thing anyway. After all, it was the first issue.

God went to the racetrack today. Put ten dollars on Lady's Underwear. Did not win, place, or show, but it was an exciting race. God loves the track. People, action, hot dogs, beer. Put another ten on Second Helping. Again no luck. But again exciting. Finally put fifty on The Holy Weasel to place. Five to one. Got it! Wow that was cool. God loves the thrill. Came home and watched the Giants' walk off win over the Dodgers. Then played poker with the regulars until three in the morning. Won some. Lost some. Enjoyed it all.

Spreading the word was to be a challenge like no other. Convincing God to acknowledge himself, herself, itself over and over was a pretty tall order. Especially since I did not really try. That is, I did not reinforce our statement with additional lines of persuasion. I did not work up any erudite articulations of philosophy or theology supporting our point of view. I only asked people to read and listen to our statement and then contemplate what it means. Either they would understand it or they would not. If they did not then probably they were not candidates for membership.

So my activity consisted mostly of driving into a town or city, finding a suitable place for me to address a small group, distributing post cards inviting everyone interested to come hear about the We Are God Society, and repeating the recitation, meditation, testimony program with whoever showed up. Sometimes that was no one. Sometimes I had as many as fifteen.

Anyone who asked for it received the first issue of The Voices of God. Anyone who wanted to join gave me their information, which I forwarded back to The Goat.

Occasionally I was confronted by various "thinkers", independent and not so independent, who wanted to debate with me on certain categories of religious principles. Some examples will illustrate.

In Mustard, Nevada, a small isolated outpost in range of nuclear test radiation, three grizzled old timers showed up for my presentation. One of them claimed to have translated both the Bible and the Koran into a language he had learned from listening to radio(active) transmissions that reflected through the atmosphere on otherwise silent desert nights. Turns out Ezekiel was a serial killer, he said.

He wanted to discuss the textual disparities between the canonized gospels of the New Testament and the apocryphal writings of Bubba and Gringo, which he believed described the sermons of Jesus more accurately, the Parable of the Left-Handed Pharoah in particular. Sorry, I told him, I was not knowledgeable enough to make a match for him.

In Tater, Idaho, members of a group calling themselves The Pickle People showed up wearing ankle-length green plastic sack dresses. They objected to my assertion that all humans are God because they were pickles, not God.

Initially stumped as to how I should respond, I then asked if they thought it possible that god could be a pickle too. They said yes. So if they and god are of the same substance, i.e., pickle, why would it be wrong to believe that you are both pickles and god? This produced looks of anguished consternation, leading to the head pickle acknowledging that I had given them food for thought. They shuffled off to discuss it.

In Lederhosen, Colorado, my presentation was disrupted by two representatives of the Avenging Angels, a militant band of Mormon apostates who wore camouflage gear and carried assault rifles. They scared everyone else out of the little hall I had rented. Then they challenged me to admit that I was not God because they could waste my sorry ass with only a small taste of their ammo.

Well gentlemen, I said. First of all, I alone am not God. We, the three of us, and the rest of your Angels, and those people you just terrorized, are God.

They puzzled over this, trying to figure out if I was the Devil.

I am pretty sure that nothing we in the Society believe is inconsistent with what your group believes. Of course, I don't suppose we would choose to invade a peaceful meeting of curious folks and brandish the Valmet M78 rifles you have there. But if you want God to shoot God, if you think God will benefit by shooting me, go ahead and do what you must.

They were impressed by my assault rifle expertise.

Besides, you have already broken up my meeting. So I would say you accomplished your mission. Which convinced them to snarl their way out of the hall.

In Zipper, Kansas, I tangled with an instructor from Boog Powell Bible College. She demanded to know my position on a number of issues. Was an unborn fetus God? What was my concept of Jesus? That is, did I believe he was God? If so, and if we are all God, then did I believe that there was nothing special about Jesus, nothing to distinguish him from the rest of humanity? Were believers in the Islamic faith God or Allah? Was Adolph Hitler God? How about Al Capone? Lucretia Borgia? Regis Philbin? Giada De Laurentiis?

I answered that the Society used the term God to refer generally to a being, power, force that we knew nothing about except as we know ourselves. We did not refer to an entity of a specific type. Thus someone could substitute a different term, like Allah, without changing the meaning of our belief.

Since we did not know anything about God except as we know ourselves, I could not distinguish one human from another as not being God. We also could not say that God had any particular characteristics, such as righteousness, goodness, evil, etc. So I had to believe that Adolph Hitler too was God, as well as the others mentioned. I also suggested, however, that the Nazi era certainly was an extreme low point for God, to do what he did to himself.

As for the rest of her questions, I said I do not know the answers. She immediately and loudly called me and the Society frauds. Pointing a bony finger at me, she declared that I was peddling a blatantly false doctrine, trying to hoodwink good people into swallowing my preposterous, evil and poisonous principles, that I should be ashamed to the roots of my soul, that the people there should hound me off the platform and chase me out of Zipper.

I was about to ask if she might prefer them to stone me for blasphemy, but I was saved from making this smartass remark by the outrage of my audience at her hysterical assault on their right to hear what I had to say. Some of them shouted at her to get out of there. One threw a tomato at her. I was amazed. Who would bring a tomato to a meeting like that?

She left. More people joined at that meeting than at any other previous one. And some of them wanted to escort me to the Villager in case she came back with violent intent. I said that would not be necessary. The only weapon she had was her tongue. God's tongue, yes, but unlikely to hurt me.

Today God stayed home with my daughter. She had a fever and a stomach ache, so I kept her home from school and I did not go into work. My partners were not happy because we had to postpone a meeting to discuss the Galvani case. But I was happy, very happy, with my – God's – decision. I read to my daughter. We watched cartoons. We took a nap together. By the next morning she was feeling much better. I thanked God. I thanked myself.

After Zipper I planned to head back west, in hopes of arriving somewhere at the same time that Angel's tour did. They were scheduled for three shows in Utah about a week out, so that seemed to be a good destination. I crossed into New Mexico and stopped in Black Chowder, a community of 27,834 residents, according to the sign at the town limit.

As I went about my usual drill setting up a presentation for the following evening, I was very surprised to be hailed by a stranger who seemed to know all about me and my mission. Pat Parrot was a news reporter for a local radio station, KDUH. Apparently reports of my meetings, Lederhosen and Zipper in particular, had reached him and he wanted to record an interview with me to play during one of the station's news segments.

It was a most boring interview. I confirmed what was accurate in the reports and corrected what was not. I talked about what the Society believed, essentially just reading our statement of belief, about The Voices of God, and clarified more than once the misinformation about me believing that I am God. You are God Pat. So is everyone listening to us. No one of us is God any more or less than anyone else.

I plugged the meeting, after Parrot assured me that the interview would air before it was set to start. But I also cautioned anyone who might think of coming not to expect any preaching or discussion of theology or even efforts to convince them. They would hear pretty much what they just heard in the interview and anything else they took away from the meeting would be a product of their own reflection.

The room I rented at the Black Chowder Inn had a capacity of twenty-five. Thirty attended the meeting. The fire marshal did not, so the last to arrive got in, but had to stand. I followed my usual procedure. Everyone cooperated. We had complete silence during the meditation. The testimony that followed was effusive and varied.

One woman spoke about trying to lose weight but never succeeding. She was excited because now it would not be her alone working on it. Another woman said that she had been training to run a marathon, that she had been growing weary of the grind, but now was inspired anew.

A guy explained how his buddies on the bowling team made fun of him because he liked to paint baby animals in water color. They poured it on so hard that he had stopped. "Screw them", he said. "What I learned tonight is that if I like doing it so does God, so I will do it even more."

My favorite that night was a young man about twenty-five who described his long search for the meaning of life and the universe and through all the multitude of beliefs as to what God is or is not. Tonight he finally figured out that he is never going to find answers to his questions because it is not possible. He would stop looking outside himself. He would learn what he could about God by learning about himself.

The comments were not all so positive. however. One lady, an elementary school teacher, said this was the same kind of trash that they published now in the *Weekly Reader*. Every time someone goes on a rampage with a gun and kills a bunch of people they devote an entire issue to covering it. She did not think the Weekly Reader was a place for sensational details about mass shootings, even if it does help improve children's reading skills.

Before I could respond another fellow rose and proclaimed himself to be an environmentalist. "So you know what I think of your Society", he said and sat down. I was about to ask for clarification when a young emaciated woman stood up and said that I had it all wrong: We are not god; we are crystalized space semen. I had no answer to that.

A very successful meeting. The more so when I heard a brief report about it on KDUH the next day. And even more when I arrived in Stonecold, Arizona just as a station there picked up the story. On a hunch I rented a bigger room and it paid off. Fifty-five souls packed it.

By the time I rolled into Fat, Utah the report had reached across the nation as a very minor human interest note. Yet it was enough to stir up the Latter Day Saints of Fat, who asked me politely to move on. So I did.

To Beryllium, Utah, home of the Last Chance Institute of Natural Healing, which provided in-patient therapy for terminally ill persons and instruction in the natural healing arts. The Institute also manufactured and distributed natural medicinal products.

As I learned from a brochure, some of its treatment methods were pretty unusual. They included immersion in precipitated sulfur moistened with bladderpod oil and beaver blood, exposing the naked body to smoke generated by burning cedar branches and juniper berries, placing high powered stereo speakers against the skin and playing a mix of thrash metal and bamboo flute music at full volume for 24 hours. I did not expect to draw too many joiners from such a place.

Fortunately, my main purpose for stopping in Beryllium was not related to the Society. Two blocks from the campus of the institute there was a club called Pop's that featured live music once a week. That week, according to the sign in front, Pop's was pleased to present Alligator and special guest Angel. I was so excited when I saw the sign I almost kissed it.

Instead I kissed Angel when I saw her as she came out of their minivan. She was stunned to see me, but full of joy. Skinnier than when I saw her last, her face sunken and pale, she nevertheless displayed an abundance of excited energy. She introduced me to the zombies purporting to be members of Alligator and, for the first time, asked a bunch of questions about what I had been doing.

My explanation of the Society and my role with it did not take hold in her distracted brain. But she could see that I was in a confident and positive state of mind, which seemed to please her tremendously. With her opening performance starting at eight, we went to the Wild Walrus for dinner.

Seeing what she ordered I discovered why she was so scrawny: A shrimp appetizer salad with a vinaigrette dressing and no croutons or cheese. That's a meal for a bird, I told her. Not a healthy diet. She laughed at my fathering.

We talked about Olivia. Angel said the last she heard her mother was enjoying the state senate, not missing the court at all, and already planning her reelection campaign. Angel was sure she was going to want me to help again.

They were nearing the end of the tour, which had been a mixed experience for her. A real grind, she said. Always with the same people. The others were ok, nice and helpful, but dull. Some of the shows had been fun; some had been miserable. Different cities different types of audiences. That's how it is. But tonight would be special, she said, with the sweetest smile I had ever seen.

And it was. Only a handful of patrons were there when she started. So I could actually hear her awesome, incredible, wonderful voice. Good too because any knuckleheads I would have had to straighten out staggered in later. So, at least for about twenty minutes, it was as if she and I were the only persons there and she was singing just to me. All the crap that had come between us over the years now seemed to have happened in some other lifetime. It was blissful.

The ultimate moment of joy for me was right before her last number. "I want to dedicate this last song to someone very very special to me. Someone who probably doesn't know how special he is. I love him very much. So this one is for you – my Ufu".

Words are worthless to describe how overwhelmed I was. Tears and everything. I wish I could have made time stop right at that exact moment, so I could live in it forever.

Today God rode the gondola to the very top of Antelope Canyon. To the summit of Monster Mountain where the Cheating Death course starts the greatest vertical drop of any ski run in the world. Fog shrouded the lower elevations. The pristine field of pure powder below disappeared into it. I pushed off. Slicing through the fine snow at greater and greater speed I felt that God had never before enjoyed excitement like I did then.

I continued my own tour. Happy for such joy as Angel brought me. Depressed for the loneliness I now experienced. And for the hostility that increasingly raged at me the more known I and the Society became. It seemed that our steady increase in membership was matched by an equal or greater increase in the number of persons who wished to disrupt my meetings, call me out in public places, or attempt to ridicule me and the Society through the media.

As it usually does, most of the vitriol was rooted in a fundamental misconception. Reports reached me of Christian radio broadcasters vilifying me because I dared to claim that I was God. It seemed not to matter how many times I tried to clarify the point. They latched onto this most inflammatory distortion because it was easily processed by the bulk of their listeners and carried an image of unspeakable sacrilege.

The other side of the coin, however, was the tremendous boost we received from the attention these commentators paid to us. Sometimes a movement is built on controversy. I began to receive more and more invitations to appear on radio talk shows originating in locations all over the country. Always I would respond that I would be happy to appear, but I would not have much to say beyond what was conveyed by our statement of belief and The Voices Of God.

And so the pattern developed. Jerry Jumpstarter, WTFM Memphis, asked me to explain the Society's principles. I read the statement of belief. "So, let me get this straight," he said. "You believe that you are God?" I believe that *you* are God, Jerry. That everyone listening is too. And me. Then I would answer most of the other questions by reiterating our belief that we cannot know anything about God other than what we know about ourselves.

I became concerned that The Goat would not be able to manage our rapidly growing membership. But when I talked to him by phone he was ebullient with confidence and swagger and told me he had everything totally under control. When he launched the second issue of The Voices Of God and sent me 10,000 copies I knew he was right.

My audiences too swelled. I needed larger venues and I needed help. I also wondered if we should start accepting donations to defray the costs. It seemed like a logical next step, maybe even a necessary one. Which led to the question of whether we could trust The Goat with the responsibility of handling these funds. I decided not to tempt him and scouted around for an alternative, ideally someone respectable who could serve as treasurer.

I am being chased down a dark alley by a mob of Puritans bent on tar and feather or drawn and quarter or a burning at the stake. The alley never ends and the mob never catches me. But only because I keep running.

I awake to clouds stinging my eyes. The fascist medical morons have instilled some kind of drops in them. They are trying to burn away the only sensory faculty I have left. So that I will not see and bear witness to their evil schemes.

I cannot bear the siren song of the dutch oven cooking stew of cobalt and chocolate or the chanting of zebras made mad by the ice that is crawling across the plain.

Hooray for the comfort of insanity. But only Coach Landry can fend off the army of flying pot-stickers swarming across Route 15 in smoke from burning benzene drifting from the plant. Where can a lunatic go nowadays to flee the waves of mutant gravity? The democrats are feeding Wrigley's into the carburetor. Commander Jenks, sir. Shall we fire on them when we have the range?

20

Last night God went to her job as an emergency charge nurse. Graveyard shift, emergency department of Monmouth General Hospital. One gunshot victim after another. Stabilized one after another. Controlled the chaos all night long. Saved many lives. Will go back for more tonight. God loves the purposeful stress.

The Villager finally broke down outside of Later, Oklahoma, bringing the "crusade" to a halt. Constant velocity joint. Not worth the cost to fix it. The vehicle had served me well and I bid it an emotional farewell as the tow truck hauled it away from the Paradise Motel, where the driver left me and my boxes of The Voices Of God. Can you wait while I see if they have a vacancy? I asked. He just laughed.

"Got a room for God?" I joked with the teenage clerk.

"One bed or two?" was her response. One.

"Smoking or non-smoking?" Non.

"First or second floor?" Don't care.

The coils in the box spring pushed back angrily when I plopped onto the bed in my room. The place smelled of cheap lavender deodorizer spray. Five channels on the TV, including one dedicated to agriculture and one that cycled through a series of still advertisements and local announcements to a soundtrack of snappy elevator music. I left the TV on the latter channel while I considered what to do next.

Actually it was not so much *what* as it was *how*. No car. Cash running low.

Al's Feed Supply. If we can't feed it you don't want it. Picture of Al in overalls, proudly waving at his abundance.

Need to find another vehicle. And a source of cash. And someone other than me or The Goat to handle it.

Drive safely. Better late at the golden gate than to arrive in Hell on time.

Suppose I could borrow a little, maybe from Olivia, enough to get me moving again. But there seemed no point in such a temporary solution.

Thursday the 13ᵗʰ Calendar of upcoming events. Kiwanis Club meeting, Friday the 14ᵗʰ, at 1:00 p.m. Silversmith Hotel ... Book Sale, Friends of the Later Library, Saturday the 15ᵗʰ from 10:00 a.m. to 5:00 p.m., Later Library ... The Later Marriott is proud to host the American Christian Broadcasters Association Annual Conference, Friday and Saturday, the 14ᵗʰ and 15ᵗʰ, 9:00 a.m. to 6:00 p.m., in the Sooner Room ...

So once again I was crossing paths with the Christian broadcasters. At a coincidental rendezvous in Later, Oklahoma. But maybe it was not coincidental. Maybe fate, or something more, some supernatural force, had cracked the constant velocity joint and deposited me close by the inner sanctum of Christian broadcasting.

Was there a design at work? Could it really have been mere random chance that brought the apostle of We Are God so close to the gravitational center of the electronic Word? No. This was a miraculous opportunity. Marooned in Later, with few prospects for progress, I had been presented with a magic lamp containing the genie of publicity.

I did not draw up a plan. I did what I did best: Inject myself into a situation and improvise.

Starting with dinner at the Marriott hotel restaurant. I walked the four blocks to the hotel and ordered the special: Grilled salamander with blueberry butter sauce, mixed vegetables, and Bronx potatoes. Added a bottle of Old Wally's Hard Cider. Then I sat back and watched the comings and goings of Christian broadcasters arriving for the big conference that would start in the morning.

A couple of faces I recognized, not from YCL, but from meetings I had attended as a Christian broadcaster myself. Catching one's eye at a nearby table, I nodded and smiled the self-satisfied smile of the righteous. He too nodded, but coupled it with a contemptuous glare. Clearly I was not popular among his set. Either they knew why I was fired from YCL or that I was the spokesman for We Are God or both. I decided to find out.

"Hey nice to see you again," I called over to him. No response, verbally or visually. He did cock his head my way as a sign to his companions that the Devil was close by and trying to communicate. So I went to their table.

"I guess you couldn't hear me," I said, trying hard to smooth out the sarcasm. Now the three faces turned upon me icy pink. My "friend" refused my hand extended for a greeting.

"We're in the middle of dinner, if you don't mind," he said with rigid politeness.

"Hey so am I," I returned jovially, ignoring their rudeness. "I'm having the salamander. How 'bout you fellas?" Now they knew I was not going to fade away. The gentleman with whom I connected rose, unctuously laid his hand on my shoulder, and drew me away from the table.

"Listen friend," he whispered. "We know about your blasphemous show. As I'm sure you are aware, we don't like it. And we would appreciate it if you would keep your wickedness to yourself."

I squared up to face him. He smelled like talcum powder contaminated with sour bubble gum. "How about that? I figured you all were here for the Christian broadcasters event. But that sure wasn't very Christian."

"Don't tell me what is Christian." His puffy cheeks vibrated.

I cut him loose with "Ok son. If that's the way you feel about it. We can take it up again tomorrow when the conference gets rolling." Grappling with the incredible possibility that I might actually be participating, he shook his head all the way back to his table. Then the three wise men engaged in an intense discussion, each periodically looking to see if I was eavesdropping.

The seed was planted. Enough scheming for the day. I finished off the special and the cider and was sauntering towards the exit when two men whom I remembered from YCL entered the restaurant. And saw me stopped before them.

None of us said anything. I sensed them looking down at me from some high exalted place. Before any of us could draw our guns, however, I was surprised by the arrival of a third dinner mate, someone I knew well: John Anderson. He saw me and immediately came forward with a smile and a handshake. He looked older, much older, than when I had seen him last.

A huge mass suddenly solidified in my stomach and anxiety charged along my nerves, all produced by the possible answer to the one question that now dominated my mind: Was she here too? The fact of Polly had never left my subconscious; it had been merely sublimated by all that had happened to me since that magnificent and wretched moment I had held her and kissed her and learned of her love and mine. John's appearance shocked away all that had obscured the pain.

He asked how I was doing, said he knew a little about the "project" I had going, but did not really understand it. His colleagues, he said, did not like it at all.

Apparently eager to talk more, he told the others to get a table while he walked me out. He guided me to a corner of the lobby where we could chat in private. At that point I asked about Polly. Was she there with him? No.

But that was what he wanted to talk about. He said she was fine, but that she had been going through some very trying stuff, was depressed even still. She had not been the same Polly for about the last two years.

It was very distressing to him. He felt helpless and did not know what to do. She and I seemed to get along pretty well when I was at YCL. Maybe I could help.

In a trance, hardly able to think rationally, I stammered something like how he thought I could help. He didn't know. Had not thought about it before he saw me.

Has she worked outside the home since she was working with me? I asked. No. That could be part of the problem. But whenever he suggested that she look for something, or come to work at YCL, she refused to even talk about it. He remembered that it was me who was mostly responsible for her coming to work at YCL. Maybe I could convince her.

I told him I would most happily do whatever he thought I could, but that I felt pretty helpless under the circumstances too. At YCL I actually had a job for her. And she was enthusiastic about working there, since it was so compatible with her faith. As he had suggested, the work I was now doing probably was anathema to her principles.

He appeared to dwell on this for a few moments, then said that Polly was not as gung ho about that sort of thing as she used to be. She even stopped going to church regularly. Then, dismissing that thought from his mind, he thanked me for listening to him and wished me good luck in my new venture.

Never before had I appreciated what the term "aching heart" really meant. The anguish I felt I would not have wished on anyone. To think of poor

Polly and what she had been through, was still going through, all because of me. On my way back to the hotel I passed a liquor store and arrived in my room with a fifth of Jim Beam and a liter of soda. After drinking a third of the the bottle I fell asleep.

I had a most bittersweet dream. I was carrying the mail. Like a real mailman, not scooting around in one of those little toy carts the wimpy letter carriers of today use. One hundred pounds of mail and a route of one thousand stops. Crisp and clear fall day. The smell of rotting apples, sewage, and football in the air.

My route took me through neighborhoods of modest two-story homes with picket fences enclosing the yards, of apartment complexes alive with younger people living the energetic life, of venerable Victorian houses from the second story of which housewives waved, to the trailer park where rottweilers growled and sodden men in dirty shirts did not bother to stand up when I handed them the mail. I did not care. I even whistled as I made my way.

But then, just past the trailer park, there was a house I had not seen there before, that appeared suddenly as if lowered into place by an invisible crane. As I neared it I recognized the house. I had seen it before. But not there. I had even been inside it, slept in it as a matter of fact. And the memory of where engulfed me like a surprise gust of wind, producing the most acute excitement.

That intensified dramatically when I saw someone waving from the second story. A woman. A woman I knew. Polly.

I called to her. She did not hear me. Or chose not to acknowledge.

Then she was standing on a balcony. Dressed in white. More beautiful than I ever remembered. Calling to me: "Do you accept Jesus Christ as your Lord and Savior?" Yes, I shouted. Yes. Yes, with all my heart. I fell on my knees. I begged her to come down. But she turned and entered the house again.

Waking up mid-morning, cold and shivering, I tried to focus again on the conference, which had been underway already for a couple of hours. My aching brain could not suggest any specific action. So I took a shower and dressed robotically, grabbed a stack of The Voices Of God, and returned to the Marriott restaurant for some breakfast. Only they were no longer serving breakfast, just lunch. Hence, instead of a beaver turd omelet I ordered beaver turd casserole and a gallon of coffee.

There were no Christian broadcasters in sight. Casseroled and jumping with caffeine, I proceeded to the foyer outside the Sooner Room. There, sitting behind a long table covered with papers, were two of the ugliest old hags that ever flew down on broomsticks from the North.

"Good morning, young ladies," I greeted them. "My goodness, I see they made sure to have Christian beauty on display." They looked at each other and giggled.

"Can we help you sir?"

"Gosh, I hope so." I introduced myself as the Reverend Patrick Teasdale. "I'm supposed to be one of the presenters this afternoon, but my flight was diverted to Cuernavaca for an emergency stop. Some young man went berserk and claimed that he was a demon hired by the United States Postal Service to crash the plane. I managed to gain his confidence and keep him controlled until we landed. But then it was too late for me to make it here, so I called to have my presentation cancelled. However, I got lucky. I was in the airport chapel explaining the situation to God, when a young man entered, overheard my prayer, and volunteered to fly me in his private jet. So here I am."

The ancient sentinels of grace swallowed the story whole, as evidenced by their popping eyes and mouths hanging open. "My goodness!" one of them stammered. "Glory Pete, what we can do to help you Reverend?"

I gently cleared a space on the table and set on it a stack of The Voices of God. "Well, if you would be so kind as to hand out these materials I had prepared, that would help tremendously. And do you have any badges or other insignia for presenters?"

Oh yes they did. Fished one out with alacrity. Did me the service of carefully marking it with my name and presented it to me as if it were the keys to the kingdom. The badge went into my pocket and I went to kill time until the afternoon session began.

First stop: the Later Historical Museum, where I was privileged to see the pen used by Homer the Horrible to draw the first panels of OklaHomer, the first comic strip published in Raccoon County. The museum also featured the medical bag out of which Dr. Delmar Dicer drew the instruments with which he performed

Later's first wart removal. As if these items were not enough, the curator lugged a special bag from a closet to show me the bowling ball used by Assistant Secretary of the Interior Scott Scowling when he visited Twister Lanes on his way to the dedication of Muskox Campground.

An edifying experience to be sure, proving that Later had many hidden attractions that were sure to enliven my stay there. At least there was more to do than I ever found in Squash. And, as far as I knew, no counterpart to Holy Peter.

The Zygote Family Restaurant was offering all you can eat corn on the cob for lunch. I ate seven ears. The record was twenty-one.

I returned to the Marriott just as the keepers of the word were reassembling. The posted agenda included a session entitled "New Challenges for the Electronic Pulpit". It seemed an appropriate forum for my contribution, whatever that might be. Having donned my badge, I entered the room to smiles and greetings all around and took an aisle seat four rows from the front.

One speaker after another whined about threats to the tax status of non-profit religious organizations, lawsuits by individuals purporting to represent religious groups seeking airtime, liberal media assaults on the integrity of faith-based broadcast content, and cultural pressure affecting language, themes, and gender attitudes. None of these topics were relevant to the Society. I needed to carve out a new one.

When the final speaker concluded and the host opened the program for questions I jumped up immediately and got his attention. "I wonder if any of the gentlemen who have spoken so eloquently would comment on this new phenomenon or movement, not sure what to call it, asserting that we, all of us, are God. The We Are God Society I believe they call themselves."

Before the host could even figure out what I was talking about someone in the audience rose and shouted "It's a stunt. Don't respond. That man is the leader of the group he's talking about." I recognized the voice and then the face of my adversary from the night before.

Hostile murmuring buzzed the room. I had to match him in voice volume. "This is no stunt. Yes I am that man. The gentlemen should at least respond to my inquiry."

I sensed that the crowd was split between those who were offended and angry, on the one hand, and those who were enjoying some entertainment after they had been drowsing through the boring session, on the other. The former faction was trying to shout me down. The host was befuddled. Something like this had never happened on his watch.

It was clear that I would not have the floor much longer, so I needed to deliver quick and sharp. I jumped on top of the chair and let loose. "If any of you would take a little time to listen or read and consider what we are all about your fears will seem silly. That's all I want. For people to hear us. And reflect. There is a stack of these outside on the table." Holding up The Voices of God. "Please take a look at one."

By then I was surrounded by gross, smelly bodies. They removed me from the chair and conducted me out of the room. My contribution was complete. I bowed to the posse and went on my way.

To nowhere. I was trapped there in Later. Without financial resources I was dead in my tracks. Without someone responsible to take custody of them I would have no financial resources. So I had no choice but to settle into the Paradise Motel as my temporary home and await developments, which I had no reason to believe were coming or would be favorable.

With nothing better to do on Saturday, I dropped by the book sale. Found a decent copy of *The Pope's Underwear* by Frederick Bohm. Also *The Autobiography of Buddy Ebsen*. Woo doggies. Also *A Comprehensive History of Organized Crime in Southwestern Oklahoma*. At least I had some riveting reading material in case my stay in Later was prolonged.

Afterwards I sauntered back over to the Marriott to be on hand when the closing ceremonies concluded. I figured maybe I could hit some of the faithful up for some spare change. Instead I ran into John again. He was waiting for a shuttle to the airport.

"I told Polly I talked to you. I also took the liberty of telling her you thought she should get out of the house and look for a job or something. She didn't react like I thought she would. She just said 'oh, does he have a job for me?' kind of sarcastically."

I forced a laugh. Then, only half jokingly I said "Tell her sure. I have a job for her. I need a treasurer for the evil Society I represent." He smiled wearily as the shuttle pulled up. Just before boarding he asked how long I expected to stay in Later. I gave him a thirty second summary of my situation, he again wished me good luck, and was gone.

Again a doleful rush of loneliness grabbed me, this one occasioned by the departure of Polly's husband of all people. At least he was somebody I knew. With him gone, the closest I had to an acquaintance in Later was the afternoon clerk at the Paradise Motel. I headed back there to my room and the bottle of Jim Beam still two-thirds full.

Along the way I passed a drive-in dispensing one dollar dogs, tubes of mystery meat tucked in a bun plus all the condiments I could fit with it, all for, you guessed it, one dollar. I bought three, loaded them with ketchup, mustard, onions, capers, and tobacco shavings, and sat down outside alone with a cup of delicious water.

I was not alone for long. A crowd of boisterous teenagers soon surrounded me, ignoring me, but making sure I could not ignore them. One of the cars they arrived in was booming KWOW radio, but it seemed none of them were actually listening.

One song finished and another started immediately. I knew the song. Angel again. That exquisite voice finding me once more where and when I least expected it. I wished the rabble there would quiet down a bit so I could hear better, but I did not cause a fuss.

Until some jerk called the song "stupid" and "whiny". My impulsive will acted before my rational mind did. I shoved the guy and cocked my fist for a blow to the jaw, but his friends grabbed my arms. "What the hell," he said. My anger must have colored my face. "What is your problem, old man?"

I did not have an answer. Only the realization of my foolishness. And the dire need to extricate myself from a dangerous situation. "I'm sorry," I mumbled. "I overreacted. You insulted my daughter's music."

"Your daughter? Angel is your daughter?" Like everyone knew who she was. A couple of the girls spoke up from the sidelines: "You're Angel's father?" The tension evaporated as my special status became known. "I love her music!"

Aware now that the guy I shoved had only been playing the asshole contrarian to provoke the girls, I apologized again to him and went back to my last dollar dog, somewhat giddy at being the center of attention because my daughter had become a minor celebrity. However, the weight of desolation had not been lifted, so I continued back to the waiting bottle of whiskey.

That was the pattern of my life for two weeks. Breakfast, lunch, dinner, sometimes only two of the three, reading about the Okie Cartel that extorted payments for smuggled corn syrup, walking around Later trying to think out a plan but getting nowhere, and ending the day in a drunken stupor watching reports on hog, wheat, and fertilizer futures.

I finally let The Goat know that I was taking a break. I also told him that financial resources had become a serious problem, that I was considering the possibility of asking for donations, and that I might want to include something about it in the next newsletter. He offered to "do whatever it takes" to raise some cash, which I took as not excluding criminal actions.

On Friday, two weeks into my sojourn in Later, the weather turned nasty. Fierce rain turning to hail. Impossible to go out. Stuck in the room with reruns of *Hogan's Heroes* and *The Dean Martin Show*. Too bad about Bob Crane. Too bad the actor who played Schultz never got an Emmy. Hard to believe Dean was not actually drunk. Makes you wonder.

Around three o'clock the front desk called to say I had received an envelope. Assuming it was from The Goat, I did not hurry down to pick it up. When I was hungry I dashed through the storm to the convenience store on the corner for some of its mouthwatering macaroni and cheese. Retrieved the envelope on my return. It was not from The Goat. It was from Polly.

Three sentences. John had told her I needed a treasurer. If I would consider her for the job she would apply. But only if she could do everything at home.

Cold and terse. I felt only anger. Bitterness. Who did she think she was? No regard for what I might be feeling holding this scrap of letter in my hands after two years. The arrogant queen bestowing her notice on a minion, granting me the privilege of her patronage.

I crumpled the paper and tossed it into the waste can across the room. Hell of a shot. Now I had no appetite for macaroni and cheese, alluring as it was turning brown around the edges and something discoloring it on top. Alternating between ignoring the letter and not even responding on the one hand and venting my hurt by letting her know how I felt on the other, I cursed my captivity.

Eventually I elected to respond in kind. I wrote an equally cold and terse note, addressed to Mrs. John Anderson, and saying only: "Thank you for stating the terms on which you would be willing to work as our treasurer. However, your curt note provided no other information. Therefore, we cannot consider you for the position."

The instant after I dropped the envelope into the mailbox I regretted it. But I probably would not have been satisfied if I did not respond as I did. A good southern Christian woman like Polly did not belong with a group like ours. Although not in any way anti-Christian, nevertheless we preached a doctrine decidedly at odds with that she had been immersed in her whole life. Even if, as John indicated, she did not worship as fervently these days, her faith in Christ was so embedded in her soul that a return to her customary life seemed inevitable.

The faint subconscious hope of rescue from North Carolina now extinguished, I decided to seek it from an alternate source. I wrote to Olivia, asking her for a short-term loan of enough money to buy the cheapest running vehicle for sale in Later, plus some to keep me fed for a couple of weeks. An envelope arrived about five days later containing a check and a note confirming Angel's report that she was hoping I would be able to help in her campaign for reelection.

I found a 1989 Ford Escort station wagon with 347,000 miles that supposedly had been substantially rebuilt. Vintage bumper stickers decorated the rear: Bob Dole for President, Meet Me in Ardmore, Give Peace a Chance, and My Kid Beat Up Your Honor Student. With seven boxes of The Voices Of God, issues 1 and 2, in the back, along with a piece of foam I bought to replace the mattress, a five-pack of Dollar Dogs, and a thermos of coffee compliments of the Paradise Motel, I finally bid good by to Later, Oklahoma.

Back on the road, I resumed the drill. Find a space, distribute cards, hold a meeting. The success I had achieved before the hiatus continued with a curious crowd of 30 in Bladder, Arkansas. Several remained after the meeting to meet me and wish us well. Nancy Smooth, a reporter for KLOL, a local radio station, described the audience as "alert" and "rapt", even though I said only what I usually did. She also passed on the comments of participants she spoke with afterward: "Something different", "refreshing not to be harangued", "he let the message speak for itself".

During my meeting in Fillerup, Texas, an elderly woman stood up during the testimonial session and thanked me for bringing her a new outlook. She explained that after her husband of 45 years died competing in an eggplant eating contest she spent her days obsessing over her loss and counting the days until she would join him and God in heaven. Now, she said jubilantly, she realized what a fool he had been. Now she wanted to make him wait by living as long as possible, especially since she can experience the presence of God here and now.

By this time my antics at the Christian broadcasting conference began to bear fruit. Reports reached me of multiple purveyors of the electronic word decrying my "depraved" behavior and my "evil" message, thus spreading my word along with their own..

Some of the increasing disparagement and hostility spawned by this notoriety was delivered live and in person at the meetings. These episodes ranged in character from polite contentiousness to one vicious attack that left me in intensive care and our message more popular than ever.

In Croak, Missouri, a team of local clerics came to the meeting bent on interrogating me into irrelevance. They were disappointed to find out that I did not claim any special anointment or divinely inspired wisdom, and that, in fact, I claimed no divine knowledge whatsoever.

Of course they were offended by my contention that they also could have no such knowledge. Their reaction was certainly understandable. After devoting years to religious learning, teaching, and counseling, it would be a horrendous affront for some smartass to come along and declare all that an illusion. These divines, however, were very polite; they were looking for a constructive discourse. Finding none, they graciously departed.

The next incident was very different. High Heel, Kentucky was the location. A sign warned travelers as they approached the town: "You Ain't From Around Here". An HHPD SUV tailed me from the town limit and everyone I passed on the main street stared at me like they were seeing a hyena driving a car. I guessed there would be trouble, but I figured that, in the line of work I was in, trouble sometimes brought results.

After failing to find a proper indoor venue, the owners of the two rooms available refusing me upon learning what I wanted them for, I opted for an outdoor meeting on a vacant lot near the end of town. A tree stump would serve as my soap box.

Next I contacted TV stations in the closest large cities, advising them of the meeting and that I expected trouble. Might get some good, possibly dramatic, video. I referred them to the previously broadcasted and published news items about me and the Society.

Everyone I handed a card to glanced at it and either gave it back, let it float to the floor, or crumpled it and threw it at me. Some added a comment, like "the devil" or "go back to hell where you came from" or "shameful".

High Heel did have a radio station, WKKK. Lester Jenkins, the owner and "voice", was hanging out in the barber shop when I tried to pass out cards to the distinguished gentlemen there scratching their balls and cussing out the Communists in the state legislature. Jenkins pulled out a small recording device when the "discussion" began.

"How many wives you got?" one crusty fellow asked. Just two ex-wives. How about you? "A smart ass, eh? Don't think yer gonna be taking any of our girls for yer harem." No intention of that, my friend.

"How about that, Ralph? He called you his friend. Guess you're one of the chosen now."

"Listen Satan, or whatever they call you, This town ain't no place for your evil message. You'll get out of here pronto if you know what's good for ya." Why is that? What do you think is going to happen? The knowing eye passed among them.

"Guess you'll just have to find out -- if yer fool enough to proceed with this séance you got planned." Does that mean you gentlemen will be attending? At that the proprietor had had enough. He told me to get out.

Jenkins did not play his recording. Instead he reported his impressions of the conversation. How this rascal who claims to be God couldn't even face up to a challenge from the town's elders, would not disclose any of his secret perverted practices, and displayed disgusting cowardice when told he better watch himself while he is within the jurisdiction of High Heel, Kentucky. Cowardice? That one almost hurt.

So at the appointed time I pressed through a crowd of at least one hundred bodies to mount the tree stump and start the meeting. I was determined to get out the major part of my speech before anything happened to disrupt it. But I was only able to state the name of the Society, the foundational belief that humans can only know about God what they know about themselves, and that everyone there was God.

At that point six men surrounded me and demanded that I stop. Wearing black jumpsuits with black hoods, they wore armbands that were stamped with the words "Mercenaries for Christ" and a blue cross was painted on each face. When I did not instantly obey they waved metal cudgels and closed in.

Why are you going to attack someone who admits he knows nothing about God? I shouted. Their ears probably were plugged with transmitters feeding them instructions from the Generalissimo for Christ. I caught sight of a fancy video camera riding someone's shoulder and emitting a blinking blue light. So I kept shouting. You, my friends, are God. You are about to attack God. With God witnessing through the eyes of all these folks.

The first blow landed just below my knee. Sharp stabbing blast of pain. But I continued to speak. A second blow struck lower with more force. I could feel my skin tearing and something snapping. I staggered and fell off the stump to the ground. Now they were beating my upper body. My last memory was metal gashing the side of my head.

Chief Wondering Soul has decreed that orange rain will wash the clay pots clean. The moon is coming to join the fire. My body rots. My mind melts like hot wax. The glittering ceiling closes in and will soon crush me into noxious powder that can be cast to the wind and carried through the gases condensing and dropping as killer snow. Yes, fire when in range, Lieutenant Ufu. Let them taste the righteousness of a sixty-pounder.

21

Dizzy and nauseated, falling through a bottomless hole lined with three-dimensional images of Pastor Davis laughing hysterically, I plunged into a brightly-lit cavern where I settled on a giant sponge and opened my eyes. I was lying on a bed, connected by tubes to bags and machines. A nurse was writing on a clipboard at the foot of the bed. I felt incredibly weak, feverish, and disoriented, too loaded with opium derivatives to feel pain.

From the nurse I learned that an ambulance brought me the twenty-five miles from High Heel to the Buzzard County General Hospital in Baconburg and that I was unconscious when I arrived. The paramedics and ER staff found multiple significant penetration wounds and lacerations, also deep bruising and possible fractures in my arms and legs, and a concussion, if not more serious brain damage. I had lost a lot of blood.

The ER staff stopped the hemorrhaging, but had to leave some of the wounds open to treat for infection. Hundreds of stitches were necessary to close the rest. Once I was sufficiently stabilized I was admitted and brought to intensive care, where I was receiving periodic blood transfusions. She and the other nurses were changing the dressings and cleaning the wounds every two hours.

Lots of people had tried to get in touch with me, she said. But the attending resident had shut everyone off until I was stable and fully conscious and could decide for myself. Like who? She did not know other than some very agitated guy calling himself a goat, someone from the District Attorney's office, and a few reporters. Reporters? Overnight I had become a national news story. Video of the incident had been picked up all over the place, so people from the media were trying to reach me.

Sharp pulsing pain now began to bite multiple portions of my body. My suffering must have been evident, because the nurse summoned a doctor, who showed up briefly and said something to the nurse about the IV dosage. Shortly thereafter the minimal awareness I had began to fade. Before fully submitting, however, I insisted that they get the Goat on the phone.

Good thing, because he was planning to come out with a posse to "teach those shithead hillbillies some West Coast justice." I told him to stay put and not risk violating his parole. He asked if the law had those "motherfuckers" in custody. I said I did not know and did not care.

His last words were about all the people calling to talk to me and asking questions about the Society and if we took donations. How about it, Boss, are we taking donations? I said I would get back to him about that.

Two new female nurses were torturing me when I woke up again. They claimed to be changing dressings underneath my scrotum, but seemed a little too gleeful yanking off the existing bandages.

Two flower arrangements had arrived while I was out. One of the nurses handed me the cards attached. Olivia and Heidi: "Very sorry to hear about what those despicable creeps did. Praying for your full recovery." Opening the other card I caught the word "Anderson" and felt a warm buzz that faded when I saw that it was from "John and Polly Anderson": "Horrified to hear about your trouble. Praying for you."

Also more calls. The Goat again three times. He's getting worse the nurses reported. When I called him back he was frantic. Too much pressure. Too many people putting him on the spot as the only available representative of the Society. Did not want to disappoint me. I told him that I was feeling better and would let them have at me. What about the donation thing? Working on it.

Angel. Crying when I called her. Could not believe what those "fucking hillbillies" did to me. I told her that I had suspected there would be trouble and brought it on anyway, which just turned up her anger at me. "Are you crazy? You could have been killed! Is that what you want, to be a martyr?" Definitely not. If I had thought they might kill me I would have moved on. Just doing what I could to sell the product.

I left messages for everyone on the list of people trying to reach me, telling them to call me the next day if they still wanted to talk. When I reached the end of the list the pain was roaring back. More drugs. Back to sleep.

Virtually every person who called back posed the same questions as the first, Jim Putzer of LIE news: What's my condition? Good, be out in couple days. Why did I think they did it? Because they did not like what I had to say and saw only one way to stop me.

Not because you think you are God? If they, and everyone else, actually listened they would know that I do not claim that I alone am God. You are God, Jim. Every employee of LIE news is God.

But what kind of God could that be if everybody is God? I do not know anything about God other than what I know about myself. Do you believe God is omnipotent? I don't know. Do you believe Jesus was God? If Jesus really lived he was God, just like you, Jim.

What's next for me and the Society, which is called what again? The We Are God Society. We publish a newsletter called The Voices of God. Most happy to send you copies of our first two issues. Next is to get back on the road telling folks about the Society.

What about financial support? Who is funding the society and my work? Thank you for asking about that, Jim, because I don't mind disclosing that I am overwhelmed. The public response to our message, and especially to the recent unfortunate event, has caught me at a time when I cannot handle it properly, seeing as how I am laid up in the hospital. And the doc says I need a few weeks rest when I get out. So I need help. And the Society needs financial help to keep me going. So I expect to hire a treasurer very soon and then we will ask for donations.

One reporter showed up in person just as the nurses were changing the dressings. He was privileged to see me grimace in pain, asked some of the same questions, and left after only about ten minutes. When they finished I asked the nurses not to put through any calls or let anyone in for a while. I was exhausted and needed more sleep.

Waking up again, still groggy, I noticed one of the nurses peeking very hesitantly into the room. She saw I was awake and entered. She told me someone was here to see me, but since I had said not to let anyone in they told her she would have to come back. Instead she had been sitting in the waiting room for three hours in hopes that I would permit her in when I woke up. Name? No. Should she go and find out? No, just bring her in.

As if angels had taken pity and banded together to bring about the one miracle that would transform me to the depths of my soul, that would elevate my spirit to unprecedented heights, a vision, a walking vision of wonder entered my room with the nurse. Polly.

How can I describe the euphoria, the ecstasy I felt just to see her? And to know that she had come so far to see me. I had no speech. I could only smile from one ear to the other and stare in disbelief.

She looked awful. That is, what I could see of her. Pretty much only part of her face. The rest was shrouded in spinster clothing, a floor-length plain brown dress and a drab raincoat, a dark blue bonnet covering her head, and a matching scarf wound around her neck. But the face peeking out was so pale and wan, expressed so much suffering and premature aging, that my heart cried.

"Oh Polly," I said, "what has happened –" then, recognizing that this was not the way to greet her, "I am so so happy to see you!"

She spoke very softly, almost like she did not want to be overheard. "I had to come." Our eyes locked in mutual sympathy.

Then I could no longer withhold. "What has happened to you?" Tears formed in her still bright eyes.

"Never mind. It is what happened to you that matters." I reached out to take her hand, but she would only shake it formally and release it. I wanted her to come close, but she remained several feet away.

"John?" At home with the children. Encouraged her to come. Said I needed her. "John is a good man. A very good man." She nodded agreement.

"Can we talk about what I am to do?" she said, forcing us to business. Holding on to her joyless soul.

Of course. I explained the circumstances in as much detail as seemed necessary. I, the Society, needed someone to take custody of any money that is donated and manage it. This would entail setting up an address or post office box and opening a bank account in the name of the Society. Yes, she could do both near her home, if that was what she wanted to do.

"It's not a matter of want," she said barely audible.

I anticipated an issue I imagined dominating her mind. As far as I was concerned, she would not need to become a member of the Society or adopt or advocate any of its doctrines. She would be just an employee, doing it for the salary. She understood.

It was evident also that, as far as she was concerned, there would be no talking about the past, about our experience together at YCL, our mutual confessions of love, our touching, our passionate embrace, or about what she had been through the past two years. None of it. Only the practical steps by which she could help me recover and move on. She also made it clear that she and I were not to spend more time together than was absolutely necessary.

Almost cruel in her fixed determination, her cold control, it was as if some fractional component of Polly had come to me, while the real woman remained safely incarcerated in North Carolina. If I had not been so desperate for help, and if she had not been the one person I believed I could trust, I would have preferred that the whole Polly had stayed home. But at one point she looked at me with deep sadness and whispered "I'm sorry".

Polly also provided the immediate help I needed to arrange for a place I could stay after I left the hospital. The Colonel George Flapjack Home: A large 105-year-old Baconburg home that housed temporary borders and provided meals and housekeeping services. I learned while there that Colonel Flapjack had distinguished himself at the Battle of the Mad Cows during the Civil War by single-handedly cooking 10,000 buckwheat biscuits for the Confederate soldiers to munch on while they shot Yankees.

As soon as she had set this up Polly was gone. And I was alone again. And horribly empty. So depressed that but for my obligation to the Society, which attached to my life like a violent crime I had committed and not yet been caught for, I surely would have taken my life. Instead I chose to see it through .. first.

I transferred to the home eight days after entering the hospital. My fellow boarders were a varied lot of itinerant educators, recovering patients like me, dudes dealing with personality disorders, and a couple of stable and harmless psychos.

One old-timer claimed to be Louis Pasteur. He regularly excused himself from the dinner table to "tend to his experiments" and asked me multiple times if I would consent to be inoculated with his latest serum so he could evaluate its effectiveness. I declined each invitation.

Another fellow was training to become a chess master. I knew how to play, but was never any good at it. Nevertheless, I played him three times and beat him in three moves each time. He was not bothered in the least, just muttered "that's good, that's good, training, learning, be ready for that next time".

These two actually were the only sociable residents. At meal time we ate and exchanged pleasantries. No substantive conversations. No one brought up what happened to me or what I did for a living and I preferred not to discuss it anyway.

The Flapjack was a good place to heal -- comfortable, very low key, and excellent meals. Even though they always featured the same dishes: scrambled eggs, bacon and Lucky Charms cereal for breakfast, homemade catfish chili and a calf brain salad sandwich for lunch, and for dinner deep fried chicken, mashed potatoes with gizzard gravy, and a buckwheat biscuit, cooked according to a secret recipe handed down by the Colonel himself.

Polly delivered. Within two days of her return home she set up a PO box and opened a bank account in the Society's name using the incorporation documents Mad Dog's assistant had prepared. I relayed the information to The Goat and wrote up an announcement for the next newsletter.

The We Are God Society is pleased to announce that we have hired a treasurer, who will retain custody of, and manage, all funds coming to the Society whether by donation or otherwise. The person we hired, whose name is Polly Anderson, has peerless integrity, ethics, and moral values. The Society is most fortunate.

Ms. Anderson will serve as a salaried employee and trustee and, to ensure her independence and objectivity, will not advocate, or otherwise be associated with, the doctrine of the Society. Now that we have such a person as Ms. Anderson to manage the Society's finances, we welcome any financial assistance our members or others can provide.

Our timing was perfect. The announcement completed the third issue. The Goat plugged it in under the Statement of Belief, added the PO Box address, and printed up 5,000 copies. At the same time I used some of the ample spare time I had to make a post card of the announcement. Then I mailed one to every person for whom I could find an address.

The response was more gratifying than I had dared hope. We had managed to take full advantage of events so that the plea for help found people while they were still outraged. Polly reported that checks were coming in by the dozens.

When I went back on the road after two weeks of very restless rest, and after being cleared by a doctor who advised, nevertheless, that I take it easy so as not aggravate any of the wounds, the crowds coming to the meetings increased dramatically. I needed bigger venues. And I needed someone to manage it all.

I found someone the same way I had found The Goat. It was at a meeting in Beard, Tennessee. During the testimony portion a young woman popped up and launched into a lengthy account of her bouts with eating disorders, circus fetishes, and grape juice addiction, her search for a meaningful life through self-help books, spiritual guides, Cosmopolitan, and the Sears Catalog, and how her career as a special event manager had begun to seem so trivial. Now, tonight, she said, it seemed like everything had changed. The We Are God Society made perfect sense. She concluded by telling me that if I or the Society needed any help she was ready to volunteer.

Her name was Maggie O'Neil and she became my bionic manager. She traveled ahead to arrange venues, distribute invitation cards, make media contacts, book accommodations, and everything else that a rapidly growing crusade like ours needed.

My audiences continued to swell. Maggie set me up in larger venues, like auditoriums and concert halls. On two occasions I appeared before more than a thousand people. Still my presentation continued exactly the same as it had from the beginning: A brief introduction, then recitation, meditation, testimony. For the larger venues we rented microphones to use for the testimony portion.

Many of those who came to the meetings clearly were motivated more by curiosity than actual interest in the message or the Society. And because of the publicity generated by the attack, I was the focus of this attention. My notoriety drove the phenomenon. Maggie had me appearing on radio and television news and talk shows and arranged interviews for newspapers and magazines. I always said the same things. Or did not say anything beyond the mantra I had adopted on day one.

Condemnations also proliferated. Pulpit protests against our sacrilegious message shadowed our progress through the states. Priests, pastors, and rabbis alike called the Society a fraudulent cult trying to pass off as a religion. They urged their flocks to denounce us and to stay clear of our hypnotic influence.

Whenever asked about this invective I responded by declaring, as I did over and over again, that the Society was not a religion. For one thing, inherent in the concept of religion is worship. We did not worship. Worship, as I understood it, was one being paying homage to another. We believed there is nothing external to ourselves that we could worship. Ours was a society of people who shared a similar belief about God. It was no more a religion than atheism or agnosticism.

Suspecting that all this controversy might be causing trouble for Polly, who was so intimately connected with a national Christian broadcasting company, I let her know that she could resign then if she needed to. She had rescued me and the Society. We were now prospering. We could find another treasurer.

She sent this brief response: "Thanks for your concern. But absolutely not going to resign – come what may." This brought me tremendous joy, initially. But as I considered the future I saw foreboding prospects. Subliminally at least, I knew that the passion we had once shared could not have simply evaporated into nothing. By not severing the connection we were tempting a dangerous fate.

One night, after a meeting in Toilet, Louisiana, I was relaxing in a hotel room with a glass of Kentucky Fried Scotch. A call was put through from someone in New York who would not provide a name. He said he was glad to finally talk with me. He had heard so much about me and the fine work I was doing.

Did not want to use too much of my time, so he went to the point of his call. It seemed that he was an officer for a large multinational corporation that he would not identify, except to note that it was a not for profit entity and its purpose was strictly eleemosynary.

They, he and the other officers, had conceived the idea of creating a great committee, a super committee, a committee that would exist outside of normal reality, but that would look into matters of normal reality. Existential investigations was one of the terms he used. Quantum conundrums was another. He understood how vague the concept was, but that the committee members would need to flesh out the details as they saw fit.

His concluding comment floored me. They, he and the other officers, wanted me to be the chairman of the committee. I told him I was greatly flattered, but would need to know a lot more about the project before responding.

Yes, he said, quite natural. However, there really was nothing more to say about it, the idea was still so abstract and would actually take shape as I conceived it. Still, I should take as long as I needed to consider the proposal, especially since they would want a firm and exclusive commitment when I was ready. I would not be able to continue in my present position.

In that case, I said, I do not need to consider. I must decline the offer right now. No problem, he said. They would not be contacting anyone else about it for the time being, so I should contact him if and when I changed my mind.

A most peculiar phone call, I thought afterwards, as the scotch melted my mind to sleep.

God had himself laughing tonight. The best was the one about a Methodist, a Presbyterian, and a kosher butcher. It was even funnier than the bowling water heater story. Felt so good to be entertaining again. Snapped a few off the cuff too. Like the Thai food bit. Knowing that it was God cracking the jokes, not just me, really made a difference.

The Journal of Theoretical Theology published a paper entitled "The Theory That All Humans Are God Analyzed By Application of Hypothetical Symbolic Reduction Principles." *Religious Concepts Quarterly* countered with "Critique of Humans Are God Theory Flawed in Form and Substance". This was followed by "Impossible Faith: Why Legitimize an Absurd Proposition", which appeared in *Divinity Today*.

Hot debate about us combusted everywhere I went. As we traveled through the southern states we triggered tempers and attempts to thwart our progress. In Bear, Mississippi, a delegation from the local chapter of the Flaming Gonad Brotherhood became angry when I refused to declare that the Society was anti-Christian. At least they did not attack me with metal clubs. Instead they occupied the platform and shouted over me, calling me a "coward" and a "fraud" and "probably gay", so that I could not be heard and had to give up.

In Wayback, Alabama, a group of fat old ladies threatened to strip if I continued the meeting. If only they had automatic weapons instead. It would have been less cruel and less effective at silencing me. Camera crews were ready to roll. I saved the well-being of America by giving in to their demand.

In Trombone, Florida, two street preachers who worked as a team, the Reverend Hobbs and the Reverend Dobbs, blasted us continuously from the moment they learned we were in town. Standing on empty fruit crates ten feet apart, they carried on a dialogue that branded us as minions of Satan, princes of egomania, and tools of evil that should be expunged from God's kingdom on earth.

"Say Reverend", Hobbs called to his partner. "Have you heard about the deadly germs that just came into town?"

"Yes Reverend", Dobbs responded. "I believe you refer to the carriers of a disease called misguided vanity, the purveyors of a diabolical doctrine intended to inflate the egos of humble men and women, and to instill in them the utterly false belief that they are the equal to almighty God."

"Yes, I do indeed, Reverend. They are here among us now, calling our good citizens to a meeting with the devil himself. What shall we tell these citizens?"

"We will tell them to shield themselves from these fiends. Do not obey their call. Stay away! Stay away!"

Seeing them going at it on the town square, I approached and offered to explain the truth about the Society. They hollered loud enough to be heard a block away: "Stay away!" Then turned to the people who had gathered: "Run! Run away! Save yourselves from this agent of the devil." Some laughed. Some looked frightened. Some obviously were mad – at me.

In spite of – or perhaps because of – Hobbs and Dobbs, we had an excellent turnout in Trombone. Picked up a few new members. After the meeting closed, a sharply dressed young woman asked if I would appear on the *Naked America* show, hosted by Ashley Skewerman. Sure. Remote camera rolling.

"Hi Ashley. I've got the man who is leading the phenomenon known as the We Are God Society, which has been picking up substantial interest lately as this man tours the country telling people about it. He just had what he calls a 'meeting' here in Trombone, Florida, where he spoke to around 125 people."

Ashley then took over the interview.

"Is it true that you are trying to destroy Christianity?"

"No, it certainly is not true."

"But you do claim to be God?"

"I also believe that you are God Ashley, and all of your viewers."

"You say there is no God separate from us, no God who did and said all that the Bible says? So how can you possibly stand there and pretend that you are not out to destroy Christianity?"

"Like other members of our Society, I do not know anything about God other than what I know about myself."

"There you have it, ladies and gentlemen, a man who asserts that he knows nothing about God, yet actually claims to be God. What is this world coming to?"

It seemed that the more popular we became the more vociferous were our critics. Yet the louder and sharper the attacks the more popular we became. After Trombone I spoke to more than 500 in Killagator, Florida, more than 1,000 in Sherman, Georgia, and more than 2,000 in Ringo Starr, Georgia, a suburb of Atlanta that had changed its name to honor a local war hero who had changed his name to honor the Beatle.

We still were not enrolling new members or receiving new donations at a pace matching the crowd sizes. But with the excitement the meetings produced it was only a matter of time.

Then we arrived in Automatic, South Carolina.

Mt. Baldy is erupting. Houses where geckos live and swallow the nightly news cascading down the embankment. The umpire is ready. He has washed the sinful sulfur from his hands. He will lead twenty mules onto the field. The team will prevail.

There is a bright flashing light and a monster mosquito diving from it for blood, my blood, God's blood. It has a Polly face. But a proboscis six inches wide. It will suck all the blood in one pull. Then explode God's blood all over the universe.

Polly and Holy Peter are dancing in radiation mist. She is giving in to his lecherous groping. I am in Hell.

22

Today God finished translating the mysterious writing found on a stretched sheep hide buried beneath layers of rock near Vladivostok in Siberia. The hide was carbon dated to 7,250 B.C.E. The writing turned out to be a medical text detailing a cure for a sickness that apparently spread from an object, presumably a meteorite, which had dropped from the sky. It took all the linguistic genius I have and a hell of a lot of work and thought. Especially since this cure possibly could be useful some day, completing this translation brought me enormous satisfaction.

I swaggered into town and stopped at the Automatic Motor Inn, where Maggie had booked a room for me. The desk clerk pointed to a dude who was waiting in the lobby. "That gentleman has something for you," she said. Overhearing her, the man came forward and handed me some court papers bearing the caption *Association for Automatic Purity v. The We Are God Society, et al.* The et al. was me.

The papers consisted of a complaint, an affidavit, an ex parte motion, and an order, signed by the Honorable Solomon Stone. This order imposed a preliminary injunction preventing us from meeting, from speaking about anything related to the Society, and from leaving the judge's jurisdiction before a hearing, set for three days hence, where the judge would decide whether to make the injunction permanent.

The complaint read like one of Pastor Rufus' sermons embellished with legal mumbo jumbo. According to the complaint, the defendants were attacking the very foundation of all religions, Christian, Jewish, and Islamic alike: Belief in and worship of a being separate and infinitely superior to humans.

Not content merely to state their pernicious beliefs and let them be buffeted by the elements of discourse, the complaint alleged, the defendants instead launched an offensive on faith, a campaign to destroy the fabric of our citizens' spiritual lives. They have traveled from community to community spewing their harmful message so as to disturb the peace wherever they go.

Now they had come to Automatic, threatening to turn its people away from God as they know Him, to worship themselves, erasing all humility and raising the ego on high. The consequences of convincing every person to believe they are God should be manifest to all. The defendants thus were a clear and present danger to the well-being of a society built on a religious foundation and dedicated to preserving it.

Garbage. Bullshit. A joke. I used every disparaging term I could think of when I called the attorney who filed the papers and obtained the order: Kate Christopher, president of the Automatic Christian Lawyers Association. Unfortunately, she was not available, so I unloaded on the receptionist and told her to pass it on.

I called Travis Small, just for advice, since he was not licensed in South Carolina. He was astounded at the judge's action. A brazen violation of the First and Fourteenth Amendments, he called it. And a prior restraint – an order preventing speech or publication *before* it occurs. Freedom from prior restraints has been fundamental for two centuries or more. As Travis saw it, the judge thought he was presiding over a medieval court where he had the power to prohibit speech and force obedience to select religious doctrines.

Armed with this pep talk, I agreed to an interview with Amanda "Sparky" Chelsey, a reporter and commentator for the Stand Up cable network. Her first question set me going: "Do you think this judge will shut you down?"

"Of course not," I responded indignantly. "Judges have not had the power to suppress speech or matters of conscience for more than two centuries. This dude obviously fantasizes that this is the Seventeenth Century and he is doing the work of the Inquisition. He will not get away with it."

"I understand that you have a rally – or a meeting as you call them – scheduled for the evening after the hearing. Do you expect that to go forward? If so, won't you just be asking for trouble like you encountered in Kentucky?"

"Sparky, the meeting absolutely will go forward – no matter what happens at that ridiculous hearing. If this rogue judge presumes to stop us I will laugh at his order and proceed in spite of it. As for any cowardly gangsters who think they can intimidate me, I invite them to attend the meeting and try their best."

Supremely confident in the outcome, initially I had no intention of retaining a local lawyer. Upon further consideration, however, I decided that disdaining the local judiciary by showing up without counsel might have some unwanted public relations consequences outside Automatic. I could defend myself. The Society should have an Automatic attorney.

Finding an Automatic lawyer who would actually help was more problematic than I expected, due mostly to the majesty and fear with which Judge Stone was regarded. Only one would even consider representing us. He was Angus Kent, the blowhard grandson of a wealthy chickpea magnate. He clearly did not pass through law school on his own endowments. It was apparent also that the only reason he was willing to take the case was because he was too dumb to know better.

In retaining him I reasoned that at least he was a hometown boy, hailed from a prominent Automatic family, who may even have had some connections with the judge, and it was an easy case. How could he screw it up?

The case brought even more of the spotlight. *The Daily Automatic* reveled in the notoriety, claiming the world was watching to see if the "craziness" would be stopped in Automatic. This gross exaggeration notwithstanding, some out of town media people hung around to see how it turned out. I barricaded myself in my room at the Automatic Motor Inn to seethe in private until the hearing.

So once again I was kicking back with a beverage, this time some of Automatic's Own Tangerine Tequila, and watching a TV movie about a cop who refuses to let go of a murder investigation, even when it turns out the victim is still alive, a dilemma the cop solves by committing the murder himself. Phone call. Same guy as before. The officer. Wanting to talk about the bizarre committee.

Did I have any new thoughts about it? No. Had not thought about it at all. Understandable. He just wanted to add that the officers expected the committee to hear from all kinds of people ... even some who may no longer be living. Come on, man, this is getting ridiculous. Some kind of practical joke, right?

No joke, although he certainly could see how it might seem that way. Ok, so how is the committee going to hear from dead people? That is something the chairman will need to figure out. I hung up on him.

Our automatic lawyer was not willing to be just a token. All Angus needed to do at the hearing was state that he represented us and object to the proceeding because the judge did not have the power to order the relief requested by the plaintiff. But he did not see it that way.

He insisted that great First Amendment principles were at stake, which he was obligated to address at length. Maybe the world was not watching, but *The Daily Automatic* was, along with a handful of other news organization. So Angus Kent would not listen to his client. He was the lawyer after all.   He would be heard.

The morning of the hearing I did not make any effort to dress other than I always did when I expected to be the star of the show: One of the off-white suits with dark blue pinstripes I wore for the meetings and a very bright colorful tie blazing with sunflowers and purple gardenias.

The object of many spectators as I marched confidently the half-mile to the courthouse, I then became the focus of the media group gathered on the steps. A News14 van was parked close by and men were lugging equipment into the building. As the reporters pressed around me I smiled and asked how everyone was doing.

"Don't suppose there will be much excitement here, my friends," I said in response to questions about what I expected. "Judge has no power to silence me. He just wants to be famous – infamous I should say."

Was I familiar with Judge Stone? "Only thing I know is that he pretends to be a judge and his signature is on the bogus injunction order."

Did I have an attorney? "Sure do. A hometown hero. He's probably waiting for me, so I better be going on in. Enjoy the show."

Angus was indeed waiting for me in the hall outside Judge Stone's courtroom. His eyes widened when he saw my outfit. "Let's get this over with," I said.

Upon entering the courtroom I noticed that the gallery was packed with people who came to watch. The uniformly nasty scowls directed at me as I passed indicated a hostile crowd. Members of the Association for Automatic Purity and their supporters.

Good, I thought, remembering the boost we had received from previous displays of such negative emotions. The patches of my skin where the Mercenaries for Christ had landed their blows still flamed on contact, but their attack had propelled us into the national spotlight.

The courtroom was unlike anything I was familiar with back at the 3rd District. The formality was forbidding. The bailiff stood at attention even when the judge was not there, did not fraternize with any lawyers, some of whom he surely knew well, and was an eager sentinel lashing out at anyone who dared intrude on the well, the area directly in front of the bench, without the judge's permission.

A sudden expectant silence announced the judge's entrance. Not to take the bench just yet. He went among the assembled guests, greeting them familiarly and bestowing righteousness left and right. He even joined in their group prayer for the Lord to "bless these proceedings and see that thy justice be meted upon the defendants".

He was an imposing figure. At least six foot five, broad muscled shoulders, an extraordinarily high forehead sloping into a full head of pure white hair; if he grew a beard he could have taken a movie role as an Old Testament prophet with no need for makeup. His stentorian voice could be heard, felt even, throughout the room even when he spoke softly to someone. It occurred to me that perhaps I had been a bit careless in my remarks about him.

Kate Christopher was a fire breather. With her hair compressed into a bun at the back of her head, she exuded powerful righteousness, supreme confidence in the correctness of her views. I thought even Judge Stone was a little intimidated.

"Your honor, we are here today to stop evil," she proclaimed. "An evil that has spread its tentacles across the land and dripped its poison into communities one after another. And now it is here in Automatic. No one has been able to stop it. But you, Judge Stone, you can stop it. The pernicious message spread by that man" – pointing to me – "is so abhorrent, so loathsome, so odious, so offensive to the good people of this righteous community that it threatens grievous harm to the public peace. Your honor, you must use the extraordinary power vested in you to hurl this devil back where he came from and to stamp out even the memory of him forever. Thank you."

Her fans applauded and cheered, until the judge called for order. The temperature in the room had risen so high I thought the courthouse was on fire.

Ms. Christopher needed several cups of water to cool the dynamo down. Judge Stone wiggled uncomfortably and looked to Angus for a response.

"Thank you your Honor. I believe it was Thomas Jefferson who said the freedom to speak is a cornerstone of the fundamental principles underlying the establishment of a democratic edifice that will endure contests and assaults and insidious subversions to thrive in a world characterized by oppression and autocratic impulses. Our founding fathers embodied these principles in our constitution when they agreed, before there was any discussion of the other components of the constitution, that the very first amendment would carry them forward. Thus did they demonstrate for all future generations the singular importance of guaranteeing the right to speak, the right to practice religion, the right to pursue happiness and property, the right to bills of exchange, the right to lay and collect taxes, duties, imposts and excises, the right to borrow money, the right to hunt game on the king's preserve, etc."

The judge interrupted him: "The right to be free from harmful and offensive conduct by others?"

"Yes yes, your Honor. That too. These are the bricks upon which our nation and our great state are built. These are the rights that will be trampled on if my clients are silenced by the court."

"What about the rights of the citizens to be protected from insulting and inciteful behavior?"

"Yes of course those rights are part of the fabric of constitutional authority as well. So in summary –"

"I agree, Mr. Kent and I will accept your contention that such rights must be protected." He cut off Angus with a hand gesture and turned back to Christopher. "Do you wish to call any witnesses?" Angus froze, stunned like an innocent man suddenly sentenced to death.

"Yes we do, your honor. We call the Apostle of the Devil himself, also known as the president, secretary, and director of defendant society, aka the man sometimes referred to as Hound Dog."

I was whispering to Angus that he must object to the proceedings when I heard the words 'Hound Dog', but did not understand the context. Angus was so befuddled he appeared catatonic. I fired him and rose to address the judge.

"Your honor, I have just relieved Mr. Kent of his role as defense counsel. I will defend myself and the society I am proud to lead. I vehemently object to this entire proceeding on the ground that it is grossly illegitimate and that you, your honor, have no power to order any of the relief requested by the plaintiff, which would be a prior restraint abhorrent to our system of justice for centuries."

Judge Stone nodded indulgently and said: "Noted. Now please come forward and take the witness chair."

Only then did I realize that Christopher had called me to testify. Surprise and confusion paralyzed me momentarily. I had not realized that she could or would do that. Before protesting, however, I perceived that, far from a bad development, she was unwittingly giving me an opportunity – to sell like I never had before.

I strolled to the chair, accepted the oath without considering the implications of saying "so help me God", and settled easily and nonchalantly into position.

Christopher was radiating eager sarcasm as she opened her questioning with: "Shall I address you as God?" Which brought titters from her fans.

"So long as you address everyone else here the same way."

She smiled scornfully. "You do believe that you are God, do you not?"

"We believe that you are God, that the judge here is God, and that all those people there are God. We are all God. And God is all of us."

"And if you had your way, all of us would believe as you do, that we are all God, correct?"

"I do not have a way, as you put it. I am indifferent to what people believe. As anyone who has actually attended one of my meetings knows, I merely state what our society believes and ask those present to reflect on it."

"You do advocate membership in your society, do you not?"

"I offer membership. I do not advocate."

"Now if, at one of these meetings, a large portion of the people attending join the society, you would consider that a successful meeting. Correct?"

"Yes. When that happens it is very gratifying."

"So when you do what you do at these meetings you are hoping that the people listening to you will accept what you have to say and join the society?"

"Well, yes, but –"

"So you are hoping that the people you are talking to will decide that they are God." Electrified sighs filled the room. Object to the line of questioning, I told myself. But that would have weakened the credibility of my confidence. Angus should be objecting. Except that I fired him.

"That's a gross oversimplification," I declared. "You are distorting my statements to fit your construction of them." My concentration faltered. I entered full defensive mode. Christopher's eyes flickered sparks of fire. She moved grandly away to open the stage and, looking at the judge then the packed courtroom, not at me, continued as if I had not spoken.

"In fact you have been traveling across the nation, stopping in one community after another, dazzling your message before their innocent and guileless citizens, trying to convince them that they are God."

"Now hold on. You are warping –"

"And now you are here in our community, bent on planting your evil seed here as well, and scheming to grow your fiendish cult among the good people of Automatic."

If she had been close enough I would have lunged for her neck and squeezed the sanctimonious pomposity from her insignificant little existence. Instead I rose in a fury. "Your honor, this is outrageous. She is not asking questions. She's making a speech. It's argumentative."

Judge Stone glared at me as if I was the most wicked being he had ever beheld. He slammed his gavel and growled: "The witness will be silent and will sit!" His wrath struck me like a sudden blast of hot wind. But the restraints had snapped. I continued.

"I will not be silent in the face of this travesty. You know you lack the power to proceed. You are operating this kangaroo court in defiance of law and the rights of me and others to be heard. There will be—"

Again the gavel crashed. The judge's ruddy face grew even more colored. "Silence!" he roared. "Sir, you are in contempt of this court. Furthermore, I have heard enough. I hereby order that the defendants are enjoined, now and forever, from speaking, writing, communicating in any manner or form, anything that concerns or relates to their so-called beliefs."

At that point I should have stood down and waited for an appellate court to intervene and chasten that judicial despot bastard. I should have simply ignored his order and dared anyone to try and enforce it outside Automatic or outside South Carolina.

But I was too indignant, too incensed, too appalled that any judge could act with such arrogant temerity. For me it was a personal attack, by a petty judge who believed he was Moses himself. As on so many other occasions, my anger and will beat my reason and sense to the controls.

I called the judge a scoundrel, a self-righteous bully, a shameful joke of a jurist. I told him his order was illegal, unconstitutional, unfair, and hurtful. I entered the well to point my accusing finger closer to his face, which was steamy with wrath.

He slammed his gavel one more time and directed the bailiff to arrest me for contempt. The bailiff tried to secure me, but I resisted, and continued shouting, telling the judge he was a fascist, mad with power and would reap the consequences. A second bailiff showed up. They finally cuffed me and led me out of the courtroom while the Automatic audience stood and shouted praise for God and Judge Stone.

My frantic mind could not grasp what was happening. Sweat clouded my vision and soaked my suit. I heard someone near me say "Holy Peter sent you a hound dog" as I was grabbed by another uniform and shoved into a cell.

For some time – I have no idea how long – I sat on a bench trying to figure out what had happened, mentally replaying the events over and over. After my heart stopped racing and the extreme agitation dissipated, I began to gain a little perspective. I was a victim. Of a preposterous farce masquerading as a legal proceeding. I had never even imagined that such an arbitrary, despotic exercise of judicial power was possible in this country.

Little by little I grew hopeful that the consequences would be highly favorable to me and our cause. The media was there. The event was captured on video and when broadcast would once again elevate me to a greater status than I yet enjoyed. This conclusion was a comfort, the only one in that isolated chamber visited that day by no one other than churlish guards.

Obviously there would be no meeting that evening. I assumed that news of my fate would reach anyone who might have attended. So I thought no more about that, except to eagerly anticipate the triumphant meeting we would have right there in Automatic once public outrage and the appellate court had cut off the judge's balls.

Late in the afternoon I was transferred to the county jail. As I was paraded through halls and tunnels I again heard voices mocking me and referring to locking up a crying hound dog.

Sleeping choppily on the crusty cot that night I dreamed that I was back in the courtroom and in place of Judge Stone was a hideous creature with sunken eyeballs that blobbed out now and then and a pointed head around which a thousand houseflies hovered. The creature leveled at me a bony hand covered in transparent flesh and shrieked "I warned you. Now it's eternal hell for you!" I woke up chilled and sweating again.

It was not until my third day in the slammer that I enjoyed any contact with a human not himself incarcerated or an employee of the prison. A lawyer came to see me. She told me that she had been retained by an unidentified person or group to work on getting me released and the injunction order lifted. Unfortunately for my conscience, she could have been the Porkupine's twin.

She also confirmed that I indeed was the subject of substantial publicity. Video of the proceedings had been aired repeatedly throughout the region and here and there about the country. Declining to say whether the publicity was positive, she restricted her further conversation to advising me that the judge would release me if I would publicly apologize for my conduct in his courtroom and sign a warrant promising to comply with his order at least until the appellate court weighed in.

Ready to hang myself from a heating pipe if I had to stay in that jail another hour, I agreed. Signing the warrant was no big deal. The lawyer predicted that the appellate court would act within a couple of weeks.

The apology, on the hand, was incredibly difficult for me. Yet I managed to mumble out a half-assed statement of "regret" to the two reporters who contacted me when I rejoined the world. It certainly was not what the judge would have preferred, but he must have been glad just to get me out of his hair.

We left Automatic behind and proceeded north. However, we were prevented by the injunction from holding any meetings, regardless of whether it was enforceable technically. I had agreed to comply and I was not about to further test Judge Stone. Furthermore, we knew that there were organizations similar to the AAP throughout the region that were ready to ask courts in every jurisdiction to enforce the order or to issue a new and identical one. Until an appellate court lifted the order we had to lay low.

Meanwhile the committee guy pestered me. Every night, just when I was coasting into serenity, he called to harass me. Any new thoughts? No. Stop calling me. We are very eager to get this thing going. Get it going without me then. This could be your big opportunity to do something spectacular, something that has never been done before. No, I am not going to do it. Look for someone else. We do not want someone else. We want you.

Polly contacted me to see if I was okay and to learn when and where we would come through North Carolina. She also said she had seen the video report on the crazy hearing and urged me to cool down a bit. I told her I was fine, that our future schedule depended on when the injunction was dissolved, and that I appreciated her advice, but it was not necessary.

Once again I urged her to consider resigning since the situation must have been extremely difficult for her. Not resigning, so stop suggesting it. Would I see her when we were in the vicinity of Greendevil? Doubtful, she said. I could not mask my disappointment. Her last words, in the sweetest and saddest tone imaginable, were "I'm so sorry".

After twenty-five days of keeping silent we received word that an appeals court had finally overturned Judge Stone's order. We prepared to renew our crusade with a meeting in Goat Balls, South Carolina. Maggie secured a 900-seat auditorium and spread the word. We considered trying to find something larger, but it seemed wise to start with a packed house.

In the end, however, we started with an almost empty house. Fewer than fifty people showed up. Most of these were there to jeer and taunt me. It was disconcerting. But I ascribed it to being off track for a month. The crowds would return once we revved up our momentum.

Between that meeting and the next, set for Kraptown, North Carolina, we received two letters with more bad news. The first was from The Goat. He reported that no one had joined for more than three weeks and, in fact, a number of members had notified him to stop sending them The Voices Of God. Not good.

The second letter was from Polly, as treasurer, notifying me that no donations had been received also for more than three weeks. The Society's account balance was running very low, especially after our hotel bills were paid. Attributing these omens as well to the broken flow of meetings and the concomitant publicity, I was not concerned.

At Kraptown, however, we discovered that recent events were producing a disturbing consequence. Multiple people there told Maggie, when she tried to distribute our announcement cards, that a month or so before they might have considered attending the meeting. But now, after my "disgusting tantrum" in Judge Stone's court, they were not interested.

This news should have made me remorseful and contrite. It should have inspired me to apologize for real in the most abject and public way possible. I should have meekly accepted the castigation and acknowledged that it was well deserved. If I had reacted the way I should have we might have moved on from the incident and continued our success. Instead, as in so many circumstances throughout my life, I became angry.

In Whiteyville, North Carolina, I was heckled by some patrons of a diner Maggie and I entered for lunch. I told them they should not treat God like that and that God might just have to kick their asses. A couple of ugly farm boys stood up to accept the challenge, while the others waited their turns. Maggie pulled me outside before anything more happened.

In Garbage, North Carolina, I called the manager of a public auditorium a "shit eating hillbilly" when he refused to rent us the place. He and the eight foot, 600-pound custodian took exception to my remark. The manager came at me with a stapler sprung open. The custodian just came at me, intending to crush my skull with his monster hands. I escaped with my head intact but stapler marks all over my face.

We set up more meetings, when we could find a place to hold them. But the attendance dwindled more each time. And many of those who were there actively expressed their hostility.

After again reporting no new members and many requests to stop sending The Voices of God, the Goat called to ask if I needed him any more. I asked him to hold on for a while. However, just a few days later he called to say he could not handle it any more. He was going to Zinac 23 with his mother.

The crusade was falling apart. When we got to The End, North Carolina, Maggie gave up too.

Bewildered by such a spectacular downfall, I charged a seedy, smelly room at the Desolation Motel to the Society's account, knowing there might not be anything left in it. The nauseating stench of stale life pervaded the room. In a box that purported to air condition the room only the fan worked; it circulated the cigarette fumes that seeped in from another room. The black and white TV showed only four channels, one of them the YCL, not surprising since Greendevil was less than 100 miles from The End.

I bought a bottle of Tar Heel Shine from a fellow who was pulling a wagon along an alley back of the motel. He advised me to "drink responsibly", especially if I had never enjoyed this brand of spirit before. I mixed some with Mountain Dew in a glass, sat on the bed watching YCL without sound, and waited for my regular caller. The Shine was awful, even diluted with Dew.

It was also potent. So I was already reeling when the call came.

"Any new thoughts?"

"You ask me that every time and every time I say no and that I will not be chairman of your fantasy committee. So why do you keep calling?"

"We are persistent when we want something."

"I still do not understand who you are, what this committee will be, and why you want me to be the chairman."

"If I told you who we are then that is who we will have to be. If I tell you what the committee will be then that is what it will be. We want you because you, better than anyone else, understand these two points."

"I don't understand shit!" I shouted into the phone and hung up.

As I rode the bumpy Shine train to oblivion I considered calling Polly to tell her how much I still loved her and to beg her for a visit. After all, she was only 100 miles away. Not even a two hour drive.

But no, I was not in any condition to talk to her, let alone meet with her.

If she saw me in that state she would gasp and run away. So I yielded to the shine.

I dreamed that I was about to address a crowd of 50,000 people who had packed a football stadium, when someone tapped on my shoulder. Was that Judge Stone peering down at me? No. I heard voices around me exclaiming that it was Holy Peter come to cast me into eternal hell.

Then Polly appeared as a shimmering figure of light. Come to rescue me? No. She clung to Holy Peter and kissed his gavel, which he then swung at my head, striking with enough force to knock me off the podium and into a dumpster filled with rattling snakes.

I could still feel the blow when I woke up. Or maybe it was Tar Heel Shine residue. Whatever, I just felt sick and my head ached horribly.

When I was able to focus my eyes I wrote a letter to Polly. I advised her of the Society's demise, told her to close the account and the PO box, and to send any related closing papers to me at the Desolation Motel, The End, North Carolina. If there happened to be any money left in the account she should keep it for herself. On the other hand, if there were debts she should pass them on to me. I thanked her for everything she had done and said good by.

It seemed there were no options left for me. With my history, much of which was public knowledge, I could not expect simply to revive my career as a political campaign manager or product demonstrator. Olivia was going to need help, but her reelection campaign would not start for another year or so and now I probably would not be a good person for her to associate with.

Reaching the bottom is pretty scary. But not as scary as realizing there is still farther to fall.

I determined to hang on there in The End until I was certain that Polly had received my letter and had time to send me any papers. Where I would go after that I had no idea.

Days passed. I did not know how many. Every one the same. Wake up. Eat a Snickers bar from the vending machine. Watch TV. Eat a Butterfinger bar from the vending machine. Take a nap. Watch TV. Eat another Snickers bar from the vending machine. Back in the Alley for some more Tar Heel Shine. Watch TV. Eat some trail mix from the vending machine. Talk to Dr. Nothing about not being chairman of his committee. Pass out.

Then one day just before Noon someone knocked on the door. Still reeling from yet another shining night I stumbled to the door and yanked it open. On the threshold of the dingiest, most decrepit motel room in America I beheld an amazing, astonishing, magnificent sight: Polly, smiling and looking healthy and well, her face once again rosy and fresh, the careworn marks of suffering I had seen the last time gone. As I expected, she gasped at the sight of me. But she did not run away.

"Hi there," she said in the assured southern voice I knew so well. Wrapped in a raincoat, she was carrying a small satchel in addition to her purse.

"Hi Polly. I sure did not expect to see you here."

"I have some papers for you. Decided to bring them instead of mailing. May I come in?"

"This isn't a place for you. It's a dump." She said she could handle it and came in, gasped again, removed her coat, set it on the bed, and sat on it.

Oh my God! The most beautiful, gorgeous, sexy, fetching vision of splendor ever seen on earth was sitting on my shabby, grungy bed. Her simple, knee-length black dress was close-fitting enough to show that she was fit and still had the womanly body any man would dream of exploring. I just stood there, stunned to gaze at something so horribly out of place.

There being no other place for my sorry ass, I sat on the floor. For a while she looked at me, examining my condition through my eyes, silently probing my soul.

"Things are not looking good, are they?" she said.

"No, they're not. But that's the way it goes sometimes."

"It happened so fast."

"Yeah, I screwed up big time." She seemed about to dismiss this admission, but looked down at her hands instead.

"Too much attention on you. Not enough on the message."

"I don't know what we could have done differently."

"Maybe use a different messenger? It seemed like your method always was to convince people how much *you* believed in something. As long as people believed in you they accepted what you believed in." I could not dispute this wisdom. But at that moment I did not want to analyze it. I wanted only to remove

Polly's shoes and socks and kiss her feet. Maybe she knew. Maybe that is why she got down to business.

"The account was overdrawn, as you probably guessed. And we owed some money. I paid the amount we owed the bank and closed the account. I also paid the debts."

"With what, if there was no more money?"

"With my money. But that is done. No need to discuss it." I started to protest, but she raised her palm in my face to stop me. "What we do need to talk about are the people who have written to demand return of their donations."

This formal, business tone of voice was hurtful to me. It seemed as if the emotion that once had driven her into my arms had been completely drained and replaced by excessively cold, rational pragmatism. As she waited for my response about the donations, I silently begged for compassion.

"I don't know what to do," I mumbled. "Why don't you just turn it all over to me, so I can take responsibility. You shouldn't have to deal with this." Powerful sadness was coating my thoughts, maybe my face as well. "Yeah, just leave it all here." Fighting the bitterness.

A spark of empathy softened her expression.

"In fact," I said, growing painfully irritated, "why did you bring this stuff? Why didn't you just mail it, with a letter saying here ya go, good luck, sayonara?" I was standing now, standing and pacing. "It would have been a whole lot easier for both of us." Tears were forming in my eyes. My fortitude was breaking down. I went to the door. Had to get out.

Her hands covered her face. She was trembling. She exploded: "I don't know why I came. I thought you would be glad. I guess I made a big mistake!" Satchel emptied on the bed. Grabbing her coat. Passing me at the door. Seeing my wet eyes and my struggle to keep from sobbing.

"Oh Polly. You have no idea how happy I am that you came. But I am not happy ... because you're just going to leave again. You're going to leave me again like the first time. Well, okay, but please hurry. Get out of here!"

Tear soaked cheeks once more suspended in an abyss. Hovering before me. Bright, bright eyes twinkling with moisture, looking deep into mine. And all at once a surrender, a cutting free of restraints, a falling away from the protecting rail, gravity finally having its way, pulling her against me, her arms around my neck, my arms around her waist, her hot red lips finding my chapped and dull ones, our tears mingling as our cheeks caressed.

"Oh God, how I love you!" she whispered. "How I have loved you for so long. And suffered for it."

"I have lived a lifetime anticipating this, but certain it would never be. So helpless and hurt. Yet praying for a chance to tell you how I still loved you. Despite everything."

How long did we remain there, in the shadow of Desperation, holding each other, clutching, grasping for more? Five minutes? An hour? I cannot say. Such a miraculous moment of perfect joy could never be measured by time.

All I can say is that it ended. Polly had to return home. Her children were expecting her. She promised to come back as soon as she could and made me promise to wait for her.

I did. A day. Two days. Three days. On the fourth day a letter arrived. She would always love me with all her heart, she wrote. But she could not destroy her family. She and I must be courageous. We must forget. She would pray every day that eventually I would understand and forgive her. Goodbye.

I drank Tar Heel Shine – straight – until my regular caller asked if I had any new thoughts. Yes, I said. I accept. I will be the chairman of your committee.

It was my only way out of The End.

www.ingramcontent.com/pod-product-compliance
Lightning Source LLC
Chambersburg PA
CBHW060324260626
47160CB00007B/2669